LORI L JACKSON

Head in the Clouds

To Cyrus, from whom hope springs eternal.

The only reliable memories, I suppose, are
the ones that have been forgotten. They are
the dark rooms of the mind. Unopened, un-
touched, and uncorrupted.

— Abby Geni

Acknowledgement

This story wouldn't exist without the unwavering support of my incredible family. To my parents, thank you for fostering a love of words and stories since I was a child. To my daughter, your constant encouragement has been invaluable. To my husband, you are my rock, my muse, and my first reader, thank you for believing in me even when I doubted myself.

To all those who care for others, you are the bedrock of humanity, much deserving of our admiration in a thankless calling. Without you, our lives would be a loathsome existence.

Clementine

I look to my left—nobody's there. I look to my right—the coast is clear. Phew. I jiggle my key into the door lock and enter my Happy Place.

Now, I know some folks might find it strange that my oasis away from the hustle and bustle of Worthy Community Home resides in a supersized linen closet. But believe you me, there ain't no other way to get a bit of peace than to hole up somewhere you can't be seen. Sure, the first few years I worked here I'd tow the company line and take my breaks in the employee lounge. And I still do on occasion. As time went on, though, it occurred to me my respites were always being interrupted by some catastrophe or another. That's when this closet became my sanctuary.

Because my moments here are precious, I've gone to great pains to fix it up real nice to maximize my comfort. I've got one of those cute, collapsible stadium chairs, complete with a pop-up table and a nifty side pocket to store my romance novels; a little crate to prop my sore feet on; a tiny fan to swirl the air when it gets stuffy; and last but not least, a handy Playmate to keep my Diet Dr. Peppers and 100 Grand chocolate bars cool—exactly the way I like them. It's the perfect spot to relax and escape for a spell.

I shake open the chair and settle my behind, pluck out my latest read, *Forbidden Ardor*—whoo it's getting steamy—then unwrap my glorious candy. Just as I place that scrumptious morsel onto my lips...rat-a-tat-tat.

"Mrs. Babineaux?" Rat-a-tat-tat. "Mrs. Babineaux?"

"Mr. Isaac? Is that you?"

"Yes, ma'am. Sorry to interrupt your break, but we've got a Code Red with Miss Margaret," Mr. Isaac replies outside the door.

"Good Lord," I sputter as I drop my book and candy bar on the chair.

"How'd you know where to find me?" I wonder, with an edge mind you, as I lock the closet behind me.

"Miss Ida Mae said you'd be here. She's in with Miss Margaret now," Mr. Isaac answers sheepishly.

Note to self: Give Ida Mae Brown a stern talking-to about revealing my Happy Place. Its whereabouts are supposed to remain strictly between us.

"What's Miss Margaret gotten herself into this time?" I ask as we trot down the hall.

"She's perched on the windowsill," he responds urgently.

"What? Oh, my goodness." I pick up my pace and leave Mr. Isaac behind me, his gimpy leg slowing his progress.

I turn into Miss Margaret's room, and lo and behold, there she is, standing on the sill, the window jimmied open with a desk chair, and her nightgown blowing in the breeze.

"Please, Miss Margaret. Get down from there. You're gonna kill yourself!" Ida Mae begs.

"Listen to Ida Mae, Miss Margaret. You got no business being on that window ledge," I say calmly as my insides knot into a ball.

"I want to climb this here tree. Daddy said I could," Miss Margaret answers.

"Miss Margaret your daddy's been dead for over thirty-five years..." I sputter indignantly.

"Nonsense. I just talked to him," she replies and reaches toward the tree some ten feet away.

"Miss Margaret!" Ida Mae, Mr. Isaac and I scream in unison.

"I can't grab it from here. Magnolia, give me a boost," Miss Margaret barks in my direction.

Good grief. She's got me mixed up with her older sister again.

"I'm Clementine, Miss Margaret. Remember?"

"Hush now and give me a hand," she mutters tersely.

"Mr. Isaac, go fetch Mama Pearl. I think she's in Mrs. Hadley's room," I direct, then turn my attention back to our wayward resident. "Miss Margaret, let me see if I can help you."

I walk slowly toward the window, so I don't agitate her. "Ida Mae, stay where you are," I whisper to my colleague.

Just as I reach Miss Margaret, Mama Pearl rushes into the room, a long syringe in tow, with Mr. Isaac close behind. The sudden movement startles Miss Margaret and she loses her balance, flailing her pale, skinny arms to keep from falling. I grab Miss Margaret's hand to steady her while Mama Pearl injects her with a sedative. Mr. Isaac comes from behind and scoops Miss Margaret into his arms, then lays her on the bed while Ida Mae and I place her in restraints. She's so slight the shot takes immediate effect, and Miss Margaret falls into a calm slumber.

"Whew," I exhale.

"That was something else," Ida Mae wipes her brow.

"How in the world did Miss Margaret get that chair up there? She's a tiny, little thing," Mama Pearl remarks.

"Miss Margaret may be losing her mind, but she's as strong as a bull," I contend matter-of-factly.

"Has she done this before?" Mama Pearl asks as if her ears are playing tricks on her.

"Miss Margaret does get pretty feisty every now and then," Mr. Isaac replies with a nod.

"She seems to get worse in the afternoons. All the residents do. Like they're bored or something. That's when they typically act out," I say.

"Does this kind of thing happen frequently?" Mama Pearl wonders.

"It sure does, and nobody on staff knows what to do about it. There isn't enough manpower to keep them occupied. I'm sure glad you were close by, though, Ruth. I don't know what we would've done. Ain't you thrilled you agreed to help out around here?" I tease.

Mama Pearl shakes her head. "We're going to have to figure out something. We can't have the residents running wild."

"Your lips to God's ears, Ruth."

Cleo

Lord. Have. Mercy. It isn't but seven thirty in the morning and it's already a bajillion degrees outside. My brow's all beaded with sweat, my new silk blouse is stuck to my shoulders, and my usually puffy coif is a frizzled mess 'cause of the humidity. Whoever proclaimed late September as the beginning of fall surely don't reside in Dallas, Texas.

The Gaston Avenue bus turns the corner and I breathe a sigh of relief. I'm moments away from blissful air conditioning and a seat to take a load off. The mighty vehicle brakes right in front of me, its hefty doors swing open, and I nab a window seat halfway down the aisle. I dab my face with a handy washcloth I always keep stowed in my bag, careful not to flub my makeup. Mama says an ounce of prevention is worth a pound of cure. That's sure enough true in weather like this.

The bus stops at the next block when, what to my wondering eyes should appear, but that dapper, tall drink of water, Brian Robinson, who just happens to be my beloved. Our eyes meet, and he grins his heart-melting smile that makes me swoon, even after three years of dating.

"Hey, baby," he says as he pecks my cheek, takes my hand, and settles in next to me.

"Hey, yourself," I reply.

"You nervous about today?" Brian wonders, his brow furrowing.

"Why do you ask that?"

"Because your palms are doing their waterworks again."

"It's hot outside," I counter, shooting him the side-eye.

"Cleovantra Empress Pearl, it's not right to blame Mother Nature when you and I both know stress makes your hands as clammy as an ice-cold pitcher on a hot day," he remarks with a chuckle.

I must admit, Brian isn't wrong. I *do* have a proclivity for angst-induced sweaty palms, especially when it comes to matters of employment. Remember that handy washcloth I referred to earlier? Well, it became a fixture in my handbag back when I began my first, real job with the infamous Chastity Lynn Worthington, and the ensuing anxiety was eating me alive. Now, I keep it at the ready, 'cause you never know.

"Don't worry, Cleo. You're going to do great." Brian wraps his arm around me and pulls me into a cuddle.

"I wish Mr. Boseman hadn't left the VR division. I really liked him," I lament wistfully.

"I know. But things change," Brian replies, as we exit the bus in front of our building.

"I'm not so good with change," I confess.

Brian squeezes my shoulder, and we walk in companionable silence to the elevator. His comforting grip eases my apprehension, so much so that I think to myself: Maybe he's right; maybe I've got nothing to worry about.

My shaky resolve all but disappears, though, as Brian winks at me and gets off on the seventh floor—where I worked not but a month ago—my stomach doing back flips while I watch the numbers tick by to my destination.

I give my hands a surreptitious wipe as the elevator opens and I head on down to the conference room to meet my new boss. As I open the door, I see that although it's not even seven forty-five, all nine of my team members are already seated. Perfect. This from a group of folks who can't seem to straggle in on a normal day till nine-thirty, ten o'clock, except for my cubicle mate, Jonathan Chu. I think Jonathan must live at the office since he's always the first one here and the last one to go home in the evening—if he even has a home. Maybe he just sleeps at his desk or sets up a cot in the break room and catnaps there. Either way, Jonathan is an enigma. But I digress.

I notice that all the chairs around the conference table are taken, so I snag the only seat remaining against the wall, right next to Jonathan. We nod our hellos and sit quietly, while our teammates laugh and joke about their weekends. I use the term "teammates" loosely, 'cause there's a definite pecking order in the Virtual Reality division.

Quinn is the ringleader of the bunch, with Hudson his wingman and second in command. They make sure the other six men in their little "Bro Club," as I refer to them, grab lunch together, go to happy hour after work, and help each other when deadlines approach. Since I started a month ago, they haven't given me, or Jonathan for that matter, the time of day. It isn't a coincidence that Jonathan, the sole Asian, and I, the only Black female, are relegated to the nether regions of the conference room this morning. They've made it obvious we ain't welcome, nor will we ever belong, to their club.

After suffering through fifteen minutes of one-upmanship as to who can drink the most beer without vomiting, Sienna Taylor, the perky, ponytailed head of Human Capital, and our new boss both breeze into the room; thank Jesus for small miracles.

"Hello, everyone. I'd like to introduce you to Ingram Singh, our new Virtual Reality Quality Integration manager. He's joining us from Google where he managed the VR department for six years. We are so fortunate Ingram chose to bring his expertise to Deep Well Technologies to help grow our business in this exciting new realm. With that, Ingram, I'll leave you to your new team." Sienna nods to Mr. Singh and glides out of the room.

"Thank you, Sienna. Good morning, VR!" Mr. Singh says eagerly in a crisp, British accent.

"Good morning," we respond in unison.

"Before I begin my spiel, why don't we go around the room so you can introduce yourselves? Break the ice a bit," he suggests.

As is usually the case, Quinn is the first one to speak up and laud his accomplishments, followed by the other Bros seated at the conference table— blah, blah, blah. The way they sell themselves, you'd think they could solve global warming and cure cancer all before lunchtime.

When it's finally our turn here in the back forty, Jonathan mumbles his name and years of service without making eye contact with anyone, let alone Mr. Singh. My heart goes out to Jonathan with how awkward he is around folks, looking like he'd rather be anywhere else than in a room full of people. It's painful to watch.

"And, last but not least, the only girl on the team," Mr. Singh nods to me. Hmm, that's a mighty odd way to start a conversation.

"My name is Cleovantra Pearl, but..." I begin.

"What?" Mr. Singh interrupts me, scrunching his nose.

"Cleovantra Pearl," I repeat.

"What kind of a name is that?" He chuckles, and the Bro Club snickers right along with him.

"The kind my mama and daddy gave me," I respond, with more of a bite than I meant.

Mr. Singh's eyes squint briefly like he's making a mental note about me. Oops, I'd better recover.

"But I go by Cleo, Mr. Singh. I've been on the VR team four weeks today," I add with my best smile, trying to win some points.

He wags his finger, "Not Mr. Singh. Ingram. I go by Ingram."

"Okay, Mr. Ingram," I nod.

"No. *Ingram.* Just. *Ingram.*" The room turns chilly as he makes his point.

"Yes, sir," I answer, and our eyes lock for a few, long seconds.

"Well," Ingram claps his hands together, "I'm excited about this new adventure. Virtual Reality is still in its infancy and there are many, many opportunities for Next Well to grow its market share in the VR space. While I'm a big believer in leveraging synergies within teams, I also think a dose of healthy competition can help motivate and bring out the best in each of us."

He writes, "THINK BIG," on the dry-erase board. "I want your ideas. Nothing is too small. Creativity needs to drive VR, not just coding, and the more unconventional your ideas, the better. The top concepts will get the most funding. And with more funding, comes a higher rank. A higher rank means more prestige within the team, and of course, more money. I'll be meeting with each of you individually in the next couple of weeks to get to know you better. Until then, start brainstorming."

My initial impression of our new boss? He can sure put together a scrumptious word salad, with lots of highfalutin words, but not say much of anything in the process. All I got out of his little speech was: Every man for himself. Like my daddy used to say, life is a contact sport. All right then, let the games begin.

Clementine

"Percy?" I wait a few beats. "Percyyyy?" I call to my husband. No reply. I cover the delectable dessert I whipped together and set off to find my willful significant other.

"*Percy Blaine Babineaux?*" I holler.

"What?" He bellows from his study.

Aha. Found him. I trot into Percy's lair where he's hunched over an enormous magnifying glass, performing surgery on what appears to be a teeny-tiny fishing lure.

"Hurry up and change your clothes. We're gonna be late," I fuss.

"Shh, I'm concentrating," he snaps.

"Now!" I pinch a chunk of his forearm.

"Ow! Damn, woman!" Percy rubs his wound, "That hurt."

"There's plenty more where that came from. Chop-chop. Let's get moving," I order.

"Why do I need to change for? We're just going over to Mama Pearl's for supper. It ain't like she's the Queen of England," he whines.

"You want another nip?" I chomp my hand at him.

Percy sidesteps my strike. "All right, all right. Keep your pincers to yourself, please."

"Don't you lollygag now. I'll be waiting in the car," I say, highly satisfied with myself I got Percy off his duff.

Not but a few minutes later, we're on the road to Mama Pearl's, aka Ruth's, home, my purse and dessert draped across my lap. "Slow down some Percy, or I'm going to lose my grip on this here bowl."

"What'd you make?" He wonders.

"Ambrosia."

Percy wrinkles his nose, "Ambrosia? Again? How many times do I have to tell you? Don't nobody like your ambrosia, Clem."

"That ain't true. Folks love my ambrosia." I scoff.

"If that's the case, why is it every time you take that nasty concoction over to Mama Pearl's, three-fourths of it's left over, huh? Then, I get the added bonus of you packing it in my lunches the whole next week. Let me tell you something, Clem. I've tried feeding your ambrosia to the stray dogs on my route, and even *they* won't eat it."

"You don't know what you're talking about, Percy." We park in front of Ruth's home behind a bevy of other vehicles. "Great. We're the last ones here. I told you we'd be late."

"Ain't that supposed to be fashionable?" Percy chuckles.

I roll my eyes at him as we open Ruth's screen door. "Hey, everybody!"

"There they are. Hey, Clem! Hey, Percy!" Ruth calls.

The kitchen is Command Central in the Pearl home, with all of Ruth's guests crammed into the pocket-sized galley. There's no doubt they're congregated in here because of the mouth-watering aroma of Mama Pearl's cooking, but it's more than that.

The first time I met Ruth, the thing that struck me most was her light; so open, warm, and loving. She lit up the room, and everyone around her. She still does, even after all these years. More than anything, I think folks just want to be near her to bask in that glow.

"Clementine, you didn't need to bring anything," Ruth takes the bowl from me, "but it's mighty appreciated." She unwraps the dessert, "Well, how about that? Ambrosia."

Percy's mocking has made me self-conscious, so I'm sensitive to her reaction. But even if Ruth ain't a fan, she doesn't let it show. She's still her bright, bubbly self. Phew. That's a load off my mind.

I peruse the room and see the usual suspects: Ruth's sister-in-law Ella along with her husband Gabe, and Ruth's son Moses and her daughter Cleo. Moses grabs some Tupperware and begins cramming it full of fried chicken.

"Moses, you stop that right now. We are civilized beings in this house. We say grace first." Ruth chides.

"But Mama, I'm late for my Investment Club meeting."

"Before we touch any food: Grace," Ruth says, and Moses reluctantly drops the dish.

"Alright, everyone. Join hands and bow your heads," Ruth directs. "Sweet, Lord Jesus, thank you for the company that fills my home, for all those who touch our hearts, and for the many blessings in our lives. We ask that you bless this bounty we are about to eat, and the love we are about to share. In Your heavenly name we pray, Amen."

"Amen," we repeat.

"Go ahead then, Moses, and finish your packing. But leave some chicken for the rest of us. We've got a lot of hungry people here," Ruth commands.

"Yes, Mama." Moses drops some more chicken and biscuits into his container and heads on out. "Bye, everybody," he shouts over his shoulder.

"That young man is something else," Gabe says, shaking his head. "He's not but fifteen years of age and he's got a larger stock portfolio than I do."

"You taught him everything he knows," Ella chimes in.

"Maybe so. But Moses is leaving me in the dust," Gabe replies.

"Fill up your plates, everybody. There's plenty of seating in the family room," Ruth interjects.

We each grab a dish, and as usual, Ruth has outdone herself. In addition to her delectable fried chicken, there's mashed potatoes, cream gravy, drop biscuits, black-eyed peas with ham hocks, and of course, my ambrosia and Ella's triple chocolate ganache cake for dessert.

I settle in next to Percy on the sofa and dig in. "Ooh, Ruth. This chicken is perfection, as usual."

"Thank you, Clem." Ruth turns to Cleo, "You all right, honey?"

"Why do you ask?" Cleo wonders while she chews a mouthful.

"Because you're sitting there moaning like you're in love," Ruth teases.

"I am in love...with this here dessert. Auntie Ella, this cake is the best thing ever," Cleo takes another bite.

"I added Bailey's Irish Cream to the frosting," Ella says.

"That's my wife. Always kicking it up a notch," Gabe kisses Ella's cheek. "Say, Ruth. How did your first week go at the community home?"

"Well, I had my hands full. I'll tell you that," Ruth replies.

"We kept her busy on the Memory Care wing," I cut in.

"My Lord are they understaffed. And how many patients are on that floor, Clem? Twelve?" Ruth asks.

"Yep. We've had two nurses quit in the past ten months, and management hasn't seen fit to replace them yet," I shake my head.

"Seems like every afternoon, the residents get restless and want to walk the halls..." Ruth begins.

"Or climb trees," I interject.

"That, too. They all have a touch of sundown syndrome. The thing is, they ain't all memory patients. Some of them, like Mrs. Hadley, are there because there's no room anywhere else," Ruth adds.

"Mrs. Hadley's in the Memory Care unit?" Cleo asks.

Ruth nods, "They moved her onto that wing after Mr. Hadley died a couple of months back."

"That's too bad. She must be terribly lonely," Cleo laments.

"We need to find *something* to keep the folks on that wing occupied. There's only so much TV they can watch, and bingo won't cut it. I just don't know what." Ruth shrugs, then takes a bite of my ambrosia.

"Cleo, why'd you leave Brian at home?" Percy wonders.

"He had to work all weekend," Cleo replies.

"Shame he's gonna miss all this good food," Percy responds.

"Don't you worry. I'll take a plate back with me and make sure he's fed properly. Speaking of work, how much longer you got at the post office, Mr. Percy?" Cleo changes the subject.

"Fourteen days, sixteen hours," Percy glances at his watch, "and twenty-seven minutes. But who's counting?" He chuckles.

"What do you plan on doing in your spare time?" Ella interjects.

"Fishing, lots of fishing. Like I do on my days off," Percy responds then turns to Gabe. "Gabe, you won't believe what I bought at Bass Pro Shops yesterday: A Stella."

"No," Gabe's eyes widen, "a Stella reel?"

"Yes, sir. I saw it in the case there, and I couldn't help but call its name. Stella! Stella!" He cries in his best Marlon Brando impression.

I pinch Percy under his arm so the other folks can't see. "Come with me. Now." I mutter under my breath. "If you'll excuse us a moment."

We rise and step into the kitchen.

"*What?*" Percy nips at me.

"When were you going to tell me about 'Stella'?"

"I just got it yesterday, Clem."

"How do you expect me to maintain a budget if you go off and buy things without telling me?"

"Clementine, you have your bank account and I have mine. Remember?"

"But how am I supposed to keep track of *our* money when you don't keep me in the loop? We've got to watch our pennies with you retiring in a couple of weeks."

Percy rolls his eyes. "I'll hand over the receipt as soon as we get home. Does that meet with your approval?"

"Okay fine," I agree, begrudgingly I might add.

Percy nods to my ambrosia, where three-fourths of it remains. "Told ya."

Margaret

Clank. Clank. Clank. "Is that truly necessary?" I ask as Mr. Isaac continues his incessant beating on my window. Clank. Clank. Clank. "We've got to keep you folks safe, Miss Margaret," he replies. Clank. Clank. Clank.

"Safe from what?" I snap, freely demonstrating my annoyance.

"The staff don't want you falling out the window and hurting yourself," Mr. Isaac responds.

"How on earth would I fall out the window?" I bark.

"In case you decide to climb a tree or something, Miss Margaret." Mr. Isaac tests the bars he installed with a good yank.

"Why would I want to do that? I haven't climbed a tree since I was ten years of age," I scoff. "What am I supposed to do if I want some fresh air? It gets stuffy in here."

"Maybe your daughter could buy you one of those oscillating fans. This room's small enough it'd stir the air around and make it mighty pleasant," Mr. Isaac offers while he stows the tools in his bag.

"My daughter's much too busy spending my money on herself to think of using it for anything practical," I grumble.

"Good afternoon, Miss Georgina," Mr. Isaac nods toward my open door.

Georgina, my oldest, breezes in. Her hair's a new color—flaming red. It fits her features better than the chocolate brown tint she wore for the better part of a month, or maybe longer, I don't remember. Why she won't wear her natural, dusty blond shade is beyond me.

"I see you changed your hair, Georgina. Again."

"Don't start, Mother." She sighs and pecks my cheek. "Hi, Mr. Isaac. It looks like you got Mother's window all fixed up."

"Yes, ma'am. It's good and sturdy." He shuffles to the door, his left leg dragging behind him. "You two take care now."

"To what do I owe the pleasure of your visit, Georgina?"

She pulls some papers out of her enormous purse and hands them to me. "I brought you the bank statements you wanted to see."

"Oh, yes. Fetch me my glasses, will you? They're on the nightstand." I point over by the bed.

"Yes, *ma'am*," Georgina responds tartly.

"Mind your tone." I take my spectacles from her and snap the case shut. "Now, let's see. What do we have here?"

"I've told you time and again, there's nothing out of the ordinary. I'm not spending your money on anyone but you," Georgina rolls her eyes, her arms folded defensively in front of her.

"I'll be the judge of that," I say, as I peruse the documents.

"You always are," Georgina retorts. I swivel my head and shoot her my patented, icy stare.

"Sorry," she mutters. "Old habits die hard."

I scan the papers, and everything seems to be in order until I see some numbers that make me sit at attention. "What in God's name is this?"

"What?" Georgina asks, bewildered.

"This!" I tap at several entries. "Why are there four checks of seven thousand dollars each made out to Hennessy Corp?"

"Hennessy Corp *owns* Worthy Community Home, Mother," she stresses.

"So?"

"You *live* at Worthy Community Home."

"I do not! I reside at 297 West Sycamore Street in Worthy, Texas, 76042. I have owned that property since 1979."

Georgina exhales deeply. "Mother, you don't live there anymore."

"That is not true! How dare you lie to me! I knew it. I just knew it. You're in cahoots with this Hennessy Corp, aren't you, Georgina? Stealing my money right from under me! I won't have it, I tell you. I won't have it!"

I hurl the documents back at her.

"What's all the ruckus in here, Miss Margaret?" A short, stocky Black woman barrels into the room. She seems to know who I am, but for the life of me, I don't recognize her.

"Mother's been reviewing her bank statements, Clementine." Georgina chimes in.

"And my daughter's been stealing me blind. It's highway robbery, I tell you. Highway robbery," I shout.

"Why don't we all just calm down? Cooler heads make better choices, I always say," the plump Black lady replies.

"I can't stand to look at her. I want her out! Get out!" I swing my arms at Georgina, ready to knock some sense into her.

"It might be best if you leave now, Miss Georgina," the nurse lady advises, holding me back.

Georgina shrugs, "Whatever you think is best, Clementine." She gathers the papers on the floor and leaves them on my bed.

"I'll see you Saturday, Mother," Georgina calls from the doorway.

"Out," I screech.

"All right now, Miss Margaret. All right," the nice lady soothes as she wraps her arms around me, and we rock to and fro. "Everything's okay."

"Georgina says I don't live on West Sycamore Street anymore."

She pulls away from me and takes my hands in hers. "No, Miss Margaret, you don't. You live here at Worthy Community Home. You have for eighteen months now."

"So those expenditures. They were genuine?" I wonder.

"Yes, ma'am. Hennessy Corp owns this facility."

"And you're Clementine. You help me?" I ask, my voice small and fragile.

"That I do. Every day. Say, I've got a 100 Grand chocolate bar in my pocket. What do you say we split it?" Clementine offers.

"I don't know," I answer skeptically. "The doctor lady that comes around says I should watch my sweets."

"Mama Pearl won't mind. Besides, a little sugar never hurt nobody. Especially after the day you've had."

Clementine loosens the wrapper and hands me half.

"Thank you," I say as she pats my knee and turns to go. "Clementine? Could you stay? Just until I finish my treat."

"You bet I will. It'll give me a chance to finish *my* half," she winks at me and smiles.

Clementine's presence is soothing, and I'm entirely grateful to her. Because sometimes, especially when I'm alone, I believe I may be losing my mind.

Mrs. Hadley

Oh, my goodness. I have *got* to go. I press the call button to the nurses' station again, but there's still no answer. I imagine they're down in that lady's room where all the commotion is coming from; Madeline, Margaret, Marjoram. Not marjoram—that's a spice. No matter her name, I suppose. She's the kind of person who sucks all the air out of a place and makes everything about her. So, it could be a while.

I don't usually need help getting to the bathroom, mind you. No sir, I'm pretty self-sufficient when my walker is close by. I suspect somebody must have moved it away from my bed while I was napping, and I don't want to risk walking that far since I'm not too steady on my feet. As such, I find myself in this predicament: reliant on another human being to complete a bodily function. It's demeaning.

Fact is, I don't belong here. I'm not afflicted with any memory problems to speak of; management just doesn't have anywhere else to put me. They moved me to this floor three days after my James passed. Said they needed our apartment for another couple moving in. I don't know what they did with all our furniture and knickknacks. I don't guess it matters much anymore.

My James and I were married sixty-two years. One Monday night, not but two months ago, I rolled over and gave him a kiss goodnight, then rolled back over the next day to whisper good morning, and he was gone.

James was my family. I got no one else, except for a couple of second cousins in Missouri and Illinois, but we're not close. I would sometimes get a card from them at Christmastime, but that hasn't happened in years. I'm not even sure I've got their addresses anymore.

As I said, I don't belong here. Truth is, I don't belong anywhere.

I press the call button again, with less urgency now. The deed is done; I couldn't hold it any longer. My humiliation is complete.

The yelling and carrying-on from down the hall has settled down, and I see Mr. Isaac in the hallway, unlocking the door to a closet.

"Mr. Isaac? Mr. Isaac?" I call.

He turns and limps into my room. "Afternoon, Mrs. Hadley. What can I do you for?"

"Would you be so kind and fetch Clementine for me?"

"I surely will. Is there anything I can help you with?" He offers.

"No, no. Just Clementine, if she's not too busy," I respond.

"I'll go get her right now," Mr. Isaac nods and smiles.

"Thank you," I call after him.

A few moments later, Clementine steps into my room. "Hi, Mrs. Hadley. Mr. Isaac said you asked for me."

"I'm sorry, Clementine. But it seems I've soiled myself," I whisper, as tears prick my eyes.

Clementine pulls my walker close to the bed. "Someone put this too far away, I see. I'll notify the others to make sure it's always next to you."

I nod, and then my sobs overtake me.

"It's okay, Mrs. Hadley. It truly is," Clementine soothes. "It's me and my staff's mistake. We were so busy, there was no one at the nurses' station to help you."

"I understand," I sniffle.

"Say, I see you finished the book you were working on," Clementine points to my nightstand. "I just got done reading *Forbidden Ardor* and let me tell you, it's good! After we get through here, I'll go and grab it for you. What do you think?"

"I'd be much obliged. I just love a good novel." I wipe away my tears.

"Me, too. And I've got a whole stack of romance novels at home. Would you like me to bring some by tomorrow?" Clementine offers.

"Yes, please. Since my James died, time hangs so heavy. I don't know what to do with myself."

"I understand, but don't you fret. I'm going to make it a point to drop by more often and check in on you. That's a promise. Now, let's get you cleaned up, okay?" Clementine smiles and pulls my walker to the edge of the bed.

"Thank you, Clementine. I get mighty lonesome at times."

"I aim to make a dent in that, Mrs. Hadley."

As I get on my feet, a surge of hopefulness runs through me, something that hasn't happened since James passed. It's a tricky thing: hope. Too much or too little of it can ruin a person. But it sure feels good to have some.

Cleo

It's eleven thirty-seven in the a.m., and Jonathan's been in with Ingram for exactly four minutes and twenty-eight seconds. Yes—I'm counting. Once he's done, I'll be the next, and last, member of the VR team to meet with our new boss. There's nothing like bringing up the rear to know your place in the pecking order.

It took no time at all for Quinn and the rest of the Bro Club to welcome Ingram into the fold. Heck, it's been just ten days since Ingram joined Deep Well and he's already a card-carrying club member, going to lunches and happy hours with the boys on the regular, with nary an invite for Jonathan and me. If it wasn't clear before where we fit in the VR food chain, it surely is now. So much for being a "team."

Jonathan wanders into our cubicle at the five-minute, eighteen-second mark, his gaze cast downward, and grabs a cup of ramen from his desk.

"How'd it go?"

He shrugs and ambles toward the break room. As usual, Jonathan's a man of few words, so I won't be blessed with any insights from him.

My laptop pings and a direct message appears: Ready for our one-on-one. I drain the rest of my Yoo-hoo and give my hands a good swipe with my trusty washcloth. Here goes nothing.

Ingram's door is slightly ajar, but before I can knock, he commands me to enter. I step inside his office and take a quick look around. His decorating scheme, such that it is, is what you might call "minimalist," with only a desk and two chairs occupying the very spacious room. Nothing more. Like Mama says, to each their own.

Without speaking, Ingram points for me to sit down while he peruses what appears to be my resume. After a few more agonizing moments, he looks up and exhales a long, deep sigh.

"You didn't attend college?" he asks.

"No sir. I earned all my programming certifications in high school. I felt college wasn't necessary for me to do what I like doing," I respond proudly.

"Huh. Interesting," Ingram replies drolly. "There's more to college than a degree, Cleo. I happen to value the networking and relationships I formed there. They've served me well over the years."

"I network here at Next Well just fine," I retort.

"Whatever works for you, I guess," Ingram says dismissively. "There's not much to your CV, is there?"

"I'm sorry?"

"You don't have a lot of work experience," he replies, cutting to the chase.

"I spent three years in Internet Security, eighteen months of that I was team lead," I counter, a bit defensively.

"But nothing in VR. Quite frankly, Cleo, I'm surprised you were hired for this position."

Ouch. That cut to the bone.

"Mr. Boseman seemed to think I have good coding and leadership skills. He said so himself," I reply stiffly.

"Mr. Boseman isn't your manager anymore. I am." Ingram settles back in his chair, "Why don't you share with me your brainstorming ideas."

"I thought the deadline was next Wednesday?"

"It is, but you have my attention now."

"I prefer waiting till then." My hands are performing their waterworks, so I wipe them surreptitiously along the sides of my skirt.

"Your hesitancy makes me think you haven't come up with anything."

"I don't want to waste your time with something rough, Ingram. Good things come to those who wait." I grin to lighten the mood.

Nonplussed, he stares at me for what seems like a good, long minute. I guess he doesn't have a sense of humor—or an appreciation for idioms.

"Cleo, we need to discuss your appearance."

"My appearance?"

"Your hair, specifically. It's not professional."

"My hair ain't professional?" I self-consciously touch my frizzed ends.

"Not in my view. And your word choice. 'Ain't', for example, isn't what I would consider business-appropriate language. Would you?"

"I suppose not. You know, there *is* such a thing as political correctness, Ingram. I wonder what Human Resources would have to say about your suggestions," I mutter sharply.

Ingram leans in, his gaze dark and menacing. "It's your word against mine. Who do you think HR would believe? I'm not going to tell you what to do. Your hairstyle and vocabulary are ultimately your decision. But some details are just as important as hard skills, Cleo. Do we understand each other?"

"Yes, sir."

"Good. We're done." He dismisses me with a wave of his hand, then turns his attention to his laptop.

My mind is reeling, so I head straight to the break room in search of my lunch—Mama's delectable chili. Comfort food is always the cure when I'm feeling low, or, as in this case, utterly degraded by my boss. Mama always makes sure my refrigerator is stocked with her home cooking, and at a time like this, I am forever grateful.

Just as I'm about to dig in, I stop myself, grab an extra plate and fork, and head back to my cubicle. I find Jonathan hunched over his laptop with his back to me, shoveling and slurping noodles with reckless abandon.

"Jonathan, do you like chili?"

He cranes his neck toward me and shrugs.

"You can't live on ramen alone. Come on, try it." I dish some out and hand him a fork. He takes a small, tentative bite, like I might be trying to poison him, and chews thoughtfully. He scoops another mouthful, this time with more gusto.

"This is good," he says with a grin. Till now, I wasn't sure he had teeth.

"Have some more." I serve him another helping and sit down across from him. We share our meal in cordial silence, chewing and savoring Mama's scrumptious cooking, when I decide to thaw some of the ice between us.

"Word is, Quinn and his posse are all going in on one, big brainstorming idea," I say casually.

"Uh-huh," Jonathan takes another forkful.

"It appears we're on the outside looking in. Have you come up with anything yet?"

"I'm a programmer," he replies evenly.

"Whatcha been working on recently?" I ask, struggling to continue our fading dialogue.

"I'm creating a VR simulation where the people and landscapes look real, not cartoonish. What about you?"

"I've been inventorying all the junk we've got lying around here. Did you know we've got thirty VR goggles just strewn about on this floor? What a waste. You'd figure they could be put to some kind of use."

Jonathan shrugs as he wipes his mouth. "That was the best chili I've ever eaten, Cleo. Thank you."

"There's more where that came from. I'll try to bring enough for two when I can. Mama'll be tickled you enjoyed her cooking."

Jonathan nods then turns his back to me, and an awkward hush settles between us. Suddenly, it hits me like a bolt of lightning, as clear as day.

"Jonathan, the simulation you're working on, how close is it to the testing phase?" I wonder.

"By next week," he replies, still facing away from me.

"Will it interface with older VR goggles?"

"It should."

"I've just had an epiphany. Want to hear it?"

Jonathan turns around, his head cocked to the side, "I'm listening."

It's finally the weekend, thank the Lord Jesus, and I'm a woman on a mission. I make the hour's long trek to Worthy and pull in front of The Weave Queen, one of Auntie Ella's salons.

Unless there's an illness or death in the family, every Saturday morning Mama, Miss Clementine, and Miss Ida Mae Browning gather with Auntie Ella for a meeting of the Hen Brigade, as they refer to themselves, to catch up and discuss all the gossip of the day in and around the town of Worthy.

They've been doing this for as long as I can remember, but Mama's made it a point to be more involved ever since Daddy passed some nine years ago. It gives her a chance to get out of the house and see folks socially, instead of tending to their needs. Everyone requires a little of that now and again, even if you were born with a servant's heart like Mama.

"Well, look who the wind blew in," Auntie Ella says as I enter the salon.

"Hey, y'all." Auntie Ella is putting the final touches on Miss Ida Mae's hair, while Mama and Miss Clementine are perched on styling chairs, sipping Diet Dr. Peppers.

"I was mighty surprised to see your name pop up on my client list this morning, Cleo," Auntie Ella mentions while dousing Miss Ida Mae in a cloud of hairspray.

"You didn't tell me you were coming by today, baby," Mama adds as I peck her on the cheek.

"I'm glad all y'all are here because I've got something to discuss." I grab a cold, chocolatey Yoo-hoo from the fridge then settle into Auntie Ella's styling station.

"What's on your mind, Cleo?" Miss Clementine wonders.

"First things first. Auntie Ella, I need to change my look."

"You want some off the top?" she asks, as she touches the perimeter of my puffy coif.

"No, ma'am. I want a weave. Smooth and straight."

"Cleovantra Pearl, you've worn an Afro since you were knee-high to a grasshopper," Mama exclaims.

"I know, Mama."

"You sure?" Auntie Ella looks skeptical.

"It's time for something different," I nod. "Now for the other item on the agenda: Miss Clementine, do you remember when you and Mama were talking at dinner the other night, wondering about how to keep your memory care residents occupied?"

"Yes, Lord. That's been front and center for a while now."

"Do you suppose you could get me and you a meeting with the director sometime early next week?"

"I guess so," Miss Clementine shrugs.

"Why do you want to meet with her, Cleo?" Mama asks.

"Your problem? I believe I've found the cure." I glance at Auntie Ella in the mirror's reflection. "All right, Auntie. Work your magic."

Clementine

I t ain't even ten till noon and it's already been one of those days. Most of my morning has been frittered away rounding up residents who refused to leave the outdoor space, running around the shrubbery like we were playing hide-and-seek or something. After forty-five minutes, and vanilla ice cream as a lure, Mr. Isaac and I successfully shepherded them safely inside. Mr. Isaac remarked it would have been easier herding cats than getting those three back into their rooms. I'd never thought of it that way, but he wasn't wrong. I swear every day is an adventure here at Worthy Community Home.

I steal a glance through the front lobby window, checking for Cleo's arrival and praying she won't be late. Now, don't get me wrong. I've got every confidence Cleo will be here; right on time. Truth be told, I've got a bit of a phobia about tardiness. Percy says I need to chill out and take life as it comes. Maybe so, but there's a reason God gave us clocks and watches. On occasion, I think Percy is slow to move on purpose, so we'll be late getting to where we're going just to get a rise out of me. I've never confronted him about it, but he's ornery enough I wouldn't be surprised.

Cleo comes through the main entrance, and I don't recognize her at first. Gone is her puffy Afro, and in its place is a long, jet-black silky mane, smooth and sleek like glass. Along with her new hairdo, she's sporting a dark pencil skirt and silk blouse, with a smart, professional leather attaché in tow. Not only is she beautiful, but she's all grown up. I hope we'll run into Ruth while Cleo is here so she can get a load of her daughter. Ruth will burst with pride.

"Cleo, girl, you look *amazing.*"

"Why, thank you, Miss Clementine. Are you ready?"

"Yes, ma'am," I nod.

"Let's do this," Cleo remarks confidently.

"One thing I need to warn you about our director: she's a bit...abrupt."

"I'm no stranger to that, Miss Clementine, believe you me."

I knock on the open office door. "Miss Jillian?"

Miss Jillian, Worthy Community Home's director, pops up from her chair like she's spring-loaded. "Come in. Come in," she motions.

Cleo extends her hand, "Cleo Pearl. Nice to meet you."

"Jillian Hennessey. Have a seat." Miss Jillian clears her throat. "I reviewed your email, so just give me the broad strokes."

"Sure. Clementine made me aware of some of the behavioral issues that arise on the Memory Care floor. As I noted in my email, virtual reality—VR for short—has been used by memory-challenged residents for about five years now. The typical resident uses VR goggles for entertainment, like traveling virtually to visit the Louvre for example, but research has shown that VR can be therapeutic as well..."

"Mm-hmm. Mm-hmm," Miss Jillian interjects.

"My team's focus is on the therapeutic aspect. Most folks afflicted with dementia have poor short-term memory and feel more comfortable with their long-ago memories..."

"Mm-hmm. Mm-hmm," Miss Jillian interrupts again.

"We've devised a virtual world where photographs of meaningful people and places can be uploaded and intertwined into a space where residents can interact just as they remember. But it won't feel like a memory. It will be as though they're reliving that part of their lives all over again..."

"Mm-hmm. Mm-hmm." Miss Jillian fiddles with her ballpoint pen, clickety-click, clickety-click.

"My team is in the next phase of the process, so we're needing test subjects. That's where Worthy Community Home comes in," Cleo explains.

"How many residents do you need?" Miss Jillian asks while working over her pen, clickety-click, clickety-click.

"Ideally, two to three."

"What about the others? We've got at least seven more that are chronic behavior problems." Clickety-click, clickety-click.

"Our team can support the remaining residents with entertainment software," Cleo responds confidently.

"And there will be no cost to us during the testing phase?" Miss Jillian drops her pen on the desk, thank Jesus.

"None. All we need are liability forms signed by the residents or their guardians. Then we're good to go," Cleo replies.

"Mm-hmm. Mm-hmm. How long for testing?"

"Around three to four months."

"Clementine, can you run point on this?" Miss Jillian grabs her pen again. Clickety-click. Clickety-click.

"Yes, ma'am. I'd be happy to," I agree enthusiastically.

Miss Jillian nods. "Okay, you have my approval. I hope it works," she mutters with a skeptical shrug.

You and me both, Miss Jillian. Good Lord willing.

Cleo

Ingram peers up from our proposal, glancing first at Jonathan, then me, holding my gaze for a good, long minute. "Your brainstorming idea is a nursing home?" Ingram remarks tepidly.

"It isn't a nursing home, it's an assisted living facility," I emphasize.

"Regardless, it sounds like you'll be babysitting a bunch of old people," Ingram replies dismissively.

"As Jonathan and I pointed out in our summary, elder care is a growing market in the VR industry. And although Next Well has a small market share in the entertainment section of VR, we think the therapeutic area is where most of the future growth will occur," I explain.

"I see that. It's just not very exciting. The other team members are working on a fascinating, new game..." Ingram retorts.

"It's all well and good to produce yet another *Logan's Run* meets *Blade Runner* gaming concept," I interject. "But that market is flooded, and the competition is fierce. If our idea works like we think it will, therapeutic software can create a growing source of revenue for Next Well and help some folks to boot. There's never a dearth of people growing old."

"It's *boring*," Ingram stresses.

"No idea is too small. Isn't that what you said in our first meeting?" I pointedly remind him.

Ingram sighs. "How many test subjects?"

"Ten," I offer.

"Two," he counters.

"Eight."

"Three."

"Six," I tender.

"Three, and that's final," Ingram proffers and taps his fingers on the desktop to stop the bidding.

"Three therapeutic subjects and seven entertainment VR goggles for the other residents," I clarify.

"Fine. How long?" Ingram asks.

"A seven-month testing window."

Ingram shakes his head. "Two."

"Five."

"Four months; non-negotiable."

I hesitate for a moment. "All right, Ingram. If you insist."

"Good. We're done." Ingram dismisses us with a wave of his hand and turns his attention to his laptop.

"Weren't we planning on two to three test subjects and four months of testing to begin with?" Jonathan asks as we head to our cubicle.

"Ingram's the kind of boss who has to think he's won."

"Hence the 'negotiation'?" Jonathan replies with air quotes.

"You're learning big guy," I nod and playfully punch his arm.

I knock with gusto on Brian's apartment door. It's been ten days since I've seen that dapper, tall drink of water and I'm in the throes of a love-deficit situation, if you know what I mean. Fortunately, my man has got the cure.

"Hey, baby," Brian says as he scoops me into his arms.

I give him a long, sweet kiss that makes my knees buckle.

"Dang, Cleo. I guess I should visit the San Francisco office more often," he smiles. "Hold up a minute. Let me get a good look at you." He steps back and motions for me to do a 360. "You said you made a few alterations to your look, but lordy, you're a whole new woman."

"You like?" I ask tentatively.

"You bet I do. I love your hair," Brian touches my sleek weave. "It makes you look all grown up."

"That's the point."

Brian takes my hands in his. "This isn't for your new boss, now? What's his name, Ingram?"

"Maybe a little," I shrug.

"Do I have a reason to be jealous? Should I go up to your floor tomorrow morning and bust out a can of whoop-ass on him?" Brian teases.

I swat his shoulder playfully. "No, it's nothing like that. He pointed out I need to be more professional, that's all. So, when in Rome..."

"Don't you go changing *too* much just to please him, Miss Cleo. I love you the way you are. You remember that. You hear?" Brian kisses my nose.

"I'll always remember," I say. "How is it you fell into my life?"

"Just lucky I guess," he shrugs and grins.

Serendipity sure is a mysterious thing. Whether it's what Brian imagines and it's all a matter of luck, or what I've been taught by Mama to believe that it's God's blessings in disguise, doesn't matter too much in the end, I guess. Regardless, Brian's devotion is a gift, and I'm entirely thankful.

Margaret

"What in God's name are *those*?" The short, stocky woman who tends to me—I can't recall her name just now—has brought along with her a slim, young Black girl to visit. They're both trying to convince me to wear some sort of contraption on my head that resembles bug-eyed binoculars. But I'm having none of it.

"They're virtual reality goggles, Miss Margaret. Cleo works for a company that's been nice enough to let us use these for a few months," the plump lady explains eagerly.

"Why on earth would I want to do *that*?"

"They take you to places you can't visit on your own," the youngster, Cleo, points out.

"I'm happy right here in Worthy, Texas, thank you very much."

"Afternoon, Mother." Georgina, my oldest, breezes in and pecks me on the cheek. "Sorry I'm late, Clementine."

That's her name: Clementine. I make a mental note to remember it.

"And you must be Cleo. I'm Georgina." My oldest shakes the girl's hand.

"Nice to meet you, Georgina. Clementine and I were just explaining to your mama what she can do with VR goggles."

"I'm telling you all right now. That thing is going nowhere near my head, and that is final."

"Don't you think it'd be fun to visit places you've never seen before, Miss Margaret? Or go back and revisit familiar memories?" Cleo coaxes.

"What do you mean by 'revisit memories'?" I ask, intrigued.

"Part of our program is scanning old photos that are dear to you and creating a virtual space, so you can relive those moments like you're actually there," Cleo explains.

"You sound like a snake oil salesman," I scoff.

"Miss Margaret! I keep care of you every day. You think I'd let somebody come in here and lead you astray?" Clementine chides.

"I suppose not." I think for a moment, "But I don't have any photographs here. They're all at the house."

"I can give them to Cleo," Georgina chimes in.

"No, ma'am. You will bring them here. Cleo can do whatever she has to do with them in *my presence*. No one handles those photo albums but me. Do you understand?"

"*Fine, Mother*," Georgina sasses, and I shoot her an icy glare.

"Why don't you try on the goggles and take a test run?" Cleo approaches with the headgear.

"No, thank you."

"C'mon, Miss Margaret. Cooperate with Cleo. I think you'll like it if you try it," Clementine cajoles.

"Not today," I fold my arms in front of me.

"Mother, you're always complaining about how bored you are in here. What is it you used to say to me and Lacey? 'Boredom is for silly whiners. Make your life interesting'."

"Don't you quote myself to me," I snap.

"Are you going to complain, or do something about it?" Georgina prods.

"Speaking of Lacey, when will my youngest see fit to come around for a visit, hmm?" Georgina and Clementine exchange glances. "What? What was that look for?"

"Things didn't go well the last time Lacey was here," Georgina mutters.

"Nonsense. We had a nice time."

"You two had an argument. Don't you remember?"

I shake my head.

Georgina chews her lip. "You said some things to Lacey that were hurtful."

"Like what?"

"You told Lacey that..." Georgina hesitates, "you wished she'd never been born." Georgina looks down at her shoes like a kid caught with their hand in the cookie jar.

"Huh. Well. Surely, she knows I don't mean it when I pop off like that." I search Georgina's face for reassurance, but she's got none to give. "I tell you what. I'll try on this newfangled gadget if you speak to Lacey for me; get her to come back?"

Georgina nods slowly. "I'll talk to her. I can't promise anything, though."

I clap my palms together. "Alright, Cleo. Hand me that gizmo."

"Yes, ma'am." Cleo passes me the goggles.

"If I should begin to die, please take these off me," I instruct.

Clementine and Cleo fiddle with the headset and get me strapped into it. Cleo gives me two controllers, one for each hand, and shows me how to move.

"Where do you want to visit today, Miss Margaret?" Cleo asks.

"Can I go anywhere?"

"Just about."

"Paris. I'd like Paris, please."

"The Louvre, a sidewalk café, somewhere else?" Cleo offers.

"Ooh, a sidewalk café. My daddy took me to Paris when I was sixteen years of age and I just loved sitting, drinking coffee in those little cups, and watching the world go by," I respond gleefully.

"I never knew you and Granddaddy traveled to Paris."

"Child, there's a lot about me you don't know."

"Okay, Miss Margaret. I'm going to turn on your viewer," Cleo alerts me as she taps on her computer. "You should be in the café setting now."

Suddenly, there I am, seated at a small table facing the street. The colors wash over me and sounds fill the air.

"Oh, yes. This is marvelous." I move my left arm and see it move in the space. I do the same with my right hand and grasp the coffee cup on the table in front of me.

"Do you want me to join you, Miss Margaret, and show you around for a bit?" Cleo asks.

No, no. I'm fine. I prefer to be alone, thank you."

"I guess I'll be going then, Mother," Georgina calls.

"Good. You go. All of you leave me be. I've got some exploring to do."

Mrs. Hadley

"How have your hips been feeling, Mrs. Hadley?" Mama Pearl gently rocks my knees to test their range of motion.

"Oh, they're a little sore. Especially the left one."

"What about nerve pain?" She helps me sit up in bed.

"It keeps me up every now and again."

"I'll increase your medication," Mama Pearl offers.

"It's all right. I don't want to be a bother."

"Irene Hadley, you are never a bother. Fact is, you're one of my best patients," Mama Pearl grins and pats my arm.

"You know, I was just thinking. How long have you been looking after me, Ruth? Fifteen years?"

"About that long. Let's see. I started at the clinic in 2008, back when I got my nurse practitioner's license, so yes, fifteen years. Time sure does fly. It seems like just yesterday I was working alongside old Doc Bradley," Mama Pearl reminisces.

"Do you find it hard shuffling between here and Heaven's Door?" I wonder.

"It's not too bad. Several of my long-time patients live here at the Home, so it saves them from having to get over to the clinic."

I have what I believe is a vested interest in Mama Pearl's non-profit, Heaven's Door. Four years ago, when the free clinic closed in Worthy, Mama Pearl bought James' and my little house and opened her own practice to serve the poor, raising the grant money herself so she and her patients wouldn't be subject to the whims of city council purse strings. Even though James and I were moving here to Worthy Community Home anyhow and needed to vacate, Mama Pearl matched the highest offer we received for our small, humble home, understanding that assisted living is expensive, and we had to watch our pennies. James and I were mighty glad someone we knew took ownership. It made the transition here less painful knowing our house was being put to good use and not just another rental property.

"Knock, knock. I have a visitor for you, Mrs. Hadley," Clementine calls from the hallway.

Cleo cranes her head around the door frame. "Hey, Mrs. Hadley."

"Cleovantra Pearl! Come over here and give me a hug," I open my arms as wide as they'll go.

"How've you been, Mrs. H?"

"I'm getting along fine, thanks to Clementine and your sweet mama."

"Are your hugs for residents only, or can mothers get one, too?" Mama Pearl asks.

"Sorry, Mama." Cleo grabs Ruth and rocks her to-and-fro while raining kisses on her cheeks.

"Okay, okay. That'll do, Cleo. I best be going, Mrs. Hadley. I've got more patients to see. I'll update your dosage before I leave today." Mama Pearl squeezes my shoulder, then turns to Cleo, "You be a good girl now."

"Always, Mama," Cleo grins, then pulls up a chair next to my bed. "Mrs. Hadley, Clementine tells me that time hangs pretty heavy in here for you. Is that so?"

"Well, yes. Since my James passed, I find most of what I do is sleep. Clementine's been nice enough to loan me books to read, but my eyes get tired, and I doze off."

"The company I work for is testing a new virtual reality concept. We scan photos that are dear to you and create a virtual space, so you can relive those moments again. We use these." Cleo pulls a headset out of her bag, "They're goggles to help you get around in there."

"Goodness. I've never heard of such a thing. But I don't know if I'll be of much help to you, Cleo. You see, I don't know where my photographs are. They didn't make it with me when I moved to this room."

"That was true, up until this morning." Clementine pulls a plastic baggie from her smock. "I found these in one of the storage rooms."

I open the bag and discover several old photos. "Why, these are from when James and I were first married. I haven't seen them in years."

"Right now, the other resident taking part in our testing is a dementia patient. If you participate, we'll use your time in the virtual space for comparison. We call it a 'control.'"

"Oh, my. That sounds important."

It's a crucial piece of our program, Mrs. Hadley. What do you say? Would you like to take the VR world for a spin?"

"Sure," I giggle. "To tell you the truth, I'm kind of excited about this."

"That's what we want to hear," Clementine grins.

"Where would you like to visit today? You can go to a museum, or visit a park?" Cleo offers.

"Either one of those is fine, I suppose."

"We have a sports model, too. There's bowling, golf..."

"Basketball?" I wonder.

"Yes, ma'am, there's basketball. Does that sound appealing to you?"

"Oh, yes. Growing up, I used to play basketball all the time. I even made the All-District team in high school. That was back when there were six girls per team on the court; three on offense and three on defense, and you couldn't pass the mid-court line. When the girls on defense got a rebound, they'd throw the ball all the way to the other end of the court. And there I'd be, standing right under the basket for an easy layup. Of course, it helped I was tall."

"Basketball it is, then. Let me get you set up." Cleo secures the headset and places two controllers in my hands.

"Do you see the basketball court, Mrs. Hadley?" I hear Cleo peck away on her computer.

"Yes," I nod.

"Okay. To walk, pump your arms up and down, like you're power walking. If you want to run, you move them faster."

I do as Cleo says, and sure enough, I'm gliding around the court until I bang into a wall.

"Oops."

"Tilt your torso left or right, whichever way you want to go," Cleo suggests.

I angle my body, slowly at first, jogging back and forth from one end to the other, until I get the hang of it.

"Why don't you go over to the ball rack and pick one up," Cleo instructs.

I lean over and grab a basketball like it's right in front of me. "Amazing."

"Great. Now, make a dribbling motion with your right hand, and continue pumping your left arm."

"I'm running down the court dribbling a basketball!" I shout in disbelief.

"To shoot the ball, stop pumping your arm, and try to make a basket just like you would in a game," Cleo directs.

I pull up next to the basketball goal and bank the ball off the glass.

"I scored! I scored!" I squeal with delight.

"Everything all right in here? Sounded like screaming going on," I hear Mr. Isaac ask.

"Things are just fine, Mr. Isaac," I assure him.

They're just fine.

Clementine

I f you had told me six months ago—shoot, even two weeks ago—I'd be supervising ten residents in the VR stratosphere, well, I would've handed you a cold washcloth and advised you to lie down for a while. But here I am. Life's funny that way, I guess.

This first day has gone off without a hitch, thank you, Jesus. Eight of our residents wandered around different museums, oohing and aahing at the sights. Most of them were so exhausted from their "travels," that they napped afterward or were content to just read or watch TV. A far cry from the usual afternoon escapades around here, that's for sure.

To keep tabs on them, Cleo showed me how to observe the various entertainment spaces without the residents knowing it. I've got to admit, walking around in a make-believe place like it's the real thing looks kind of fun. Maybe I'll take it for a whirl myself when I get the chance.

It was mighty fortuitous Cleo's VR experiment began this afternoon because Percy's last postal route is today and I'm fixing to cut out early to surprise him with a scrumptious, celebratory dinner. Of course, when I stopped by the store this morning before work, I had to fan myself to keep from fainting while the checkout clerk rang up my groceries. Steak was almost ten dollars a pound. And Percy's favorite beer? Twelve dollars for a little old six-pack. The total for seven items: sixty-seven dollars and thirteen cents. Lord have mercy, but inflation sure does trample your wallet.

I've been so busy, what with the VR implementation and all, I haven't had time to write down my expenditures for the day. I like to do it when no one's around, which is a rarity on this floor, because, truth be told, the other nurses tease me about it. See, I have a tiny notebook in my pocket and carry it wherever I go, so I can keep account of my spending. It don't matter how small the purchase is, I jot it down. The other ladies think it's funny I record every single thing, so I'm skittish about doing it when they're nearby. But it helps me watch our pennies, and with Percy being such a spendthrift, it makes me feel more in control. It drives him crazy, though. I guess that's what marriage is all about—putting up with your spouse's peculiarities.

Since Mrs. Hadley and Miss Margaret are part of Cleo's actual testing, she asked for them to spend longer in the VR space so they could get accustomed to it. I snap on my VR headset in Mrs. Hadley's room and see her practicing free throws.

"How's the shooting coming along, Mrs. Hadley?"

The ball clanks off the rim. "I was always cursed at the free throw line."

"You've been at it quite a while. Ready to call it a day?"

"Can I come back again tomorrow?" Mrs. Hadley asks gleefully.

"I don't know why not. Cleo may have other plans, but I'm sure we can make time for you to get a little practice in." I place my hands on her shoulders, "All right. I'm going to remove your goggles now."

Mrs. Hadley blinks. "Ooh, my eyes are foggy."

"Cleo said it might take a bit for your vision to adjust," I explain as I take off my headset.

"That was amazing. Who would've thought, an old lady like me, with a walker no less, playing basketball!"

"There'll be more where that came from. You want me to fetch you a book to read before I go?" I ask.

"No, no. I'm going to rest awhile I think," Mrs. Hadley says as I pull a blanket over her. "Thank you, Clementine," she mumbles and dozes off.

I enter Miss Margaret's virtual space and there she is, still seated at a little café table in Paris. "Miss Margaret? It's time to go."

She shakes her head. "I'm not leaving."

"Miss Margaret, you've been in here for over two hours. Cleo said you shouldn't stay any longer than that."

"I don't care. I'm not going anywhere," she folds her arms defiantly.

I reach out and grasp her forearm. "C'mon, Miss Margaret. It's almost dinner time. Let's get on back. It's Taco Tuesday tonight; your favorite."

Miss Margaret yanks away from my grip. "You'll have to catch me first," she retorts and takes off running down the street.

"Miss Margaret! Miss Margaret! Get back here!"

She veers around cars and pedestrians in the street while I crash into a trash can and some tables trying to follow her; moving in here is much harder than it looks.

Miss Margaret turns to see if I'm behind her, then cuts into an alleyway.

I pump my arms faster and get the hang of tilting my body so I can navigate obstacles. I turn into the alley and gain on her when Miss Margaret suddenly stops: it's a dead-end.

"Please don't make me leave," she begs, her face overcome with despair.

"We've got to, Miss Margaret," I say, huffing and puffing.

"I don't like it there." Her voice quivers, "I can't remember who I am."

"I know, Miss Margaret. I know." I wrap my arm around her. "We'll come back here tomorrow. I promise."

"You're not just saying that to get me to leave, are you?"

"No, ma'am. I wouldn't do that to you."

Miss Margaret exhales deeply and wipes her eyes, "Oh, all right. You win."

"Good." I remove our headsets. "Say, I happen to have a 100 Grand chocolate bar in my pocket. Want half?"

She nods. "But that doctor lady says I should watch my sweets."

"Mama Pearl won't mind. A little sugar never hurt nobody."

I rush home, pushing the speed limit, since I'm running late after my detour in the virtual world with Miss Margaret.

"Percy? Percy? You home?" I call as I turn on the kitchen lights.

Taped to the refrigerator door is a note:

You weren't here. Went out with the boys to celebrate my last day.

P.

I sigh, grab a frozen dinner from the freezer, and pop it into the microwave. Another night spent in front of the TV: the story of my marriage.

Cleo

"Then Miss Margaret took off running down the street," Miss Clementine flails her arms as she reenacts her virtual misadventure from the previous afternoon. "I was able to catch up with her—after a spell mind you—but I sure hope that don't become a habit. It was almost as bad as what she does out here for real," Miss Clementine huffs.

"Did you try turning off Miss Margaret's headset?" I ask gently.

Miss Clementine stops mid-motion and mulls over the question. "Hmm. Well. Truth be told, it never occurred to me."

"You've always got that option if Miss Margaret becomes a handful, or any of the residents for that matter."

"Won't it be harmful to them?"

"It might be disorienting, but it'll stop them from getting more agitated in the VR space."

"Miss Margaret sure didn't want to leave, I tell you that."

"That's good and bad, I guess. From now on, I'll be with you two in there, Miss Clementine. You won't be alone again with her, I promise." I give her a big, old bear hug to seal the deal.

"It's no matter. I shouldn't complain. I think this VR stuff will make my life around here a whole lot easier in the long run."

"Is Miss Margaret in her room?" I wonder.

"Buried in pictures," Miss Clementine quips.

"Say a prayer for me," I reply as I take off down the hall.

Sure enough, Miss Margaret is seated in front of a table piled high with photo albums.

"Hey, Miss Margaret. How're you this bright, sunny morning?"

Miss Margaret looks up from the snapshots on her lap and stares at me like she doesn't know me from Adam.

"I'm Cleo Pearl, ma'am. I'm here to help you relive your memories. I see you've got plenty of pictures to choose from."

"That I do," she responds, then returns her gaze to the album.

"Mind if I join you?"

She nods to a nearby chair, "Pull up a seat."

I settle in close to her and see that this particular group must be from long ago since all of the images are Polaroid.

"Is this you, Miss Margaret?"

"Yes, that's me at my high school graduation."

"Look at your red hair!" I exclaim.

"I hated that color. I didn't like being different. The blondes always got the boys. I learned quickly that peroxide is a redhead's best friend."

"Are these your people?" I point to the various folks surrounding her.

"This is my daddy, Braxton Worthington; that's my sister, Magnolia, and her husband, Ashby..."

"I didn't know Miss Magnolia was your sister. She was a mighty fine lady. If it wasn't for her generous donation, my mama's health clinic would've never gotten off the ground."

"Magnolia was always a benevolent soul, especially with Daddy's money," Miss Margaret sniffs.

"I worked for her daughter, Chastity Lynn, for a bit while I was in high school," I offer.

"I've never met Magnolia's daughter," Miss Margaret mutters softly and turns the page.

My, oh, my. There's a story there, I'm sure.

"Here it is," she taps a picture. "I loved this old house. It was the cutest little thing you ever saw. Daddy bought it for me right after I flunked out of college," Miss Margaret reminisces.

"It's adorable; shaped just like a gingerbread house," I remark.

Miss Margaret nods. "That's what I called it; my gingerbread house. And there's my car out front. A 1970 red Corvette. Daddy bought it at cost from his dealership. I didn't want anything prissy like the other girls in town, so I asked him for an automobile with some flair. I'd say he did me proud."

"Yes, ma'am. I can imagine you zipping around town in that."

"Such fun I had back then," she muses.

"Would you like to begin there, Miss Margaret?"

She claps her hands excitedly. "Oh, yes. As quickly as I can."

"If you'll hand me the picture, I'll scan it. And in a few minutes, you'll be on your way."

Margaret

pring, 1970

S My living room's the same. Nothing's changed. My canary yellow sofa, the sunburst clock hanging above it, the huge color console TV in the corner that weighed more than me, and the swirly green shag rugs to tie the room together since Daddy was of the mind hardwood floors were a better investment than wall-to-wall carpeting; he was right, of course. It's all here. Just like it ever was.

I reach out and touch the rainbow-colored afghan Mama crocheted for me before she died. It's so soft and plush. I rub it along my face and breathe in the scents. It still smells like her. The memory I'm now in is so much richer than the little café I visited yesterday; fully developed, three-dimensional. Don't misunderstand, anything is better than the hell on earth I'm currently living through, even a cartoon cutout resembling Paris. But this space—this is the real thing. At least it feels like it, anyway.

The front door opens, and I'll be, Daddy walks in laden with groceries.

"Daddy!" I holler and throw my arms around him.

"Good Lord, girl. I can't keep hold of these sacks with you slobbering all over me," he cries as I shower his cheeks with kisses.

"What's gotten into you? You're acting like you haven't seen me in a blue moon. You do something I need to know about?" Daddy bends his head and peers skeptically over his glasses.

"Can't I be happy you're here without there being a crisis?" I grab the groceries and set them in my avocado green kitchen.

"Maybe so, but I know you, Margaret. Everything all right?"

I take his hand, "Things are more than fine. C'mon and sit for a spell."

Daddy pulls out a handkerchief and wipes his brow. "It may only be April, but it sure is warm outside."

"Is it the weather, or could it be you've packed on a few pounds?" I poke his belly playfully.

He lightly taps my hand. "Behave now. We've got an item of importance to discuss."

"Yes sir," I salute and tuck my legs under me on the sofa. "What is this 'item of importance' you speak of?" I mimic his tone.

"I'm going to cut right to the chase: Magnolia's nanny quit on her today, so I want you to watch Billy while she's working down at the dealership."

"Daddy, I don't want to be a babysitter. That's all I've ever done. Can't you help Magnolia find somebody else to look after Billy? What about Clarice?"

"Clarice is *my* housekeeper. Her job is to tend to me. Besides, she's too old to watch a four-year-old."

"How about this? Why doesn't Magnolia stay home with Billy, and I take her job at the dealership?"

"Can you do bookkeeping?" Daddy asks pointedly.

"Well, no."

"Can you type?"

I peer at the floor and shake my head.

"That's what I thought."

"But I can learn," I say emphatically as I jump to my feet.

"Come here, child." Daddy beckons me and I fold into his lap.

"You watch Billy for six months, and we'll see about getting you a position at the dealership."

"Why do I have to wait?" I whine.

"You need to prove to me you can handle responsibility. Your track record hasn't been exactly stellar in that regard." He gives me a knowing glance.

"But Daddy..."

"Margaret, that's final."

I nod dejectedly, understanding that our discussion is finished.

"You are a stubborn old man, Braxton Worthington."

"And you are a maddening, yet decorative creature, Margaret Anne Worthington," Daddy says as he kisses my forehead.

The doorbell rings and I jump up from his lap.

"You expecting company?" Daddy wonders.

There on the stoop stands the most beautiful man I have ever laid eyes on, Ashby Brooks, Magnolia's husband.

"Hello, Ashby. To what do I owe the pleasure of you gracing my doorstep?" I can't help but blush.

Ashby peers around me. "Is Braxton here? It's urgent I speak with him."

"Please come in," I say brightly and move aside.

"Magnolia said your telephone hasn't been installed yet, or I would've called," he offers, as his delicious cologne wafts through the air.

"What can I do you for, Ashby?" Daddy asks.

"Mr. Johnson is threatening to back out of our deal if we don't throw in flowered floor mats," Ashby explains.

"Flowered floor mats? In a Cadillac DeVille?"

Ashby shrugs. "The wife wants them."

"Does Cadillac even *make* flowered floor mats?"

"I've never heard of them. I tried explaining it to Mr. Johnson..." Ashby begins, but Daddy waves him off.

"Let's get back. I can't afford for that sale to go south." Daddy gives my forehead a peck, "You be a good girl now, you hear?"

They leave me standing in my living room, without so much as a 'goodbye' from Ashby. It kills me he won't pay me any mind. To him, I'm just Magnolia's little sister; I'm not a woman yet.

I go into the kitchen and begin emptying the grocery bags. Daddy left my list on the top of the counter, and I notice 'Peroxide' written among the sundry items. I dig through the sacks and, sure enough, I find it.

I wrap a tea towel around my neck and stick my head under the faucet. To some, diamonds are a girl's best friend. But I beg to differ. To this flaming redhead, peroxide is worth its weight in blonde.

Mrs. Hadley

Seeing as though I've only got four photographs to choose from, Cleo and I thought it a good idea to upload all of them and see where my mind takes me. Clementine scoured the remaining storage rooms in hopes of finding more of my past, but there was nothing to be found. It's as if my pictorial history just vanished into thin air; poof—without a trace. Or, more likely, my keepsakes were thrown away by a careless moving crew. Either way, we're making the best of what we've got.

Cleo adjusts my headset. "You ready Mrs. Hadley?"

I sit up straighter and roll my shoulders. "As ready as I'll ever be."

"Here we go," Cleo says and her voice drifts away.

I look to my left. There he is; my James. But not like he was those last months when his health was failing. He's young now; vibrant, alive. What my father would call "a strapping young man" back in the day.

We're driving along a highway somewhere, the trees just beginning to change colors to red, orange, and yellow.

"What day is this?" I ask.

"Friday," James answers evenly, his eyes on the road.

"The *date*?" I emphasize.

"October 2, 1960," he replies.

I reach out and touch his shoulder, gingerly at first, testing to see if he's real. Satisfied with my senses, I run my hand along his forearm, stroking the fine, dark hairs that grace him.

"That's feels mighty nice. We've got about ten more minutes before we get to Dayton, though, so bottle that craving you got, and we'll uncork it later." James glances my way and winks.

His small gesture makes my heart ache, and tears well in my eyes, pricking my cheeks. It's harder than I thought to be close to him, knowing he's no longer living.

"Irene? What's the matter? Why're you crying?"

"Just happy is all," I smile bittersweetly and hastily wipe my face.

"Me, too." James takes my hand, caressing my fingers with his thumb. "You missing Texas? My mama warned me it can be tough on a newly married woman leaving home for the first time."

I shake my head, "It's nothing like that."

"You sure? We're beginning our lives together: a new state, a new job, a fresh start. But it ain't worth nothing if you're heartsick, honey."

"I'm fine, James. Really." I squeeze his hand reassuringly.

"Good," James nods his head, "because we're here. Wright-Patterson Air Force Base."

My eyes widen and I watch in awe as we pass enormous transport planes parked on the tarmac, dark gray and imposing, with pallets upon pallets of equipment waiting to be loaded.

James points to a group of hangers. "That's where I'll be. Hanger ten. Supposed to be the best group of mechanics there is."

"Is that because you'll be working there?" I tease.

"You know it," James chuckles and stops the car. "Well, this is it. Home sweet home."

I peer at the little house that resembles more of a shack than the proper home I grew up in, its red paint peeling, and the yard overgrown with weeds.

"It isn't much to look at I'm afraid," James speaks aloud what I'm thinking. "It *does* have indoor plumbing, so it's got that going for it."

"Wonders never cease," I chuckle.

"C'mon woman. Let's christen this place right." James picks me up and carries me to the front stoop.

"Put me down!" I giggle as he lugs me over the threshold.

As we enter, my perspective changes and I'm no longer wearing the same white blouse and blue slacks as earlier, but a yellow gingham dress and heels. I'm standing in the small kitchen spooning coffee grounds into a percolator.

"Irene, we're going to be late," James calls to me.

I shake my head, struggling to get my bearings. "Don't you want coffee?"

"No time for that. Let's get moving."

I step into the tiny living room and James is waiting by the front door in his mechanic's uniform. Even in coveralls, that man is a sight for sore eyes. I kiss him long and slow like I'm never going to stop.

James drags his lips away. "Hey, now. We best not start something we don't have time to finish. You look beautiful, by the way. There ain't no way General Phillips' wife won't want to hire you."

"What's this job for again?" I ask as we get in the car.

"Housekeeping, cooking. Like you've done before."

We leave the base and turn onto a tree-lined street with huge, dignified homes, mansions really, on either side. James pulls up to one at the end of a cul-de-sac.

"Here we are," he puts the car into park. "Like I said, her name is Mrs. Phillips. And don't you worry. You're going to do great."

Pangs of sorrow and longing run through me. I grab his shoulders and give him an urgent kiss goodbye.

"What's up with you?" James smiles skeptically, shaking his head.

"Just something to remember you by," I reply ruefully.

I shrug and open the car door. My heart sinks as I watch him drive away, then I begrudgingly trudge up the steps and ring the front doorbell. Moments later, a petite, slender woman appears, wearing a navy A-line dress and pearls, the spitting image of Jackie Kennedy.

"Are you Irene?" she asks with a pleasant smile.

"Yes, ma'am. I'm here about the housekeeping job."

"I'm Mrs. Phillips. Please, come in." I follow her through the foyer into the living room, with its matching floral chintz sofa and chairs, the dark wood floors so buffed and shiny you can see your reflection.

"Have a seat," Mrs. Phillips directs. A tea set rests on a nearby coffee table, and she pours two cups, handing one to me. "So, Irene. How long have you been in Dayton?"

"Two days."

"I understand you're newly married," Mrs. Phillips says as she sits on the sofa across from me.

"Yes, ma'am," I nod.

"If you don't mind me asking, how old are you?" Mrs. Phillips drops a sugar cube into her teacup.

"I turned eighteen last month, ma'am."

"Have you ever been to Ohio before?"

"To be honest, I've never been *anywhere* before." I fiddle with the handle of my cup.

"I see. That must be difficult; a new marriage, a new home. Tell me, Irene. Do you have any experience with cooking and cleaning?"

"I sure do. I took care of Mrs. Rafferty's house every day after school there in Worthy, tending to her children, doing the laundry, getting supper on the table, and such," I reply.

"Well, we don't have children to care for anymore; they're all grown. But there's plenty to do around here." Mrs. Phillips looks me straight in the eye. "I do have a question for you, and it might seem rather impertinent."

"Yes, ma'am?"

"Are you and your husband planning on starting a family soon? The reason I ask is we've had two helpers leave us in the past thirteen months to stay home with their children. I'm afraid we need more continuity than that."

"No, Mrs. Phillips," I shake my head vigorously. "James and I got married just four days ago. I'm not ready for any kids, I'll tell you that."

Mrs. Phillips claps her hands together. "Splendid. Irene, the job is yours. When can you start?"

"I can start right now if it's all the same to you. Thank you, Mrs. Phillips."

"Call me Sondra. Mrs. Phillips reminds me of my mother-in-law."

Cleo

Lord. Have. Mercy. Mama's done it again. I take another bite of her double battered, twice-fried pork chop and my head about explodes from flavor overload. I scoop up a spoonful of her famous collard greens—made with fatback instead of bacon as her secret ingredient—and I nearly pass out. I'm telling you, if I had my druthers, I'd fall into a vat of Mama's collards and do my dead-level best to eat my way out or die trying; they're that good.

Jonathan moans as he chews at his desk. "Is your mother a chef?"

I shake my head. "No, sir. She's a nurse practitioner by trade."

"She should be. Her cooking is incredible. I've put on eight pounds since you've been bringing lunch for us," Jonathan says and shovels a forkful of macaroni and cheese.

I look his skinny frame over. "You could stand to add a little more weight, so I'll keep it coming."

He wipes his mouth and throws his paper plate away. "I rewatched your session with Mrs. Hadley. It's fascinating how her mind took over from the installed memory and went to a completely different location."

"I figured Mrs. Hadley would just stay in the virtual spaces her photos provided. She mentioned it was a little disorienting to suddenly be someplace she wasn't expecting to go, but it wasn't difficult for her to shrug off," I offer. I'm tempted to lick my plate clean, but I fight the urge.

"This data point opens all sorts of possibilities. Who knows where a person's mind can take them from a single photo," Jonathan adds.

"And it feels so real to them. Mrs. Hadley said her sensations of sight and touch were the same as they are out here among the living." I tuck my laptop into my bag.

"That means the VR environment is vibrant enough to tap into her sensory recall. Interesting." Jonathan drums his fingers on his desktop, mulling things over.

"There are leftover pork chops in the fridge and a container of Mama's pot roast. Why don't you take them home so you can have some proper meals over the weekend?"

"Hey, I eat okay," he says a tad defensively.

"Ramen isn't what I would call a substantive meal. Would you?"

"I suppose not. You taking off early?" Jonathan asks.

I nod. "Mama's throwing me a surprise early birthday party."

"If it's a surprise, how do you know about it?"

"My younger brother, Moses, has the loosest lips this side of the Red River. That boy can't keep a secret to save his life."

Jonathan chuckles. "Tell your mother 'Thank you' and happy birthday to you, Cleo."

"It ain...it's not for another week. So, you still have time to get me a present," I flash him a sassy grin.

Whew, that was a close one. I dang near broke my twenty-three-day "no aint's and better grammar" streak. Like Daddy used to say, old habits sure do die hard.

Brian and I are putt-putting down the highway in my little Ford Festiva, affectionately christened Miss Sybil when I was gifted her five years ago by Mama and Auntie Ella for my eighteenth birthday. Why that particular name? Well, it could be because of her dayglow red hood, scuffed-up white body, and orangey-red trunk. Or the fact that I have to gun the engine to get her to start and jiggle the keys to get her to shut off.

She's all sorts of unpredictable, just like that girl Sybil who had around sixteen personalities and her poor Mama never knew which one she was going to have to tangle with. So, I figured Miss Sybil was the perfect nickname since it describes this car to a T. But I digress.

"Cleo, the CD player isn't working again," Brian says as he tries to force-feed a disc into the changer.

"Just bang on top of the dash. That'll loosen it up," I direct.

Brian thumps the dashboard, and sure enough, the CD pops in, with the rich, velvety voice of Aretha Franklin filling the air.

"Baby, I don't mean to sound indelicate, and I know how much you love Miss Sybil, but don't you think it's time you bought yourself a newer vehicle? Like one from this century?" Brian wonders.

"Why would I do that for?"

"Because nothing in this car works right, and I don't want you stranded on the road all by yourself, especially at night."

"That's sweet. But I could be stranded in a new car just the same."

"It's less likely though." Brian leans back, then does a double take, like a lightbulb's gone off. "You don't want to spend the money."

"Bingo." I smile at him broadly, teeth and all.

"You make great money, Cleo. I know you can afford it," he argues.

"That's not the point. I don't *need* to when this a perfectly good car."

"You are a stubborn woman, Cleovantra Pearl," Brian sighs.

"But you love me, anyways," I tease.

Miss Clementine's and Auntie Ella's cars are parked along the street in front of Mama's house, so I pull in behind them.

"This get-together is supposed to be for Mr. Percy's retirement, and not my birthday, so I've got to act surprised. How's this?" I demonstrate my best shock and awe pose.

Brian rolls his eyes. "Don't quit your day job," he says and grabs Mr. Percy's gift from the back seat.

I practice various expressions as we make our way to the front porch. "I'm ready for my close-up, Mr. DeMille," I purr.

"Girl, you're crazy." Brian opens the door, "Hey, everybody. We're here."

"Happy Birthday!" rings out from the living room as Mama, Moses, Miss Clementine, Mr. Percy, Auntie Ella, and her husband Gabe jump to their feet.

Mama takes one look at my face and isn't buying my acting job. I guess I won't be winning an Oscar anytime soon.

"Did you know about this?" Mama asks, her hands on her hips.

My silence answers her question and Mama turns to Moses.

"Moses Marshall Pearl, you and your mouth," Mama scolds.

"Sorry, Mama." Moses peers down sheepishly.

"It's all right, Moses. It's hard to keep a secret." I playfully punch his arm.

Auntie Ella and Gabe carry trays of drinks into the living room, handing champagne to everyone but me and Moses, where we are offered Yoo-hoos. Now, it's not that I'm against imbibing. I've been known to have a sip or two of a cocktail every now and then. But to me, a cold, chocolatey Yoo-hoo is the nectar of the gods, so why mess with perfection?

"All right, everyone. Raise your glasses," Mama begins. "To Percy, congratulations on your hard-earned retirement…"

"Hard-earned is right," Mr. Percy interjects, and everyone chuckles.

"And to my precious girl, Cleo, happy birthday, baby. May you both have good health and many blessings to come."

"Hear, hear," Gabe says, and we all take a sip to seal the deal.

"Can we eat now? I'm starving," Moses groans.

"What about grace?" Auntie Ella asks.

"Lord, bless the food. Amen," Moses offers, then rushes off to the kitchen.

"He's a man on a mission," Brian chuckles and follows Moses' lead.

"Gabe, you're not going to believe what I've got being delivered on Monday. My very own fishing boat," Percy beams.

"A fishing boat?" Gabe and Miss Clementine exclaim at once.

"Yes, Lord. And she's a beauty." Mr. Percy beams.

"Why is this the first I've heard of it?" Miss Clementine mutters.

"I was going to tell you. It just slipped my mind." Mr. Percy winks at her.

"I'll bet," Miss Clementine scoffs.

"You planning on taking it out Monday?" Gabe asks.

"I sure am. You want to join me?" Mr. Percy offers.

"It's supposed to rain Monday," Miss Clementine says with a bite.

"Well then, I'll do something else, Clem," Mr. Percy sasses.

I sense World War III is about to break out, so I think fast on my feet. "You know, Mr. Percy, we've got all sorts of virtual reality goggles lying around at work. I'd be happy to bring you by a pair to use when the weather is bad."

"I don't know, Cleo. I'm not much good with technology."

"You can say that again," Miss Clementine mumbles. Mr. Percy shoots her the evil eye, so she turns on her heel and heads to the kitchen.

"It's real easy, and I'd be happy to show you how to use it. There's even a fishing space where you can catch anything from a goldfish to a whale," I add enthusiastically.

"A whale? Well, ain't that something. On second thought, why don't you bring one of those things over when you get a chance."

"Sure thing, Mr. Percy."

"Oh, and Cleo, a little advice from a long-suffering married man: No matter what kind of love you got, never, *ever* get hitched."

I nod my head, "I hear that. There's no place on my hand for a ring."

As I utter those words, I steal a glance at Brian returning from the kitchen holding two dishes of food, his expression a mixture of hurt and confusion. Right then, I wish I could snatch those words out of the air and take them back like they never existed. But it doesn't work that way.

"Thank you, Brian," I smile thinly as I take the offered plate. Brian and I eat in silence after that, because what is there left to say when you've spoken your truth?

Clementine

'My dear, Rebecca, there is nothing I would cherish more on this earth than to call you my own. But you are betrothed to another.' Rebecca places her fingers on his lips. 'My darling Reginald, it is of no consequence who my father chooses for my hand in marriage. My love will endure for you forevermore. Kiss me, Reginald. Claim me as your own.' Reginald grips Rebecca's arms and pulls her into a frantic embrace, kissing her with an urgency and fervor he can no longer ignore.'

Ooh, Lord. I turn on my little battery-operated fan to swirl the air around and cool myself, all steamed up from reading *Love Everlasting*, the latest dime-store novel by my favorite author, Eliza Ferguson.

Ever since Cleo introduced virtual reality to the Memory Care wing, my life has been so much easier around here. The afternoon jailbreaks have all but stopped and the residents are calmer, not just when they're flitting about the VR domain. As such, I've been able to spend more quality time in my Happy Place among the sheets and pillowcases.

I let out a hefty sigh. Though I hate leaving my comfy lair, I best make an appearance on the floor and take care of some much overdue paperwork. I pop the remainder of my 100 Grand bar into my mouth, stow my paperback, and hide my stadium chair in the corner. My Diet Dr. Pepper is about half full, so I head down to the break room to store it in the fridge. Waste not, want not, as the saying goes.

As I turn the corner, the clickety-clack of Miss Jillian's heels echoes behind me down the hallway.

"Clementine. A moment, please," Miss Jillian says, as monotone as ever.

I turn and Miss Jillian is wearing her standard uniform—a black pencil skirt and jacket —but instead of her usual ponytail, her hair is flowing around her shoulders.

"Well, don't you look pretty today, Miss Jillian? You should wear your hair down more often," I praise.

"My image consultant suggested it." She touches the ends of her hair, "Do you really like it?"

"Yes, ma'am. It suits you well."

She nods stiffly, like she's uncomfortable accepting a compliment. "Great feedback from the Memory Care residents and their families regarding VR. Staff, too. What are your thoughts?"

"I'm very pleased. It's gone off without a hitch. Do you think Hennessey corporate will consider making virtual reality permanent once Cleo's testing is finished?"

"I don't know. I don't know." Miss Jillian responds in rapid-fire fashion.

"If everything goes as planned, won't you make a recommendation for it to continue?"

"Perhaps. Perhaps. I'm not going to be the director here for long. This is a training stop for me. Father wants me to spend time in all facets of the business before I'm promoted to the board," she explains at her usual breakneck speed.

"But it would benefit the residents' quality of life. Don't you agree?"

"Sure. Sure. We'll see. Keep up the good work, Clementine," Miss Jillian responds, and then she's off to the races.

"Thank you," I call, shaking my head, and wander into the break room.

My phone pings. It's a text from Percy with the total amount for his boat purchase—finally. Sweet Jesus: $4,200 for a used fishing boat.

"Lord have mercy. That man drives me crazy," I sputter as I reach into my pocket and pull out a notepad.

"You okay, Mrs. Babineaux?" Mr. Isaac asks as he limps up next to me.

"I'm all right, Mr. Isaac. Just my husband spending us out of house and home," I quip as I write down Percy's expenditure.

"What you got there?" Mr. Isaac points to my notepad.

"Oh, this? It helps me keep track of our money is all," I reply sheepishly.

"Nothing wrong with that. Of course, you could do it on your phone," he offers as he buys a package of crackers from the vending machine.

"How's that?" I wonder.

"They got all kinds of apps for budgeting and such. You just download them and away you go." Mr. Isaac settles himself at a nearby table.

"I prefer something I can hold onto. What happens if I lose my phone, then all my records would be lost."

"All that data gets stored on something called a cloud. It never goes away or gets misplaced, like your notebook could," he replies.

"Well, thank you for the suggestion, Mr. Isaac." I purposefully change the subject. "Is that all you're going to eat for lunch?"

He nods slowly. "Yes, ma'am. I didn't get a chance to make anything at home, what with my wife in the hospital and all."

"I'd heard she'd taken a turn for the worse. How's she doing?"

"Not well, I'm afraid. The doctors are recommending hospice." Mr. Isaac's voice cracks.

"I'm so sorry, Mr. Isaac. Cancer is rough."

"It surely is," he laments.

A light bulb goes off in my head. "Now, I know I can't do anything to help your wife, but what I *can* do is make sure you're fed." I open the refrigerator and retrieve my Tupperware.

"I've got leftover beef stew and ambrosia I made the other night, and there's plenty here for both of us. Would you like to share?" I ask brightly.

"I do love me some ambrosia salad," Mr. Isaac smiles.

"That's music to my ears. My husband Percy hates the stuff." I grab some dishes and silverware from the cupboard and pop the stew into the microwave. I spoon our lunch onto the plates and hand him one.

"I sure do appreciate this, Mrs. Babineaux." He takes a bite of my salad. "Mm, mm, mm. That's the best ambrosia I've ever had."

"There's more where that came from, I assure you. I've got almost an entire container in the fridge you can take home if you like."

"Clementine?" Ida Mae pops her head into the break room. "One of the VR headsets ain't working right. Can you give me a hand?"

I shake my head. "We can't have that. It's back to the salt mines, I suppose." I grab my plate, "You take care, Mr. Isaac."

"Thank you, Mrs. Babineaux. For everything." He smiles bittersweetly.

I pat his shoulder, hoping my small gesture will ease some of his pain, if only for a little while.

True to the weatherman's prediction, it's raining buckets while I'm driving home, such that I can't see but two feet in front of me even with the windshield wipers going at full throttle. As I turn into the driveway, Percy's truck is parked to the side and a ginormous fiberglass boat sits in our garage, leaving no room to spare for my little Toyota Corolla.

I make a mad dash to the back door, cursing Percy and his new toy under my breath, and end up completely drenched by the torrential downpour.

"Percy?" I holler.

No response.

"Percyyyy?" I yell louder.

"What?" he snaps from the living room.

"Why is that God-forsaken boat taking up my parking space?"

"I didn't want it to get wet," Percy barks.

"It's a *boat*, Percy. They live in the *water*. They're *supposed* to get wet."

"I don't have a cover for it yet, and I don't want to have to bail water out of it. If you haven't noticed, it's raining outside," he chides.

"Course I've noticed. Look at me." I spread my arms to reveal how soaked I am. "Ain't you going to have to get the water out of the truck bed?"

"I'll just open the tailgate and it'll drain right out," Percy answers nonchalantly. He sips a beer, his third from the empty cans sitting on the tray next to him.

"Is this all you've been doing all day? Drinking beer and watching the Fishing Channel?" I growl.

"Naw. I strung some new lures and took a nap, too." He turns his gaze to the TV, where two men are casting rods off a dock.

I shake my head. "You know, Percy. I don't think this boat is such a good idea. You don't even know how to swim."

"You just don't like me spending the money. It's got nothing to do with my safety," he scoffs.

"That's not true," I say defiantly. "Promise me you'll at least wear a life jacket out there?"

"I'd have to buy one. Will it fit in our budget?" he mocks.

"If it'll keep you from drowning, it will." I snark right back at him. "So, you'll get one?"

"Yes."

"Tomorrow?" I needle him as I make my way to the kitchen.

"*Yes*, Clem. Now shush. I'm trying to watch."

I search the fridge for the meat I planned to prepare for supper tonight.

"Percy, where's the hamburger I asked you to thaw?"

No reply.

"Percyyy?"

"I forgot to get it out of the freezer," he replies meekly.

I sigh, yank out two frozen dinners, and plop them onto the counter. "You want Banquet Salisbury steak or Stouffer's lasagna?"

"Salisbury steak."

I pop it into the oven, and after a few minutes, deliver Percy his dinner.

"Here you go." I place a plate and fork on the tray next to his recliner, without so much as a peep from him.

"You're welcome," I reply to myself.

I wait for a beat; no response. Desperate times call for desperate measures they say, so I give his bald spot a good thump.

"Ow! Damn, woman. That hurt!"

"Say 'Thank you, Clementine'," I order, my middle finger and thumb poised for another strike.

"For what? Thumping me?" he cries, soothing the crown of his head.

"For your *dinner*."

"*Thank you*, Clem, for turning on the oven."

"Like you mean it." I flick him again.

"Ouch!" Percy wails. "Fine," he exhales, defeated. "Thank you, Clementine. Is that good enough?"

"That'll do," I nod. "And you can forget watching fishing while we eat. Turn it to the Hallmark Channel, please."

"Not a sappy movie, Clem, for the love of all things holy," Percy begs.

I hook my thumb and fingers together. "Want another one?"

He raises his hands defensively, "All right, all right. You win," then points the remote at the TV.

I smile knowingly, satisfied with my small victory. As I've learned over forty-two years of marriage, reigning in your husband is a never-ending war, but it's nice to win a few battles every now and then.

Margaret

April 1970

Cleo and her memory machine take me for another whirl, plunking me down this time in my little Corvette while cruising down Highway Six. The T-tops are off, and the sweet, spring air kisses my face, filling my lungs with its heavenly scent. I steal a glance in the rearview mirror. My newly dyed hair is pulled back in a scarf with a few strands of blonde peeking out across my brow, stylish Wayfarers adorn my eyes, and my lips are painted bright red while a cigarette dangles from them; Virginia Slims—my favorite. With me all dolled up like this it must be Sunday and time for Daddy's happy hour.

Growing up, Mama always insisted on a proper Sunday sit-down meal. But ever since she passed a couple of years ago, Daddy decided a more informal cocktail hour would better suit him, with plenty of booze to go around, something Mama wouldn't dare let in the house while she was alive.

I park behind the bevy of cars already there—I'm fashionably late as always—shed my scarf and check my hair in the side-view mirror. Perfect. Just perfect. I let myself in and find Clarice, Daddy's septuagenarian housekeeper, lining a tray with champagne glasses and shakily topping them off with the fizzy foam.

"Hey Clarice," I say as I breeze in.

Clarice straightens and peers over her glasses. "Miss Margaret? Ain't you a sight for sore eyes. Come here and let me get a good look at you."

I do as I'm asked, with Clarice giving my new hair color a closer inspection.

"It suits you, Miss Margaret. You're the spitting image of Marilyn Monroe," she observes.

I point to my right cheek. "I even added a beauty mark, just like Marilyn's," I muse.

"And your dress, Miss Margaret," she steps back to get a better view of my red V-neck midi dress, "simply beautiful," she remarks.

"Why thank you, Clarice." I twirl the hem.

"Be careful now, Miss Margaret. You're going to turn some heads."

"That's the idea," I wink and grab a glass of champagne.

Out on the manicured lawn, the usual guests are here: salesmen from Daddy's dealership and their wives, Daddy's poker buddies, my sister Magnolia, her boy Billy, and last but certainly not least, Ashby, Magnolia's ruggedly handsome husband. They're gathered in clusters making small talk, but while I stroll through the yard sipping my cocktail, I can feel their glances turning my way. As I meet some of their gazes, the men quickly look away for fear of being caught leering, but their wives fearlessly stare me down with silent warnings to leave their husbands alone.

Magnolia breaks away from a grouping and approaches me, her eyes amused, yet her expression's unreadable, as is her custom. My sister and I couldn't be more different, like night and day. Where I cut loose and thirst for life, almost drowning in all its possibilities, Magnolia's old school, matronly and proper. Daddy says Magnolia was born an old soul; me—I'm a free spirit, going wherever the wind blows.

"I see you decided to make a splash today, Margaret. How unlike you," Magnolia remarks dryly.

"What, this old thing?" I point to my dress.

Magnolia smirks. "You know what I mean. Mother's rolling over in her grave, what with you and your blonde hair. I can't imagine what Daddy's going to say."

"I don't believe my hair color is on his mind right about now," I respond and nod toward Daddy seated at a table, a buxom brunette thirty years his junior draped across his lap.

"You've always had a flair for the dramatic," Magnolia needles.

"And you're as jealous as ever," I counter.

"At least we're consistent," she muses. "So, I hear you're going to be taking care of my Billy."

"It was Daddy's idea," I say evenly.

"You'll be careful with him, won't you? You'll watch him closely? He's a curious little boy and quite a handful. Are you sure you're up for it?" Magnolia asks earnestly.

"Of course, I'm up for it. I've babysat Billy hundreds of times."

"But not all day, every day," she stresses. "Promise me you'll keep a good eye on him?"

I roll my eyes. "I *promise*, Magnolia. You worry too much, sister."

"And you don't worry enough," she cautions.

Ashby leads Billy by the hand, and they mosey over our way, dressed in matching blue seersucker sport coats and red ties. I glance at Ashby and our eyes lock. Never before has he acknowledged me as a woman. But the way he considers me now—the spark in his gaze—I know that bottle of peroxide has done its job. Mission accomplished.

Mrs. Hadley

November 1960

My eyes flutter open, and snowflakes dance across the window, lightly dusting what remains of the tree's leaves and dormant lawn. It's early, just about dawn given the few snippets of light reflecting off the snow. I turn to James lying beside me breathing deeply and steadily, our blanket pulled up to his chin to keep warm.

"Hey, sleepyhead. It's snowing out," I say and kiss his cheek.

"Hmm. Okay," he replies sleepily.

I nudge his ribs. "Let's go out and play in it."

"Nuh-uh. I want to sleep." James rolls over.

I lean up on my elbow and poke his back. "I've only seen snow but once in my life. Make your girl happy and come join me before it all melts away."

He turns around to face me. "This is Ohio, Irene. There'll be plenty more where that came from. Before long, you'll be praying it'll stop." James covers his head with his pillow. "So, let me be."

"C'mon, James." I lift the pillow and nuzzle his ear. "Pretty please."

He sighs and peeks at me. "You're not going to leave me alone, are you?"

"No sir," I grin.

"All right. I'll go outside with you, but you've got to do something for me first," James counters, a devilish smile crossing his lips.

"I've got a feeling I know what that is," I reply as I pull him closer. "Give me a little kiss, will you please, Mr. Hadley?"

"Coming right up, Mrs. Hadley." James wraps me in his arms and places his mouth on mine.

Suddenly, my perspective changes and I'm no longer in James' embrace but in Mrs. Phillips' kitchen.

"Irene? Are you in there?" Mrs. Phillips calls.

I shake the cobwebs out of my head to get my bearings. "Yes ma'am. I'm on my way."

Mrs. Phillips is in the family room, seated on the sofa in front of the TV.

"What can I do you for, Mrs. Phillips?"

She wags her finger at me. "How many times do I have to tell you, Irene; call me Sondra."

"Sorry, yes Sondra. You're looking better; you got the color back in your cheeks," I notice.

"That medicine Agnes Westbrook brought over this morning is a godsend. Her doctor's part of a new drug trial and she's been taking it for the past month. Agnes calls them 'miracle pills'; she says they can cure anything from nerves to morning sickness," Sondra explains.

"What's it called again?"

"Kevadon. But it also goes by Thalimide, or Thalidomide, something like that. I can't remember."

"It sure seems to have done the trick for your migraine," I reply.

"Thankfully, yes. Fingers crossed." Sondra glances at the wall clock. "Oh, my. It's almost time for *As the World Turns*. What did you prepare the General for dinner last night?"

"Chipped beef on toast, ma'am."

"Is there any left?"

"Why yes, as a matter of fact. You feel like eating some lunch?"

"I believe I do," Sondra nods. "Why don't you fix yourself a plate too, Irene? We can eat together in front of the TV."

"I can't wait to see what Bob is going to say to Lisa about their divorce," I clap my hands excitedly.

"I'll get the TV trays set up," Sondra offers.

"Be back in a minute, Mrs. Phillips. I mean Sondra."

Cleo

oodness me but Auntie Ella has outdone herself this time. Apparently, she was futzing around in the kitchen not long ago, playing with different flavor combinations until she concocted her newest confectionery creation: spiced double chocolate ganache truffle balls spiked with Cointreau orange liqueur. Each little nugget melts in your mouth, sending a flavor explosion that rocks your taste buds. It's as close to a religious experience as I've ever had when it comes to desserts, and that's saying something given Mama's culinary expertise. I just won't mention anything to Mama for fear of initiating a kitchen war with Auntie Ella. On second thought, I might benefit from any epicurean one-upmanship that may occur between them since somebody would have to taste their wares. Hmm, I'll ponder this prospect further. But I digress.

I peek over at Jonathan who whimpers in ecstasy as he chews the last of his truffle. "I think your aunt may be a better cook than your mother, and that's saying something."

"Auntie Ella can bake a mean sweet, that's for sure."

Jonathan raises his hands defensively. "Please hide those from me, or I'll OD on the rest of them."

The funky strains of Stevie Wonder's "Superstition," my snazzy new ringtone, fill the air. It's Miss Clementine on the other end.

"Hey, Miss Clementine. Everything all right?" I ask.

"Cleo, I hate to bother you, but something happened today that I think you should be aware of," she begins.

"What was it?"

"Well, three residents had to be cajoled into using the VR entertainment space this afternoon. They're complaining about visiting museums and whatnot without anyone to talk to. They want to interact with others, like at a park or a mall or something; somewhere they can meet new people," Miss Clementine explains.

"That's understandable."

"Is it possible to do? VR has been such a blessing for the residents and staff. I'd hate for it to get stale and they lose interest."

"I don't see why Jonathan and I can't create some new settings specifically for the residents to talk and get acquainted in. They'll probably need more supervision than what they require now, though, to make sure everybody gets along. Are there enough staff for that?" I wonder.

"Oh, yes. We can manage. I'll make sure of it."

"It's kind of slow here, so we'll get to work on it today. Hopefully, I'll have something to offer them by tomorrow afternoon," I offer.

"Yes, time is of the essence. I don't want them roaming the halls again if it can be helped. Thank you for your help, Cleo."

I ring off and turn to Jonathan. "You catch any of that?"

"I gather there's dissension in the ranks?"

"The residents are getting bored with visiting places on their own. Miss Clementine wondered if we could create some areas where they can get to know each other, supervised of course."

"Sure. There's enough memory to generate four or five domains," Jonathan nods.

"Domains? You make it sound so fun," I tease.

"Realms?" he suggests.

"How about 'social gathering circles?'"

"'Social gathering circles.' I like it. I'll go ahead and apportion the memory now. With both of us working on it, we can devise at least a couple of them before the end of the day," Jonathan replies.

"Knock, knock." Ingram, our "bro boss," pokes his head into our cubicle.

"Bless your heart, Ingram. I didn't think you knew where our little cubbyhole was located. Wonders never cease," I say drolly.

Ingram stares at me, his eyes unblinking and jaw set, mulling over whether to engage me or not. He turns his attention to Jonathan—I guess Ingram thought better of it.

"Sorry to interrupt, but Quinn and his guys need some programming help with their VR app."

"Since there are eight folks on their team, I'd imagine they've got plenty of brain power available to figure it out," I respond, with a bit of a bite.

"It's all hands on deck on this one, Cleo. Need I remind you that we're a *team*," Ingram emphasizes.

"So will Jonathan and I get a piece of their bonus for this project, since we're a *team*?" I needle.

"I've explained this before, but I guess I'll have to do it again for those of you who're slower than the rest. Bonuses are based on the totality of the project, not individual contributions," Ingram responds, visibly irritated.

"It sure seems to me we're all a *team* when the others need something. And when they don't, well, it gets mighty lonesome in this neck of the woods." I stress the obvious.

Ingram holds my gaze for a good, long minute. "Can I count on you, Jonathan?" Ingram asks, not taking his eyes off me.

Jonathan nods silently, fixated on his laptop.

"Great, I'll have Quinn send the files over. Needless to say, I expect *both* of you to pitch in. Oh, and as a reminder, quarterly reviews are coming up soon," Ingram replies pointedly as he leaves.

"You know, Jonathan, it might have more of an impact on Ingram if we're a united front," I say, keeping my voice low.

"I'm sorry, Cleo. I'm not brave like you. Ingram scares me," he responds, still facing his computer.

"What Ingram's doing isn't right, Jonathan. You know we'll help Quinn and the Bro Club and not see so much as a crumb of acknowledgment when all is said and done."

"It's not about accolades, Cleo; it's about making VR better for Next Well," Jonathan answers meekly.

"Is it? Because the way Ingram's got things set up, it's going to be every man for himself."

Jonathan sighs and swivels his chair toward me. "There's no sense in arguing about it now. Let's just get our social gathering circles set up, and then pivot to Quinn."

I nod begrudgingly. Within me, my resolve hardens, and my determination grows. I may have lost my latest skirmish with Ingram, but I'm not about to bend to his will. In my mind, the battle lines have been plainly drawn.

Clementine

True to her word, Cleo and her partner worked up a couple of "social gathering circles" — as they call them—capable of resident interaction, and in the span of just twenty-four hours. According to Cleo, each area is built around an existing template: the café where Miss Margaret lounged for a spell has been transformed into a park with walking paths and a little pond; and the basketball court Mrs. Hadley enjoyed can now host games between the residents and resembles an actual arena, with bench seating and a scoreboard to boot. It's truly a wonder what technology can do these days.

"The first thing the residents will need to do is select an avatar," Cleo explains to me and Ida Mae.

She shows us a whole slew of physiques to choose from, with just about any facial color, body size, and clothing type you can think of.

"Can the staff pick out a special avatar, too?" I ask.

"It would be best for all of you to select something that resembles what you really look like. We want the residents to recognize you as an authority figure if something goes wrong or an incident occurs," Cleo explains.

"Let them know we're keeping an eye on them," Ida Mae nods.

"Like you do now; nothing intrusive," Cleo replies.

"I sure wouldn't mind taking a spin as someone else, though. Can we do that, Cleo, when we're on break or something?" I wonder.

"I don't see why not. But be sure to switch back to your real persona if you need to keep the peace," Cleo responds.

"This ought to be fun. I always wanted to be 'Chantal' in another life," Ida Mae dreams aloud.

"'Rebecca' is my go-to. And sweet Reginald would be my knight in shining armor." I clutch my heart wistfully.

"Are those characters from your romance novels?" Ida Mae asks.

"You know it; the *Love Evermore* series by Eliza Ferguson—my favorite books of all time," I say.

"You two crack me up," Cleo shakes her head, chuckling. "Now remember, if you run into any problems, you can always turn off a resident's headset. And you know I'm just a phone call away."

"Got it." I flash Cleo the OK sign.

"All right, then, I'm off. Big squeezes everybody." Cleo hugs the daylights out of me and Ida Mae, grabs her computer, and heads out the door.

Ida Mae bends close to me and whispers, "Did you hear about Mr. Isaac?"

"No, what?"

"Wife passed away last night. Heard he's all kinds of broken up over it."

I shake my head. "Mm. Mm. Mm. That poor man. She was ill, for what? Three years?"

"I believe so. Cancer sure is a hard way to go," Ida Mae opines.

"You ain't kidding. We should send some flowers for the funeral. I'll take up a collection," I offer.

"Good idea," Ida Mae agrees.

"Losing your spouse after a lifetime together. I can't imagine," I ponder as much to myself as I do to Ida Mae.

I open the back door carrying my empty lunch bag and purse, feeling mighty cloudy after learning of Mr. Isaac's wife's passing. Much like when one of my residents leaves this mortal plane, I'm touched with sorrow and reminded how short our time is on this silly little planet, and how often we choose to waste it instead of making it count.

I set my things down in the kitchen and notice the pork chops on the counter I asked Percy to thaw earlier. He remembered this time and my heart swells tenderly.

As usual, he's in the family room, but instead of watching TV, Percy's wearing VR goggles and making a casting motion with his right wrist into the air.

"Percy? Where did you get those?"

"Cleo," he responds.

"What are you doing in there?"

"Fishing. What else?" Percy imitates reeling in a catch.

"Take those off now, would you please?" I command.

Percy sighs, shuts off the headset, and drags it from his face. "Yes?"

We stare at one another for a bit, each of us wondering who will make the first move.

"I got the pork chops out. Did you see?" he asks tentatively.

I nod, then slowly walk over and place my arms around him, clutching him to me like I'm never going to let him go.

"Clem? Are you all right?" Percy wonders, his voice concerned.

"I will be. Just hold me, okay?" I murmur into his chest.

"Okay," he replies and grips me tighter.

Sometimes, that's all you really need.

Margaret

April 1970

Eggs, milk, orange juice, cheese, hot dogs and buns, Wonder Bread, peanut butter, and tomato soup; the refrigerator and cupboards are well-stocked with Billy's favorites. I double-check my spare bedroom one last time where Billy will nap, making sure the twin bed is properly made with squared corners tucked in tight like a hospital bed, so Magnolia won't find a reason to complain.

The living room is chock-full of brand-new toys from little green army men to balls of every shape, color, and size. I straighten everything once more, hoping Billy's new stash will meet with Magnolia's approval. It's funny in a way because Billy would be content playing in a cardboard box; he's so easy to please. Make no mistake: all these airs and graces are for my insufferably picky sister. Things have to be just right, or she'll never let you forget it.

The doorbell rings. I smooth my skirt, check my hair in the mirror, and take a deep breath. I throw on my best smile and open the door.

"Billy boy!" I exclaim.

"Maggie!" Billy grins brightly.

Magnolia jerks Billy's hand, glowering at him. "Young man, you will refer to my sister as Aunt Margaret. Do you understand?"

Billy flinches. "Yes, mother." He jams his hands in his pockets and looks at me sheepishly, "Hi, Aunt Margaret."

"Maggie is just fine with me, Billy," I say, glaring at Magnolia who scowls right back at me.

"Come on in, Billy, and take a peek in the family room." I step aside and Billy runs into the house, making a beeline for the toys.

"Wow!" Billy grabs a small, orange ball from the pile.

"What in God's name is that?" Magnolia asks.

"A Nerf ball!" Billy cries. "My friend Jack has one. You can play with them in the house and not break anything." He throws it at the wall, and it bounces right off without making a dent.

"Wonders never cease," Magnolia replies wryly. "May I see where Billy will be napping?"

"Of course. The spare room is around the corner," I reply.

Magnolia sniffs around for a bit, inspecting the bed as I knew she would, and scrutinizing my food inventory. I smile to myself, knowing I've covered all the bases which leaves nothing for her to grumble about.

"Everything seems to be in order," Magnolia nods. "Billy, your father will pick you up this afternoon—at five sharp." That last comment was aimed at me no doubt.

"Come give your mother a kiss, please," Magnolia directs.

Apprehensively, Billy pecks her cheek, as if he'd rather be doing something—anything—else.

Magnolia sees herself out and my shoulders relax. My sister has a way of bringing out the worst in people.

"Well, Billy boy, what would you like to do today?"

"It's my daddy's birthday. Can we make him a cake?" he asks brightly.

"Why sure we can. How about that? I plumb forgot it was your daddy's birthday. But we'll need to go to the grocery store and buy some flour and baking soda."

"Can I bring my Nerf ball, too?"

"You bet." I grab my purse and we hustle out the door. "It's a beautiful day. I think I'll take the T-tops off."

"Okay," Billy replies as he tosses the ball around the yard.

I unhinge the panels and place them on the front stoop. As I turn back around, a gust of wind blows Billy's toy into the street. He chases after it just as a car appears around the bend, barreling toward him.

"Billy! Hurry! Run!" I warn.

Billy snags the Nerf ball and makes it to the other side, as the car's tires screech and come to a stop.

"Watch your kid, lady. You're going to get him killed," the heavyset driver complains from his car window.

I rush over to Billy who's grinning from ear to ear, happy to have retrieved his ball before it got away from him.

I squat down so we're at eye level. "You can't run into the street like that when you're not supervised, Billy. It's dangerous," I caution sternly.

"But I *was* supervised. You were outside," he points out innocently.

"Don't play coy with me; you know what I mean. I was busy with the car. You have to look both ways, Billy. You just have to," I remind him. "Let's go on and get to the store."

"Can I still bring my ball?" he wonders.

"Sure, but hold onto it. You don't want it blowing away again."

The supermarket is busy, filled with housewives doing their weekly shopping. We find the flour, the baking soda and add cocoa to the mix, then decide that some chocolate ice cream would be nice as a treat.

While at the checkout counter, the woman waiting behind us comments, "Your little boy is so handsome. And he's the spitting image of you."

"Why thank you, ma'am. I have to agree," I say as I pay for our items.

Billy turns to me as we walk to the car, his expression confused. "Maggie? Why did that lady back there say I was your boy?"

"She was just being nice." I place the sack in the back seat.

"But I'm not your boy."

"Sometimes, it's easier to agree with someone than to make a big deal about something. It's called a 'white lie.' They don't hurt anybody."

"A white lie," Billy repeats.

"Don't tell your mother you learned that from me, though, or I'll never hear the end of it. Let's keep what happens while we're together just between us, okay? They'll be our little secrets."

"Our little secrets," Billy nods.

After several hours and two failed attempts, Billy and I put the final dabs of frosting on his father's birthday cake. We stand back from the kitchen table to get a better look at our masterpiece.

"It's lopsided," Billy observes.

"It turned out better than the other two. Here, I'll add some more frosting to even it out."

I scrape the bowl and plop a few dollops on the left side of the cake, then swirl them around. "What do you think?"

"Much better. It looks like a real cake now," Billy decides.

The doorbell chimes. "Billy, go get the card we made for your daddy," I instruct and carry the cake plate to the foyer.

"Ready, Billy?" He nods earnestly. "Okay, open the door."

Billy does as he's told. "Happy Birthday!" we say in unison.

Imagine our surprise to see Magnolia standing on the front porch, alone.

"From the looks on your faces, I believe you're both surprised to see me," Magnolia muses. "Ashby had a last-minute sale to attend to. Oh, my. Allow me to inspect this lovely confection of yours," she replies tartly.

"Bless your hearts, you must've beaten the batter too long," Magnolia grins smugly, like the cat who ate the canary.

"That's our best one. The other two sunk in the middle," Billy points out.

"Well, we can't serve a crooked cake for your father's birthday, now can we, Billy?" Magnolia steps over to the garbage can in the driveway and dumps the cake inside.

"Come along, now. You and I will bake him a proper one at home." Magnolia hands me the empty plate, wraps her arm around Billy's shoulder, and shepherds him away.

Weary and defeated, I fish the chocolate ice cream from the freezer and curl up on the sofa, prepared to satiate my dejection one heaping spoonful at a time.

Mrs. Hadley

January 1961

The dining room begins to spin, so I brace myself against the china hutch as a cold sweat dots my forehead. With all the gumption I can muster, I wobble into the powder bathroom, just in time, before unleashing what little I ate for breakfast. The floor tiles are nice and cool. I lay my head down for a bit to get my bearings, praying the nausea will quiet down soon.

Tap. Tap. Tap. "Irene? Are you all right?" Sondra asks worriedly from behind the door.

"I will be," I reply weakly.

"When you're feeling up to it, come into the kitchen please," she responds.

I sit up after a spell, and once I'm confident there won't be a repeat performance, I join her in the other room.

Sondra has placed two cups on the breakfast table and is pouring what looks to be tea for the both of us.

"You poor thing. Have a seat."

I fold into a chair and rest my weary head in my hands.

"Try some of your tea; it's peppermint. It will help calm your stomach," Sondra suggests.

I nod gratefully and take a small sip. "It's good. Thank you."

"Third time this week, Irene?" Sondra asks gently.

"Yes, ma'am."

"How far are you along, dear?"

I shake my head and look away, embarrassed by my predicament. "I don't know. I ain't been to a doctor yet."

"Well, we'll get you in to see my doctor as soon as we can. You need proper care now."

"I don't want to put you out," I resist.

"Nonsense. It's the least I can do. I'll be back in a moment." Sondra leaves the table and returns with a medicine bottle in hand.

"In the meantime, I'll give you some of these." She counts out a handful of pills. "They've worked miracles for my friend Trudy's morning sickness. And you've seen how they've cured my migraines."

I pick up a tablet and look it over. "What's the name of it again?"

"Kevadon. Some call it Thalidomide. Go on, take it. You'll feel better in no time," she urges.

I place the pill on my tongue and wash it down with some tea.

"Soon, you'll be right as rain," Sondra smiles and squeezes my arm.

I tear the VR goggles from my head. "I can't go on, Cleo. I can't do it," I cry.

"What's wrong, Mrs. Hadley?" Cleo asks, her face full of concern.

"This memory; all it's going to do is lead me on a path I'd best not go down. Not again." I say, shaking my head.

Cleo places our headsets on the table in front of us. "That's okay. You don't have to do anything you don't want to."

"It's been wonderful being so close to James, really it has, even if it's only in my mind. But this..."

Cleo takes my hands in hers. "Would you like to talk about it? Sometimes getting things off your mind can do wonders."

"James made me swear never to speak of it to anyone," I reply uneasily.

"But he isn't here now, Mrs. Hadley," Cleo responds gently.

I sigh deeply and think about it for a moment. "You're right. Ain't no use in keeping secrets any longer. I shouldn't have kept it *this* long, I suppose."

I lean forward in my chair and take a deep breath. "That remembrance you saw? I surely was with child, yes indeed. And those pills? Thalidomide? I took them all throughout my pregnancy. They worked like a charm, too, I tell you that. No more morning sickness. Then, when the labor pains began, James took me over to the base hospital and Sondra's doctor met us there as a favor to her. In that day and age, men weren't allowed in the delivery room, so it was just me, the doctor, and a nurse."

"The doctor gave me something called 'twilight sleep.' It took the pain away and made me feel like I was floating in the clouds. It felt nice. There was some pulling and tugging down below, and then a loud, healthy cry; my baby's cry."

"I heard some commotion, and the nurse left and came back into the delivery room with another doctor. They talked for a bit, then the nurse rushed off carrying my baby in her arms. After a while, I was wheeled into a hospital room where James was waiting, and the doctor broke the news: our baby girl was born with normal arms, but tiny, little legs. He said they looked like flippers. She'd never walk and would no doubt be retarded, if she lived at all. The doctor said it was best if we sent her to an orphanage where they had the means to care for her. So, James and I signed the paperwork and that was that."

"I never saw my baby. I never held her. Sondra had her husband, the general, fast-track a transfer for James back to an Air Force base here in Texas, and we left within the week. James swore me to secrecy, and we never spoke of it again. I learned some years later that drug was responsible for thousands of birth defects. If I had only known."

I wipe a tear from my eye. "Somehow, I was able to forget. I pushed her into a corner of my mind where she stayed hidden, until now. I'm all alone, Cleo. And I sure do wonder what happened to my girl. Is she alive? And if she is, how is she? What's she like? If I could find her, would she even want to see me?"

"Well, Mrs. Hadley," Cleo begins, "I can look for her if you like. The internet is chock-full of information. Maybe there's something out there about her."

"Would you do that for me, Cleo?" My heart swells.

"Yes, ma'am. I'll do whatever I can."

Clementine

Most of last evening and much of my early morning has been spent chopping, mixing, and cooking away, laying up enough food to tide Mr. Isaac over for the next week. Today will be his first day back at work since his wife passed, so it's the least I can do. Ida Mae and I attended the funeral last Saturday to pay our respects, and I was reminded once again that death is never easy—for anybody.

Now, if I could find my wayward husband to help me carry all this Tupperware to the car.

"Percy?" I call.

No response.

"Percyyyy?"

"What?" he shouts from his study.

"Come out to the kitchen and help me, please," I answer.

I wait a couple of minutes, then force the issue. "Percy, don't make me have to hunt you down."

"All right, all right," he hollers.

Percy trudges into the kitchen and looks around at all the containers. "Are you feeding an army or something?"

"I told you last night, remember? It's for Mr. Isaac," I scold.

"Oh, yeah. Your boyfriend," Percy says dryly. "What all did you make for Prince Charming?"

"Ham, baked chicken, pork chops, macaroni and cheese, collards, and ambrosia," I reply as I gather my purse and jacket.

"You made that poor man ambrosia?"

"Mr. Isaac *likes* it, Percy," I argue.

"He must have a death wish, then," Percy mutters.

"Can you stop with the commentary and take these to my car?" I snap.

"Okay, okay. Keep your cool."

"What's on your agenda today? Let me guess—fishing," I snort.

"You got that right," he nods. "I think I'll take the boat out this afternoon."

"Did you buy a life jacket?"

"C'mon, now. I don't need one of those," Percy protests.

"Percy Blaine Babineaux, we discussed this..." I grumble.

"But..." he interjects.

"No buts. Which would you prefer? A pinch," I chomp my left hand at him, "or a thump?" I ask while flicking my fingers on the right. "Because you're getting one or the other if you don't pick up a life vest *today*," I stress.

Percy steps back defensively. "Fine, Clem, fine. Just keep your hands to yourself." He sighs. "How is it you always seem to win these arguments?"

"Because I'm *always* right," I nod, satisfied with myself.

The morning passes quickly as I monitor the residents in the new VR spaces Cleo and her partner arranged. Cleo tells me that soon they'll be able to visit museums together and interact while they are there. It adds such a rich dimension to their experiences to connect with people, even if most of them don't remember who they met the day before. That's dementia for you.

What's funny is how carefully the residents selected their avatars, with some trying to appear as they normally do, while others chose a face and body type resembling someone completely different. The residents got such a kick out of creating their virtual identities, that I decided it was too good a deal to pass up.

As such, I'm off to my Happy Place to take a spin in the virtual realm as someone other than Clementine. I know I probably shouldn't of, but I get mighty bored watching folks interact, going on and on about their families, former careers, and whatnot since as their nurse I've heard most of their stories before. So, I toyed around and created a new, alternate avatar for myself: Rebecca.

After perusing the many personas available, I settled on an image much younger than me, with a tall, slim physique, long, flowing chestnut hair, and caramel-colored skin; a far cry from my actual dark, splotchy face, cropped Afro, and squatty build.

And let me tell you, my adrenaline gets to pumping when I think about strutting around as someone anonymous. Now, I realize how silly it is to be excited about playing make-believe, but a little daydreaming never hurt anyone, and I could sure use some sparkle in my life, even if it's all pretend.

Just as I open the door to my Happy Place, Mama Pearl sees me as she turns into the hallway.

"There you are, Clementine. I was wondering where you ran off to," she says with a grin.

"Hey there, Ruth. I'm on break and thought I'd give the land of virtual reality a spin." I wave my headset at her.

"With how much time you spend in there with the residents, I would've thought you'd be tired of it by now," Mama Pearl observes.

"Not when I'm Rebecca." I bat my eyes and run my hand through imaginary long locks.

"You're going to use an alias?" she chuckles.

"Yes ma'am, I surely am."

"Well, I'll be. What's in there you're hoping to find, Clem?" Mama Pearl wonders curiously.

"I don't have the faintest idea. But I'll let you know when I find out." I flash her an impish grin and head off for a new adventure.

Cleo

Work has been a beatdown these past two weeks, what with Jonathan and me burning the midnight oil keeping up with our own VR systems while helping the Bro Club with their God-awful project. I use the term "project" loosely, given how little the Bros had accomplished before Jonathan and I came in. It makes me wonder whether they attempted any real programming at all; maybe that was their plan from the start.

Because of the grind, there's been no time for me to help Mrs. Hadley in her quest to find her daughter. But I made Mrs. Hadley a promise, and I'm a woman of my word. So, this bright, chilly Saturday morning I'm holed up in Brian's apartment working in companionable silence right alongside him; me in exploratory mode and Brian in computer gaming mode. How some boys can play that stuff day in and day out is befuddling, to say the least. Brian says he does it purely for work research, to sharpen his skills so he can get better at securing client networks. Yeah, right. But I digress.

On the relationship front, things have been a bit chilly with Brian since he overheard me speak of my hesitancy toward marriage. I've done my best to reassure him with all the love I've got that he's the man for me, up to, but not including, becoming his wife. I know it sticks in his craw, yet I can't lie to him. And so it goes.

I begin my investigative journey into Mrs. Hadley's past and thank the good Lord that Ohio is an open record state; meaning I can search birth and death certificates without them being unsealed. Since Mrs. Hadley's daughter was born in 1961, I first check Ohio's Department of Health to see what's available, but they don't have a searchable database. Boo. After a bit of Googling, though, I find a non-profit outfit called Family Search that has a robust collection of records divided by county. It also allows me to narrow my query by parent name. Bingo. A few keystrokes later and voila, there in black and white is the name of Mrs. Hadley's daughter: Jane Smith. And according to this, she's still alive.

So, I pivot to Google once again and use the White Pages website this time, filtering by state and age. Sure enough, I discover a Jane Smith living in Cleveland, Ohio, in her sixties, with Dayton as one of her former residences.

"Well, I'll be damn," I say out loud.

"What?" Brian asks, his gaze still fixed on his game console.

"I think I've found Mrs. Hadley's daughter." I flip my laptop around to show him.

"Really?" He lays his controller on the table to give me his undivided attention, then peers closely at the screen. "Jane Smith is her name, huh?"

"It sure seems like it," I nod.

"That didn't take you very long. I thought it would be months before you discovered anything. You make it look easy," he adds.

I shrug. "Beginner's luck, I guess."

"What's the plan now?" Brian wonders.

"Let Mrs. Hadley know what I've found and go from there," I reply.

Brian's expression turns serious. "Is getting involved in this a good idea, Cleo? It's one thing to do some internet sleuthing, but if Jane Smith is truly her daughter, things are fixing to get real. How far are you willing to go?"

"I guess that's up to Mrs. Hadley. She doesn't have anybody, Brian. If I can help her, I don't see how that's a bad thing."

"This ain't no VR game, Cleo. These are people's lives. You just can't play around with them," Brian remarks soberly and leaves the family room.

Why do I get the feeling he isn't referring solely to Mrs. Hadley? I think about it for a while and wonder if he'll ever let this marriage thing go. One thing I *do* know through all of this: Love sure is hard sometimes.

Margaret

ay 1970

MIt's one of those days here in North Texas where you'd swear it was the middle of August instead of May, with the blazing heat stifling your senses and the humidity so thick you wish you could wring the wetness out of the air like a washcloth. I've opened every window in my little home in hopes of getting a cross-breeze between the kitchen and family room, and box fans are already blowing full steam ahead to make the interior more bearable.

Magnolia's car pulls up in front of the house and she and Billy tumble out onto the sidewalk. Although I can't hear her, by Magnolia's actions I can see she's put out with her young son, pulling him by the hand to hurry him along, her lips moving like a magpie and her expression full of frustration.

That poor boy. Magnolia's got Billy wound so tight he's petrified of making a mistake, even around me. Case in point: Not long after I began looking after him, Billy woke up from his afternoon nap and came out into the family room in a flood of tears.

"What's wrong, Billy boy?" I asked.

"I... I... made... a... mess, Maggie," he whimpered.

"How's that?" I wondered.

"I... wet... the... bed," Billy wailed.

I scooped him into my arms to soothe him. "Well, accidents can happen to any little person, Billy. I did it myself when I was your age."

"You did?"

"I sure did."

"Don't tell Mother, okay? She whips me when I wet the bed. Can it be our little secret?" he begged.

"You bet. It'll be our little secret. I promise." I set Billy down and took his hands in mine. "Everyone makes mistakes, sweetie. Even your mother."

Billy's eyes grew wide. "She does?"

"I promise you she does," I nodded.

Billy considered this a moment. "Thank you, Maggie," he said and threw his arms around me. Right then, I understood just how difficult it must be for Billy and his father, Ashby, to live under Magnolia's constant criticism, and my heart ached because I knew that disapproval all too well.

The doorbell rings, interrupting my thoughts. I open the front door and see Magnolia and Billy waiting on the stoop, with Magnolia holding a large paper bag.

"Good morning, Billy boy!" I exclaim.

"Hi, Aunt Margaret," he replies sullenly, without his usual spunk.

"Why the long face?" I ask.

He shrugs and peers down at his shoes.

"Billy's none too keen on learning his letters and colors. But we all have to at some point, don't we Billy? So, I brought you some workbooks to help him along." Magnolia thrusts the sack at me. "No time like the present, right young man?"

Billy shrugs again and jams his hands into his jean's pockets.

"I'll just take a quick look around before I go." Magnolia sidesteps me and makes her way inside.

Now you would think after five weeks of watching her son without incident that Magnolia would be more trusting of me and let her guard down a little. Yet each morning and evening she inspects my home like a drill sergeant, checking to make sure things are just so and complaining when they don't meet her lofty expectations. It's enough to drive me batty.

"You know, Magnolia, nothing's changed in here since yesterday afternoon. Could you give it a rest for once?" I ask tartly.

"Why? Do you have something to hide?" She cocks her brow.

"Of course not," I reply testily.

"Then you shouldn't mind if I do," Magnolia quips.

She noses around my kitchen, looking through my cabinets and the refrigerator, then digs around in my laundry basket for God knows what.

Satisfied, Magnolia brushes by Billy and me toward the door. "Well alright then, I'm off. Have a good day. Oh, and Margaret, if Billy plays in the water would you make sure he's properly dried? I don't want my leather seats getting wet."

And just like that, she's gone.

"Mother didn't hug me goodbye," Billy remarks softly.

Try as he might, Billy can't hide his hurt. I don't understand people like Magnolia sometimes. Affection is such an easy thing to share, but some people can't be bothered.

I scoop Billy into my arms and shower his cheeks with kisses.

"Stop, Maggie!" he giggles.

"What do you say we take a peek inside this bag and see what we've got."

"Do we have to?" Billy pouts.

"Only to see what we're up against."

We sit on the sofa, and I dump the contents onto the coffee table.

"Hmm. *ABC's and Me. Colors, Colors, Colors.*" I thumb through the workbooks. "These look pretty dull."

"They are," Billy agrees.

I think for a minute. "Well, your mother's right. You do need to know this stuff. But there are other ways to learn."

I grab a stack of magazines from the end table. "We can use these instead."

"How about we start with colors?" I fan my fingernails in front of him. "What color is this?"

"Ah… um…" Billy hems and haws.

"Red. This is red."

"Red," he repeats.

"Good. Now I want you to find pictures of red in here." I hand Billy a *Cosmopolitan* with a half-naked lady on the cover and think better of it. "On second thought, use this one." I give him a *Vogue*. Sometimes discretion is the better part of valor.

Billy flips through a few pages and then stops. "Here's red!"

"That's right. Now, tear it out," I instruct.

"But that'll mess up your magazine," Billy counters, wrinkling his nose.

"Don't you worry, I've got plenty more where that came from. Go on; let 'er rip."

Billy tugs the page, and it comes out in one piece.

"Great. Once we've got a bunch more, we're going to make something called a collage."

"What's that, Maggie?"

"It's where you glue pictures onto paper to create something beautiful, and you'll learn about colors in the process. Before long, you'll have your very own art gallery."

"Neat!" Billy replies.

We work together the rest of the morning, tearing and pasting images of every shade in the rainbow onto construction paper and hanging them throughout the family room. Billy can now name each color without hesitation. How about that? Billy's become an expert in less than a day.

I do hope Magnolia will praise Billy's success. Even though I shower him with all the love I have in me, Billy thirsts for his mother's approval. Even at four years of age, her disappointment pains him so.

The afternoon air is stifling, so we change into our swimsuits, and I attach the garden hose to a fun new toy I bought: a Slip 'N Slide. Billy and I take turns running and splashing through the water until our fingers are good and pruney. I make us some proper lemonade—with real lemons, not from concentrate—and serve it on the front porch along with animal crackers and peanut butter cookies for sustenance.

Once he's reenergized, Billy devises a game where he hits a whiffle ball off a tee, slides down the Slip 'N Slide to retrieve it, and then repeats the process. Since he's in hog heaven, I decide to take a breather and paint my nails a different shade; chartreuse this time.

As they dry, a late-model car appears around the bend—Ashby's car. He slows to a stop in front of the house.

"Daddy!" Billy runs into Ashby's arms.

"Hi there, Billy! Are you staying cool on this blistering day?"

"I sure am. Do you want to play?"

"Not right now. Why don't you show me how it's done?" Ashby sets Billy down, revealing a huge water stain that marks his suit jacket.

Ashby saunters to the porch. Our eyes meet and my heart skips a beat.

"Hello, Ashby."

"Hello, Maggie."

"Would you like some lemonade?" Before Ashby replies, I busy myself pouring him a tumbler so he can't see his effect on me.

"Sure, I'll take a glass. Thank you." He shrugs off his jacket and settles onto the porch steps.

"Here you go." I hand him his drink and sit beside him; close enough to touch but far enough away to not arouse suspicion.

Ashby takes a long draft. "This is good; so refreshing on a hot day." He looks me over from head to toe. "I don't believe I've complimented you on your hair. Blonde suits you well."

My cheeks blush. "Thank you, Ashby."

He drains the glass and sets it aside. "I want to thank you for looking after Billy. He just loves coming over here."

"Really?"

"You're all he talks about at home. It drives Magnolia stark raving mad," he snorts in amusement.

"I'm happy to help."

"Listen, Maggie." Ashby grazes his hand across my knee and my heart skips a beat. "I was wondering if I could stop by during my lunch hour to see Billy. I don't get a chance to spend much time with him in the evenings, what with work and all. So, how about it?"

"I think that's a fine idea. Billy usually eats around noon and takes a nap right after."

"A nap, huh? For how long?" Ashby cocks his head, his lips curling into a flirty smile.

"Hour, hour and a half," I say casually.

Ashby nods slowly. "Good to know."

"Why Ashby Conrad, what's going on in that mind of yours?" I tease.

His expression turns serious, and my pulse quickens.

"Lots of things, Margaret Worthington. Lots of things."

Mrs. Hadley

A few weeks ago, Mama Pearl ordered physical therapy for me to invigorate my lower body, in hopes I could slowly transition to a cane instead of using my cumbersome walker. I'm mighty grateful to her since the exercises and treatments have energized my muscles and been a welcome distraction while Cleo searches for my daughter. As I lie on my back, Mama Pearl tests my leg strength and I silently pray for good news.

"You're much improved, Mrs. Hadley. I think you're ready to try a cane," Mama Pearl remarks as she helps me into a sitting position.

"Praise the Lord," I clap my hands in delight. "The faster I can get rid of that old walker, the better."

"Now, this will be a gradual process, Mrs. Hadley. And I don't want you using the cane without a therapist or a nurse around. Nothing good comes from breaking a hip," Mama Pearl warns.

"I understand."

"Hey there, Mrs. Hadley; hey, Mama," Cleo says brightly as she breezes into my room.

"You find anything, Cleo?" My anxiety surrounding my daughter is such that I overlook the normal pleasantries and get straight to the point.

Cleo's gaze darts between me and Mama Pearl, silently requesting my permission to answer.

"It's okay, Cleo. You can speak in front of your mama. I don't have anything to hide." I assure her, and then I turn to Mama Pearl. "Cleo's helping me find my daughter."

"Well, I'll be. Isn't that something?" Mama Pearl wonders in amazement. "Was that part of Cleo's project?"

"Yes and no," I shrug as my uneasiness rises.

Mama Pearl pats my arm and gathers her black bag. "Well, I'll leave you both to it. I'll write the order today, and hopefully, by tomorrow you'll be practicing with a cane, Mrs. Hadley." She kisses Cleo's forehead and heads out the door.

I don't rightly know why I suddenly got cold feet when discussing my daughter in front of Ruth. But good old Mama Pearl: Where most others would ask a million questions, she understands her boundaries, letting her patients open up to her when they're good and ready, and not a moment before. For that, and so many other things, I thank the Lord daily for the blessing that is Ruth Ada Pearl.

"Well?" I ask Cleo anxiously.

"I think I've found her," she nods.

My eyes widen. "Is she alive?"

"Yes, ma'am." Cleo steps forward and hands me a printout. "Her name is Jane Smith. She lives in Cleveland, Ohio."

I draw in a sharp breath as my heart pounds a mile a minute. There on the document are my daughter's particulars: her name; her address; James and I listed as her parents. It's overwhelming. I bury my face in my hands and begin to weep.

"Oh, Mrs. Hadley, I thought you'd be happy," Cleo says with alarm as she wraps her arms around me.

"I... am... happy. I... am," I choke between sobs.

"Okay," she replies, none too convinced, and rocks me gently.

After a little, I'm able to calm down and catch my breath. "Sorry about that." Cleo hands me a tissue and I wipe my tears away. "Do you know anything more about her?" I ask.

"That's as far as I got. I thought we could do some sleuthing together. How does that sound?"

I nod and blow my nose.

"It might be easier at the table. Let me help you over there," Cleo offers as she scoots my walker in front of the bed.

Once we're settled, Cleo pops open her laptop. "There's a website called TruthFinder that we can use. It'll show where Jane has lived, any relatives, all kinds of things. Do you want me to go ahead?"

"Yes, please," I reply as my nerves do the jitterbug, swing dancing to and fro and back to front.

Cleo works her magic on the computer, typing away until she finds what we're looking for.

"Jane resided on St. Joseph's Avenue in Dayton for eighteen years. After that, there are various addresses in Cleveland listed for her," Cleo remarks.

"Was she adopted?" I wonder.

"I don't think so, or there would be other names noted here as relatives," Cleo points out.

"Then who raised her?"

"Let me search the address in Dayton." Cleo does her thing and then shares the results. "It looks like Jane grew up in St. Joseph's Orphanage."

I sigh and shake my head. "That poor girl. She's what, sixty-one years old by now?"

Cleo nods. "She is. There's not much more information on this site. I'll try Facebook and see if Jane has a public profile there."

Cleo continues her detective work, and after a bit, she meets my eye as a grin crosses her lips.

"Mrs. Hadley, this here is your daughter."

Cleo turns the laptop around and there she is, right in front of me: Jane. My Jane. She's smiling brightly, with James' eyes and my high cheekbones. I would recognize her anywhere.

Cleo comes around the table to join me. "It looks like Jane enjoys playing basketball, too." She points to a photo of Jane and her teammates, sitting in wheelchairs under a basketball goal and sporting large, gold medals around their necks.

I peer closely at the picture, noticing that Jane's arms are normal, but her legs appear childlike, not fully formed, just as the doctor warned me so many years ago. Still, Jane didn't let that stop her, and my heart swells with pride.

"I can print some of these off for you if you like, Mrs. Hadley," Cleo offers.

"That would be wonderful, Cleo. Thank you," I reply.

As I gaze at my girl, reality settles in, and melancholy shrouds me like a thick blanket.

"Is something wrong, Mrs. Hadley?" Cleo asks.

I turn to her and wonder out loud, "Oh, Cleo. What do I do now?"

Clementine

Well, fiddlesticks, I say to no one in particular since I'm holed up alone in my Happy Place. I pluck off my VR goggles and sigh loudly, disappointed with my second foray into the virtual realm as Rebecca. To say my experience in there left something to be desired is an understatement.

On my first go around, I was flirted with unmercifully by two octogenarians; today there was no one about, so I meandered a bit and then called it a day. I guess it never occurred to me that the only folks inhabiting this little oasis would be the residents I care for daily. Even though they're cognitively impaired, they're not too far gone to notice that the cast of characters is small in there. Note to self: Speak to Cleo about opening the space to other people outside of Worthy Community Home, or the natives may grow restless, including yours truly.

I return to my desk at the nurses' station and notice a large stack of Tupperware and a beautiful bouquet of pale pink and lavender peonies wrapped in tissue.

"Where'd these come from?" I ask Ida Mae.

"Mr. Isaac dropped them off earlier."

"Well, ain't that sweet of him." I bring the flowers to my nose and inhale their wondrous scent. "I should put these in some water. Do we have any vases around here?"

"In the break room, I believe," Ida Mae replies. "Did Rebecca have a pleasant stroll in the metaverse today?" she teases.

I shake my head. "Don't ask."

"Pretty dull?"

"You can say that again," I remark, and head off down the hall.

As I pass through the residents' wing, the echo of singing fills the air, faintly at first, but crescendos as I near Miss Margaret's room. I allow Miss Margaret to finish her solo, then give her a round of applause.

"That was wonderful, Miss Margaret, and kinda sassy I might add," I praise her from the doorway.

"Why thank you, Clementine. I've always liked songs with a little swagger to them."

"I didn't know you could sing?"

"Oh, yes. I was quite the songstress back in the day. And I just love music; it makes me giddy."

"You seem so much happier these days, Miss Margaret, and livelier, too."

"It's all because of that contraption Cleo lets me wear. It takes me back to the most amazing time of my life—when I met my one, true love. I feel like I'm getting a second chance," Miss Margaret says wistfully.

"It's done wonders for you, I tell you that," I marvel.

"Georgina promised to bring my record player and some of my albums the next time she visits. Would it be all right to play them?"

"I don't see why not, as long as the other residents don't complain."

Miss Margaret claps her hands together. "Marvelous. Say," she points to the bouquet in my hand, "where did you get those lovely flowers?"

"Mr. Isaac gave them to me."

"Clementine," Miss Margaret clucks her tongue jokingly, "and I thought you were a married woman," she teases.

"Don't you be ornery now, Miss Margaret," I chuckle. "I'll come by and check on you later."

I swing down to Mrs. Hadley's room and find her working intently with a physical therapist using only a cane for support. She's another resident who's shown much progress in the past weeks. Since Mr. Isaac's office is just across the hall from her, I decide to pop in and thank him for the flowers.

But I'm not prepared for what I find.

Mr. Isaac is seated behind his desk, his head leaning as far back as it can go, his body rigid and stiff. Oh, sweet Jesus.

I set the bouquet down and touch his arm cautiously. "Mr. Isaac?"

No response.

"Mr. Isaac?" I say louder and shake his shoulders.

"Aah!" Mr. Isaac snaps to attention and jumps straight out of his chair.

"Aah!" I scream in reply.

Mr. Isaac clutches his chest. "Oh, Mrs. Babineaux you gave me a fright."

"I thought you were gone, Mr. Isaac," I remark.

"Gone where?" he wonders.

"Gone, gone." I nod my head for emphasis.

Mr. Isaac considers this for a moment, then begins to giggle. "You... thought... I... was... dead?" his giggles grow louder.

"Why yes, I did," I chuckle.

His cackles progress into a full-fledged belly laugh, and since laughter is contagious, I join in right along with him. We hee-haw for a minute or so, to the point where we grab our sides and gasp for breath.

"I'm sorry Mrs. Babineaux. I know this ain't a laughing matter," he sighs. "I haven't been sleeping much lately and I'm a bit off my head."

"That's understandable, Mr. Isaac, what with all you've been through." The air grows awkward between us. "Thank you for the flowers," I say to change the subject.

"It's the least I could do for all that delicious food you cooked for me."

"There'll be plenty more where that came from until you get back on your feet, Mr. Isaac."

"I appreciate that, Mrs. Babineaux. You know, I grew those flowers myself," he offers proudly.

"Did you now?"

"Peonies were Lily's favorite. When she got sick, I tilled up the whole backyard and planted peonies in every color I could find. That way, she could look out our bedroom window and see them blooming if she didn't have the strength to go outside. They were my love letter to her."

"That's beautiful, Mr. Isaac," I reply softly.

"I thought it would be easier, a comfort even, now that Lily's out of her pain. But it's so hard," his voice breaks. "There's nothing harder."

I wrap him in an embrace. "Bless you, Mr. Isaac. God bless you."

Some may judge me for putting my arms around another who ain't my husband. But this man is hurting, and I happen to believe the good Lord didn't put me on this earth to look the other way. So, I hold him and let his tears wet my shoulder, until there's no more left to spill.

Cleo

After what seemed like an eternity and a day, Jonathan and I finally put the finishing touches on the Bro Club's project yesterday so they could begin testing. Just as I suspected, the Bros had done little in the way of programming, leaving it up to Jonathan and me to mete out the parameters and logistics. Of course, Quinn and his crew took all the credit, shocking I know, so in turn, Ingram heaped praise on them with nary a "Thanks" aimed in our direction. It's enough to make my head explode, but as Mama says, what doesn't kill you makes you stronger; I feel like Hercules right about now.

Because we've been knee-deep in someone else's weeds, Jonathan and I have had no time to touch base on our own enterprise. More importantly, I've had zero opportunity to restock my refrigerator with Mama's delectable cooking. So, in an act of desperation, I fished through my freezer this morning and found the last of any semblance of food in my apartment; pork chops I fried at some undocumented time in the past.

I hand Jonathan his portion and settle into my desk chair. He picks up his utensils and commences sawing into his meat as if it were a forty-year-old piece of pine wood. I inspect my pork chop, pale gray and dry, and knock it against the side of my desk like a hammer; it's that stale.

"Did your mother make this?" Jonathan asks meekly.

"No, these would be my handiwork, and they are inedible." I grab our plates and dump their contents into the trash. "I need to remember to date my freezer food."

"There's always ramen," Jonathan adds cheerfully, attempting to make me feel better.

I curl my lip at the thought.

"Since I've got you here, we've got a few items to discuss about our project," I begin. "First off, we need to come up with a name. Calling it a 'project' doesn't have much pizzazz."

"It's necessary to have pizzazz?"

"Yeah, you know, something cute and catchy," I add.

"Do I look like someone who concerns himself with 'cute and catchy?'" Jonathan gestures to his scuffed loafers, rumpled khakis, and weathered plaid shirt.

"Fine, I'll do it. Let me think." I consider our predicament for a moment, then the spirit moves me. "How about 'Head in the Clouds?' Most folks think the metaverse is up there somewhere." I point to the heavens.

"Not bad," Jonathan shrugs halfheartedly.

"Do you have a better idea?"

"'Head in the Clouds' is fine. Let's move on," Jonathan replies.

"All right. Miss Clementine suggested we open the VR spaces to persons outside Worthy Community Home."

"That would add interest but comes with more oversight. Our original task was to explore memories, not to amuse the masses," Jonathan emphasizes.

"True, but the entertainment areas would be less expensive and easier for institutions to use. It could become a viable revenue stream for Next Well."

"Memory investigation is more compelling."

"And we'll still be exploring Miss Margaret's recollections. Think of it as a way to fund our memory research after Head in the Clouds ends."

Jonathan nods begrudgingly. "Okay. Since Mrs. Hadley won't be participating any longer, I guess we could use some of the budget to expand the designs to accommodate more people."

"Now you're talking," I say as my stomach growls.

"Want me to heat up some noodles?" Jonathan asks.

"It's Friday. Let's go out for lunch—my treat," I offer.

"Where should we go?"

"Smokey's Barbecue is just down the street, and they cook up a mean rack of ribs and some tasty brisket."

Jonathan scrunches his nose. "Barbecue?"

"Come on, Jonathan. Live a little."

"Mama, where're you at?" I holler as the screen door slams shut behind me.

"In the kitchen," she calls.

I lug three bags of Tupperware through the family room and dump them onto the kitchen table.

"Well, ain't you a sight for sore eyes," Mama remarks. "Come over here and give me some love."

Mama wraps me in a bear hug and kisses the daylights out of me.

"It's so good to see you, Cleovantra. I know we bump into each other at the Home, but we haven't talked in a blue moon it seems. Come on, let's sit for a spell. You want anything?"

"I'm good, Mama. I should be coming around more often since work has settled down."

Mama carries her coffee cup over and takes the chair next to me. "How's that project of yours going?"

"It's got a title now: 'Head in the Clouds'. Miss Margaret's taken to it like a duck to water. Mrs. Hadley, on the other hand, met up with some memories she didn't want to relive, so she's paused for the time being."

"Is what Mrs. Hadley said the other day true, Cleo? Did you find her daughter?" Mama wonders.

"Yes, ma'am I surely did. I'm amazed Mrs. Hadley could forget such a thing as the birth of her child."

"It all depends on what you can bear, Cleo. You'd be surprised at how far the mind will go to protect the heart. What's Mrs. Hadley going to do?"

"I guess try and get in contact with her, but Mrs. Hadley hasn't said anything definite," I shrug.

"Are you planning on helping her?"

"If she wants me to."

"Is that a wise idea?" Mama asks cautiously.

"What do you mean by that?"

"Cleo, sometimes it's best to create boundaries with people. It's all well and good to assist Mrs. Hadley with her search, but you don't want to get tangled up in a situation where you don't belong," she counsels.

"That's a lot like the pot meeting the kettle, Mama. Look at how you burn the midnight oil caring for folks, using your own money to buy their medication and such."

"That's different, Cleo. It's a matter of life and death for some of my patients," Mama argues.

"How do you know it isn't for Mrs. Hadley? She doesn't have anyone left, Mama. You sound just like Brian," I scoff.

"How *is* Brian by the way?" she asks softly.

I sigh deeply. "Fair to partly cloudy."

"You want to talk about it?"

I shake my head. "Talking won't do any good."

The air grows uneasy between us.

"Times like these, I wish your father was here." Mama strokes my hair. "He always knew what to say to you."

"Mama..." I interject.

"It's true. I'll never forget when we brought Moses home from the hospital. You took one look at that screaming bundle and ran off to your room, slammed the door, and stuck your head under the pillow. Swore you'd never come out again. But Gus went in there and whispered his magic words, and sure enough you came around to your brother. Your father had the Midas touch with you."

"I love you, Mama," I say and clasp her hands in mine.

The truth is tricky sometimes. It'll come up and pinch you when you least expect it and leave a little mark in its wake. Like now for instance. What Mama said about Daddy and me was genuine and true. I just don't have it in me to speak it out loud. That would hurt Mama so, and I could never do that to her. Not to Mama.

Margaret

My heart is light, my soul airy, and my anticipation great. Cleo and her magic time machine will soon be here to whisk me away for another glimpse into my beloved past and, fingers crossed, Ashby. In the meantime, I waltz around my room, humming as I go, with an old dust broom as my partner, until my adventure resumes.

"Mother? What are you *doing*?" Georgina cries from the doorway, her expression aghast.

"Why, I'm dancing is all," I reply as I spin across the floor.

"With a broom?" she asks, chagrined, her arms laden with record albums.

Mr. Isaac limps in behind her lugging my stereo and speakers.

"I was wondering where that went to. I've been looking all over the place for that sweeper." He sets the equipment on my bureau against the wall. "I never figured it'd end up a dance partner," he chuckles.

"You don't mind if I use it, do you, Mr. Isaac?" I purr charmingly. "It comes in handy when I get the urge to take a whirl."

"I've got another one I can make do with," he replies as he plugs in the sound system.

"That's very kind of you, Mr. Isaac," Georgina chimes in.

"It's no bother. You're all fixed up now, Miss Margaret. Mrs. Babineaux wanted me to remind you to keep the volume low, so you don't disturb the other residents."

"Will do. Thank you, Mr. Isaac."

Georgina drops the albums on my coffee table with a thud.

"Careful now," I scold.

"*Sorry*," she replies irritably.

I shoot her an icy stare, then thumb through the records until I find an oldie but goodie by Dolly Parton.

"C'mon. Let's shake a leg. It'll help get you out of the funk you're in." I offer her my hand.

"No, thank you." She holds up her palms to resist.

"You'll feel better," I insist.

"No, mother. I don't want to dance with you. God, you never stop, do you?" Georgina shouts.

"What's eating you, Georgina? Is it Lacey? You two have an argument?"

Georgina folds her arms and turns away from me.

"That's it, isn't it? You bickered over me, didn't you? She still won't come to visit me here and you gave her an earful. I bet you told her it wasn't right to treat her mother that way. Well, I thank you kindly, Georgina. You've always been such a good daughter..."

"*It has nothing to do with you and Lacey, mother. Not everything revolves around you*," she roars.

I stop mid-diatribe when it finally dawns on me that something deeper is bothering my oldest girl.

"Sit down, Georgina." She hesitates. "Please?" I ask softly.

Begrudgingly, she joins me at the table.

I take her hand in mine. "Tell me."

"It's Kevin," she sighs deeply. "We aren't getting along; we haven't been for months. Nothing I do is right, whether it's the kids or the house or the finances, everything that goes wrong is somehow my fault."

"How's your sex life?" I wonder matter-of-factly.

"Mom!" Georgina exclaims.

"What? It's important."

"That's my fault, too, apparently," she mutters.

"Is he stepping out on you?"

"I don't think so. He works from home like I do, so he's not out running around. We just don't connect like we used to."

"Are you happy? Because it sure doesn't seem like you are."

"No," her voice quivers as she looks away.

"Then leave him," I offer pragmatically.

"Leave him?" she turns to me, stunned.

"What good does it do to stay in a miserable marriage? I should know; I've been married three times. And in every one of them, I hightailed it out of there at the first sign of cracks."

"I can't leave. What about my kids—your grandkids? What will a divorce do to them?"

"Would you have preferred me to stay with your father? Remember all the knockdown-drag-out fights we had? And how relieved you were once your daddy and I separated?"

"I still love Kevin, Mother," Georgina replies just above a whisper.

"Love is overrated, in my opinion. Try and work it out, I guess. Give yourself an end date, though. Don't let it drag on. It'll make it worse for everybody in the end. Take it from me, Georgina. If there's one thing I'm an expert in, it's how to break up an unhappy marriage."

Mrs. Hadley

"Focus, Irene. Focus. Get to that chair over there across the way," I say to myself. It's not but ten feet in front of me, but it might as well be ten miles with how tired I am right about now. The physical therapist worked me for an hour this morning on exercises to strengthen my "core", whatever that is, then using my walking stick, yet not enough to satisfy my impatient spirit. So, I'm doing what I've been warned not to: taking a stroll with my cane all by my lonesome.

I'm thankful for the distraction. It helps keep my mind off Jane, at least for a bit. It's a bitter, double-edged sword, finding my daughter: my heart sings knowing she's alive, but how to contact her is another matter entirely.

Okay. I made it to the chair. I plop down to rest for a moment, then take a deep breath, plant my cane, and try to pull my considerable girth into a standing position. But my stick slips out from under me, and I teeter to and fro, struggling to keep my balance.

"Oh, Lord," I exclaim.

"Mrs. Hadley?" Cleo drops her bag at the doorway and hustles over to help steady me. "Let's get you back in the chair." Cleo eases me down gently.

"Whoo, Cleo. That was a close one. A split-second more and I would've been greeting the floor with my face and breaking a hip besides."

"Didn't Mama caution you not to walk alone?"

"Why yes, she did. Can't we keep this just between us, though? I don't need Clementine or your mama fussing at me."

"Miss Clementine and Mama are right, Mrs. Hadley. You're not steady enough to do this by yourself."

"I've got to occupy my mind somehow or all I'll do is fret over Jane."

"Have you come to any decisions?" Cleo asks delicately.

I shake my head. "I don't know where to begin. I can't exactly get on an airplane and go introduce myself; not in my condition. So, what do I do? Call her on the phone and say, 'Hi Jane. This here's your mother. You know, the lady who turned tail and left you behind sixty-some-odd years ago. Want to be friends?'"

Cleo nods. "I understand. I've been doing some thinking myself and I have an idea. I poked around a bit more and found out that Jane is very involved in her wheelchair basketball team. In fact, she runs the team and has been for five years now. Since you both love the sport, maybe that's a way for the two of you to meet."

"I'm afraid I'm too old to push a wheelchair around, Cleo. Besides Jane lives hundreds of miles away."

"Jane lives far-off on *this* mortal plane, but not in the virtual world."

Suddenly, a light bulb flickers inside my head and all becomes clearer.

"You want to use those funny-looking goggles to bring us together?"

Cleo smiles knowingly. "Yes, ma'am."

"You think Jane would actually do it?"

"It's a long shot, I'll admit. But Mama's always said I can talk the paint off the walls down to the studs to get what I'm after. So, I like my chances."

"Well then, let's give it a try, Cleo," I nod with a smile.

Cleo

Of the many blessings I have to be thankful for, the one that is most serendipitous at present is my dear Auntie Ella, and by extension, her delectable Oreo peanut butter pie. Since this is a 911 situation, Auntie prepared her mouthwatering concoction yesterday evening for me to bring to the office in hopes of softening up Jonathan by way of his sweet tooth. If I've learned anything about my cubicle mate in the short time we've known each other it's that a food-induced coma is the best way to wear him down to get what I'm aiming for.

True to form, Jonathan is already in the office at seven-thirty in the morning, hunched over his laptop, banging away at the keyboard like his life depended on it.

"Careful now. You're going to wear those keys down to the nub pounding them like that," I caution as I place the pie and my bag on my desk.

"Did your laptop do you dirty again?" I tease.

"I type with purpose and intentionality," Jonathan replies.

"That phrase would look great on a greeting card," I reply tartly.

"There's nothing wrong with how I type," he says defensively.

"Of course not." I unwrap the pie and hold it under his nose for him to observe. "Think you can pull yourself away from murdering your keyboard for a piece of Auntie Ella's Oreo peanut butter pie?"

His eyes narrow. "What are you scheming, Cleo?"

I feign outrage. "Can't I share some of Auntie's love and blessings with my project partner for no reason?"

"I'm onto you. You bring sweets to the office whenever you want something from me."

"Not *all* the time," I maintain.

"So, you admit it," he counters.

"Okay," I confess. "I have an ulterior motive."

I set the dessert down and take a seat.

"I think it would be a good idea to make the outdoor and basketball areas appear more real like they do in the memory recall space. That way, all the residents can enjoy an enhanced experience."

"That requires money, Cleo…"

"I know, I know," I interject. "But look," I pull a large spreadsheet from my bag and hand it to him, "I ran the numbers last night and we can swing the extra cost."

Jonathan considers my proposal for a moment, which gives me just enough time to slice a humungous piece of pie and set it next to him as a lure to reel him in. He shovels two large bites with reckless abandon, then moans softly.

"I'm a sucker for your auntie's charms," he mutters.

"It won't take but a few hours to program the changes. And, since we can cover the expense, why not make their interactions the best they can be? Come on Jonathan."

"Fine, you win," he sighs, "as long as I get the rest of the pie."

"I can't even have a sliver?"

"All's fair in war and desserts," he contends.

I curl my lip as I mull over his proposition, then begrudgingly hand it over.

Jonathan smiles broadly, like the cat who ate the canary. "Nice doing business with you."

"I've got to be more careful around you Mr. Chu or you're going to learn all my tricks."

"One thing you need to know about me, Cleo; I'm a very quick study," Jonathan replies as he stabs his fork into the center of the pie.

It doesn't take Jonathan and me long to make the adjustments, and we set the program to update tomorrow morning. To be honest, Jonathan could've finished it up on his own, but it helped me productively procrastinate from my next, looming task: emailing Jane.

Using my ninja-like sleuthing skills, I found where Jane works and her contact information. I figured it would be less creepy to reach out to her there than her personal address. But finding Jane was the easy part; now I have to work out what to say.

I first try the homegirl approach:

Hey there, Jane! This here's Cleovantra Pearl from way down in Dallas, Texas. Guess what? I know who your mama is. Hit me up for a chat, will ya?

Call me crazy, but somehow, I don't think that's the right tone.

I then attempt a cryptic style:

Miss Smith: I have important information regarding your next of kin. Please respond at your earliest convenience. Thank you.

Hmm. Still not it. Since the third time's typically the charm, I opt for a more direct route:

Dear Miss Smith. My name is Cleo Pearl, and I am a virtual reality developer with Next Well Technologies in Dallas, Texas. Currently, my team and I are testing a virtual basketball environment in hopes that disabled individuals might enjoy a more enhanced experience in the metaverse than what they are normally accustomed to.

After much research, I discovered your wheelchair basketball team, the Cleveland Comets, has enjoyed much success competing in the National Wheelchair Basketball Association. Since you are the Comets' liaison, I am reaching out to you to gauge your and your team's interest in taking part in our project. All equipment would be provided by Next Well, and there would be no traveling involved. All interactions would be done virtually and in the privacy of your own homes.

This is an evolving design, and your participation would greatly enhance our sampling data. Please let me know if you would like to engage in this new and exciting cutting-edge technology.

Regards, Cleo Pearl.

All right, then. No muss, no fuss, and straight to the point. I like it. I give my email the once-over and then send it off into the stratosphere in hopes of attracting Miss Jane Smith's attention. Fingers crossed.

Clementine

Oh, my. I never figured the metaverse would look quite like this. Miss Margaret has described her experiences in the VR realm to be akin to the real thing, right down to the slightest smell and touch. But I wasn't prepared for how vibrant the space would be since Cleo's enhancements. She and her partner put some forethought into the changes as well, with the residents' avatars giving off a slight glow so the staff can easily spot them among the newcomers milling about.

It's a welcome diversion, too, because this morning one of our longtime inhabitants went home to Jesus. She'd been in the throes of dementia for the past three years, but deteriorated rapidly in the last couple of months, unable to walk, to speak, then finally, to eat. I wish I could say she died peacefully; truth is, she thrashed about unmercifully before she went like she wasn't going to let go without a fight. In the end, though, grace and peace finally found her, and she chose to let them in. She folded her arms across her chest, and that was that.

It goes this way for most of the folks I've looked after over the years. I get to know them, care for them, love them, then they leave. And a little piece of my heart passes right along with them.

As I stroll through the park space now, the sun feels warm on my skin and a slight breeze flutters the trees' leaves like they're dancing in the air. I pass others along the walking paths, exchanging "Hellos" and pleasantries about the weather. It's nice to see new faces, even if they're masquerading as someone else. It helps lift my spirits and adds a bit of mystery to the place.

I come to a small pond in the center of the park and admire the tranquil, crystal-blue water. I step closer to its banks, reaching out to run my hand through the calm waters, when my feet give way and I slide down the muddy banks and into the pond.

"Lord have mercy," I exclaim.

"Ma'am? Are you all right?" a tall, husky gentleman shouts from the path.

Try as I might to lift them, my feet are stuck to the pond's floor.

"I'm fine," I reply. "I just can't move is all."

"Here, let me help you." He quickly removes his shoes and wades in.

"Lean on me, then I'll tug your legs to see if we can't get you free."

He bends down and I brace against him. My Good Samaritan pries my limbs from the muck, then delivers me safely to shore.

"There you go. All better now," he grins.

"Except for my shoes. They got left behind, I'm afraid." I glance at my bare feet.

"Want me to fish them out of there for you?" he asks.

"No, no. I can just conjure up some new ones," I chuckle.

He nods. "Ain't that the truth."

I'm close enough to get a good look at his features: his soft, brown eyes tinged with laugh lines, his complexion the shade of brown sugar, his warm, open smile.

"I do so appreciate your help. I'm Rebecca," I say and offer my hand.

"Gregory," he replies, and we shake, his grasp firm but soft to the touch.

Across the way, two men begin arguing, their voices aggressive and threatening. I look over, and sure enough, they're residents of mine in some sort of a spat over a park bench.

"Ooh, Gregory. I'm sorry, but I have to go."

"Already?"

"I'm afraid so. It was nice meeting you," I respond.

"Will you come back someday?" Gregory calls after me.

"I'm sure I will," I nod and scuttle away.

"When?"

"Soon," I holler over my shoulder, then sneak around the corner so he won't notice my avatar change from Rebecca to Clementine.

Fiddlesticks. And I was just getting to know Gregory, too. Sometimes these residents of mine can be a real pain in the neck.

After diffusing World War III over squatters' rights in the virtual realm, my afternoon proves much quieter, thank the sweet Lord Jesus. While I pull my purse and lunch bag out of my car, I notice the distinct smell of burning flour as I near the garage.

"What's Percy gotten into this time?" I mutter aloud, shaking my head.

I open the back door and, sure enough, there's Percy, covered in white powder, with fish guts on the counter and scorched fillets in a cast iron skillet.

"Percy? What on earth are you doing?" I cry.

"I'm making dinner. What's it look like?" he replies and scoops the burnt bits onto plates.

"You ain't cooked by yourself not one day in the forty years we've been married, Percy Blaine Babineaux. Why'd you decide to start now?" My eyes narrow. "Something happen to that boat of yours?" I ask suspiciously.

"Naw, Clem. It's nothing like that." He sets the food on the table and takes me in his arms.

"You work hard all day and I'm retired now. I thought making us a little dinner was the least I could do," Percy explains.

"Well, isn't that something? Wonders never cease, I suppose."

"There's a first time for everything. Give me a little sugar now," he pulls me closer and kisses me long and deep, enough to make my knees buckle like when we were young.

"I could get used to this, Mr. Babineaux."

"There's plenty more where that came from," Percy grins devilishly, takes my hand, and leads me toward our bedroom.

Margaret

May 1970

Yesterday it was hot as blazes outside; today it's raining buckets with no sign of letting up. Daddy likes to say there are four seasons in Texas: heat, drought, floods, and twisters, which is pretty accurate as far as I can tell. It's a funny thing about sayings; there's always a kernel of truth to them.

Days like this when Billy can't get out and shake around to burn off some of his fireball energy are challenging for me, since I've got to get creative to prevent the doldrums from setting in.

"I'm tired of looking through magazines, Maggie. Can't we do something else?" Billy whines.

"We need to find a few more examples of the letter 't', then we can take a break," I reply.

"But I don't *want* to," he shouts and swipes the magazines off the coffee table in one fell swoop.

"That wasn't very nice, Billy," I say evenly with a disappointed gaze.

Billy shoves his hands in his pockets and stares down at his shoes. "I know. I'm sorry, Maggie."

"You pick those up and place them nicely on the table while I think about our next project," I instruct.

"Won't you help me?" he moans.

"No, sir. You made this mess; it's your job to clean it up."

"*Okay*," he mutters begrudgingly.

While Billy busies himself, I begin thumbing through my record collection when an idea hits me.

"I know what we'll do," I spin around to face him. "I'm going to teach you how to dance."

"Isn't that for older folks?" Billy wonders.

"Anyone can learn to dance, and there's no time like the present. Come on over here," I direct.

"Which one am I going to learn?"

"The Jitterbug. And this song," I place a record on the turntable, "is perfect. It's called 'At the Hop.'"

I take his hands in mine. "Okay, just follow what I do, and you'll have it down in no time. First, we're going to swing our arms back and forth and step forward and backward like this," I demonstrate.

It doesn't take long for Billy to get the hang of the rhythm. "Good. Now, let go of my left hand."

He does as he's told, and we continue moving without missing a beat. I twirl him around and he shouts with excitement.

"I'm dancing, Maggie!"

"You sure are," I reply.

Billy and I swing and sway through another six songs until we're both gasping for air.

"Ooh, I'm tuckered out." I wheeze while holding my sides.

"That was fun," Billy exclaims, "but my tummy is growling," he says as he grabs his stomach.

"Why don't we have something to eat? What are you hungry for?" I ask.

"Peanut butter and jelly."

"Peanut butter and jelly it is. Put that record back in its sleeve, would you Billy? And I'll make our lunch."

Just then, there's a knock and the front door opens.

"I didn't miss anything, did I?" Ashby asks, grinning from ear to ear.

"Daddy!" Billy hollers and rushes over to hug Ashby, rain-soaked jacket and all.

"Hey, there Billy boy."

"You're drenched, Ashby. Take that coat off and I'll hang it up to dry. Then you both can have a seat in the kitchen while I make our sandwiches," I order.

"Yes, ma'am." Ashby nods and whispers to Billy loud enough so I can hear, "I think Aunt Margaret means business."

"You've got that right." I turn on my heel and get to work.

After we've satisfied our inner beasts with peanut butter sandwiches and celery sticks, Billy yawns and rubs his eyes, struggling to stay awake.

"I think it's time for someone's nap," I suggest.

"Do I have to?" Billy fusses.

"You know how crabby you get when you don't get your rest," I reply.

"I'm a little hellion in a teacup?" Billy offers.

"That's right," I agree. "Give your father a hug, then I'll tuck you in."

I lead Billy by the hand to the guest room, turn on the small fan next to the bed to stir the air around and add some white noise, then kiss his cheek. By the time his head hits the pillow, he's out like a light.

Ashby has settled himself on the family room sofa, his arms splayed across its back and his tie loosened and askew.

"Come over here and sit with me for a bit," he commands, patting the seat cushion next to him.

I join him, with my hands sweaty and my pulse quickening. Ashby pulls me closer so our legs are touching, while casually wrapping his arm around my shoulders.

"Was that your idea?" Ashby nods toward the far wall that's covered in Billy's artwork.

"Billy was a bit resistant to flash cards, so I thought something more tactile would suit him better," I reply nervously.

"Your hair smells wonderful; like a bouquet of roses." Ashby runs his nose along my neck.

I shudder at his touch, and it's all I can do to keep calm.

Ashby kisses me softly at first, then more deeply, our intensity rising. He lowers me so we're lying down, our lips never parting.

He fumbles with his pants' zipper, pulls my panties aside, and before I know it, I feel a pinch, a few thrusts, and then he's done. I lay there, wide-eyed and motionless.

After a bit, Ashby sits up to adjust himself. "Whew. That was great, darlin'. Was that your first time?"

I nod, still speechless.

"Well, it'll get better as you do it more," Ashby casually assures me. "I've got to get back to the dealership. Fetch my jacket for me, will you?"

I do as I'm asked, still in a fog. Ashby shrugs on his coat, kisses my cheek, then lets himself out.

A clap of thunder jolts me out of my haze, and Billy cries out to me from his room.

"Maggie!"

I rush to his side and wrap him in my arms.

"It's okay, Billy boy. It's just a little storm is all," I say and rock him gently.

"Sing to me, Maggie," he begs.

So, I oblige him, softly, with "You Are My Sunshine," his favorite.

The melody calms Billy's spirit and I lay him back down.

I've heard it said you're supposed to feel different, like a woman, when you lose your innocence. But that's not how it is for me. There's a distance, a hollowness, I can't shake. And I'm left to wonder: What's love supposed to be like? Because that sure wasn't it.

Mrs. Hadley

Oh, lordy but I'm sore. Ever since my near miss the other day walking with my cane, Clementine's been showing up to my room twice daily, once after my physical therapy appointment in the morning, and then later in the afternoon, to take me for a stroll up and down the hallway. My hunch is a little bird named Cleo whispered in Clementine's ear about my close call even when I asked her not to. No mind, though; Cleo's heart was in the right place. And the upshot is, the more practice I get with my walking stick, the quicker I can leave that godforsaken walker behind.

"All right, Mrs. Hadley. Once more down the hall and we'll call it a day," Clementine says.

"Good. I could use a break," I agree, as we amble to my room.

"Mrs. Hadley! Mrs. Hadley!"

Clementine and I turn around to see Cleo running toward us full steam ahead, in heels mind you, frantically waving her arms.

"Is there a fire somewhere we don't know about, Cleo?" Clementine muses.

Cleo catches up to us, gasping for breath. "It's Jane, Mrs. Hadley. She's interested in our VR project. And she can Zoom with me now!"

Cleo rushes into my room lugging her hefty bag.

"What's a zoom?" I ask Clementine, befuddled.

"It's where folks talk to other folks on the computer," Clementine explains.

"So they can hear each other?" I wonder.

"And see each other, too," Clementine nods.

"Oh, my. I'll have to put some makeup on. How's my hair look?" I ask Clementine nervously as I run a hand through my short locks.

"Jane ain't going to see *you*, Mrs. Hadley, unless you want to confess who you are on a video screen," Clementine stresses.

"But I'll be able to hear her, you think?"

"Probably so. Let's get on into your room and find out," Clementine prods, and I move as quickly as my old legs will carry me.

"All set up, Mrs. Hadley," Cleo says, seated at my small table in the center of the room.

Cleo's angled her computer so it's facing a blank wall; I suspect to hide the fact that Jane will be conversing with Cleo in her elderly Mama's room and not some fancy office building.

"Why don't you and Miss Clementine sit over by the bed, Mrs. Hadley?" Cleo suggests.

We settle ourselves and Cleo gets down to business.

"All right, you two, here goes. Fingers crossed," Cleo says and punches away on her keyboard.

After a bit, some noises arise from the laptop's speakers.

"Hi, Miss Jane! It's nice to see you. How are you this fine afternoon?" Cleo asks enthusiastically.

"Good, good. Nice to see you too, Cleo," Jane replies.

"Ooh! Ooh!" I exclaim, excited to hear my girl's voice.

"Shh!" Clementine shushes me as she presses a finger to her lips.

"Sorry about that, Miss Jane. Open-concept seating here at the office sure makes it hard to have a bit of privacy," Cleo explains, thinking on her feet.

"Oh, I understand. I've got the same setup here. It annoys the dickens out of me," Jane chuckles. "I must say I was surprised to receive your email the other day. I discussed your proposal with my teammates, and we're very interested. We'd like to give it a try."

I mouth "yay," and quietly clap my hands with glee.

"I'm so pleased to hear that, Miss Jane. As I mentioned previously, Next Well will supply the VR headsets, and I'll train you and your teammates on how to use them," Cleo responds.

"When can we expect the headsets?" Jane wonders.

"I'll send them overnight to your business address, so hopefully sometime tomorrow; the next day at the latest," Cleo replies.

"And how long will the testing go on for?"

"Two months."

"Our team practices on Wednesday nights. Would you be available to give us a demonstration at that time?" Jane asks.

"I sure would. How about next week?" Cleo offers.

"Perfect. Okay, then. We're looking forward to it," Jane remarks.

"I am, too, Miss Jane. Your participation will really change things up. Talk to you soon." And with that, Cleo signs off.

"Is the coast clear?" I ask hesitantly.

"All done," Cleo confirms.

"Oh, my gosh! Oh, my gosh! Oh, my gosh! Oh, my gosh!" I flap my hands excitedly, then wrap Cleo in my arms. "Thank you, thank you, thank you, Cleo! I'm going to be with my girl now!" I say as I sway her back and forth.

"It sure looks like it, Mrs. Hadley. One step at a time, though."

"I know," I sigh happily. "Just let me cherish this for a moment. At my age, it's the little things that make *all* the difference."

Cleo

rue to my word, I gathered up eight VR headsets from the office—
Miss Jane only asked for seven, but I threw in one extra for good
measure—and scrounged around Brian's apartment for boxes since
he's such a packrat. Much of the software and computer games he buys come
in large packages, so I figured I could use a few of them and declutter his
space at the same time; what my daddy would call a win-win situation.

"Are you going to use *all* of those?" Brian asks, annoyed at the disruption
of his personal space.

"They're just gathering dust," I retort.

"What if I need to return something?" he argues.

"These boxes are from stuff you bought before the pandemic, so I think
it's safe to assume they're out of warranty," I counter.

"Maybe I just like having them around," Brian mumbles disagreeably.

That's it. I've had enough.

"When are you going to stop punishing me?"

He exhales deeply and peers down at his shoes.

"I've been paying a penance to you for weeks now, ever since Mr. Percy
said his piece on marriage. The fact is, you and I've never talked about it;
we've just been dancing around the subject. And I think it's about time we
cleared the air."

I prop my hands on my hips like I mean business. "I love you with all that
I've got, Brian Robinson. You make my knees buckle and my heart sing, and
I can't imagine my life without you. You had me way back in high school,
and you'll have some kind of hold on me until the day I die."

I inch closer to him, my anger softening.

"We aren't but twenty-three years of age, you and me. Marriage is a big deal, Brian, and I'm not ready for that yet; the operative word being 'yet.'"

I slowly wrap my arms around him, his gaze still downcast.

"Let's allow the idea to marinate for a while, then we'll see about trying it on for size. Okay?"

I nudge Brian to look at me. "Please don't be angry with me."

He shakes his head. "I'm not angry. I've never been angry."

"What is it, then?" I ask gently.

"I'm scared," he whispers.

"Scared of what?" I coax.

"Scared that I'm not enough for you anymore, and you'll look around for someone better. You've turned into somebody else these past few months: new job, new hair. You don't even speak like you used to," Brian laments.

"What's wrong with the way I speak?"

"'Ain't' used to be your favorite word," he remarks, cocking his eyebrow.

"Just because I've cleaned up my speech and straightened my hair doesn't mean I'm leaving you, Bri," I chuckle.

"Really?" he asks anxiously, his brow furrowed with worry.

"*Now hear this, Brian Eugene Robinson. I am not going anywhere,*" I shout. "*Get that through that thick head of yours,*" I tap his forehead for emphasis.

"Okay," he replies, unconvinced.

I offer my hand. "Let's seal the deal: Pinky swear."

Brian breaks into a smile.

"You know I mean business when I whip out my pinky. Say it," I command, and grab his finger with mine.

"Pinky swear," he shakes his head and laughs.

"Good. It's official now," I decree, then rain kisses all over his face.

"C'mon and help me wrap these headsets so I can send them off tonight," I direct.

I toss a box to Brian and get back to the task at hand.

"Hey Cleo, I forgot to tell you. I was pinged on LinkedIn by a recruiter from Google. They're hiring for an Internet Security manager," he offers casually.

"Ooh, baby. You're attracting the big guns. Did you set up an interview?"

"Not yet. You see the thing is, it's not for the Dallas office. The job's located in Austin."

I pause what I'm doing and meet his gaze.

"I don't want to move. So, I'm going to tell them, 'Thanks, but no thanks,'" he shrugs.

"No sir, Mr. Robinson. You set up an appointment with them ASAP and see where this thing goes," I counsel.

"You think?"

"I *know*," I emphasize. "You can't let an opportunity like that go to waste."

"Will do, then. Thanks for the encouragement, baby."

We exchange small, wistful smiles, quietly acknowledging that all is fine on the surface, but recognizing deep down, uncertainty and turbulence still linger below.

Clementine

I look to my left—nobody's there. I look to my right—the coast is clear. Thank the Lord for small miracles. I jiggle my key into the door lock and enter my Happy Place, in hopes of taking a break and continuing my metaverse adventures. It seems like everybody, residents and staff alike, wants a piece of me today, so ten minutes is about all I can spare. I snap on my headset, set my avatar to Rebecca, and away I go.

The space is just as beautiful and alluring as before, like the prettiest spring day you've ever seen; seventy degrees, blue skies, a gentle breeze. I'm near the pond, so I walk closer to see if I can't run into Gregory again, that fine specimen of a man who helped me out of the water the last time I visited.

Sure enough, I spot him among a clump of trees near the path surrounded by a gaggle of women, no doubt competing to attract his attention. Since my time here is short, I decide to sidestep the swarm, and quietly resolve to connect with Gregory another day.

"Rebecca?"

I spin around.

"I thought that was you." Gregory smiles at me then turns to the others, "If you'll excuse me, ladies," he says and quickly joins me by my side.

"I like your shoes," Gregory remarks teasingly.

I chuckle and peer down at the red, sequined heels I'm sporting, just like Dorothy wore in *The Wizard of Oz*. "It's amazing the selection you can choose from in this neck of the metaverse."

"They suit you," Gregory compliments.

"Why, thank you, kind sir. I like these shoes better than the ones I lost in the pond, anyway."

"Did you hurt yourself the other day, you know, for real?" Gregory asks.

"No, no," I assure him. "Only my pride."

"I guess what happens here, stays here," he replies.

I nod. "That's the idea, I think."

"Do you mind if I ask you about yourself?"

"You mean, who I am on the other side?"

"Yeah," Gregory shrugs. "Too much?"

"I'd like to keep my selves separate for now."

"Fair enough," he agrees. "What does Rebecca do for fun?"

"Rebecca's discovering herself, so that's to be determined."

Gregory stops and turns to me, his expression genuine.

"Well, speaking for Gregory, I can safely say he sure does enjoy walking in this beautiful oasis with Rebecca, whoever she decides to be."

"And speaking for Rebecca, the pleasure is all hers."

Gregory's face brightens and his smile gleams.

Out of the corner of my eye, I see Ida Mae across the way, waving her arms to flag me down and pointing to her watch.

"Ooh, Gregory. It's time for me to go."

"So soon?"

"I'll try to visit tomorrow," I reply.

"Same time?" he asks.

"Same place," I nod.

I take off down the path, cut through a grove of trees, and return to my storage closet. I whip off my headset and lock the door behind me.

"How are you this fine day, Mrs. Babineaux?" I hear behind me.

I spin around and see Mr. Isaac cradling VR goggles in his hands.

"I'm blessed as always, Mr. Isaac. Are you trying out the metaverse as well?" I ask.

"Yes, ma'am. Miss Cleo showed me how to get in there the other day; she said it might keep me from being so lonesome."

"How's it working out for you?"

"Better than I imagined. And you?" Mr. Isaac wonders.

"It's got possibilities," I shrug. "But time will tell, I suppose."

Margaret

July 1970

It's been about six weeks since Ashby's first visit, and we've established a routine of sorts. Every Tuesday and Friday Ashby stops by for lunch. After we've eaten, I put Billy down for his nap, Ashby has his way with me on the sofa, then he returns to the dealership, all in the span of an hour, as if it were any other normal day.

It *has* gotten better, the private part that is, just like Ashby said it would. But what used to be uncomfortable from a physical standpoint, is now troublesome from an emotional point of view, because guilt rears its ugly head every once and a while. Ashby *is* Magnolia's husband, after all.

I've mentioned my remorse to Ashby a time or two, but he tells me to put it out of my mind and not give it another thought; that's what he does to rest peacefully at night, and he can, he says, without a care in the world.

At Daddy's Sunday gatherings, Ashby and I are rarely in the same room together and we hardly ever speak. Yet now and then, Daddy's caught the lingering glances Ashby and I exchange, which makes me wonder if he's getting wise to us. Daddy hasn't let on like he suspects anything, but doubt persists in the corners of my mind.

As for Billy, most days he's as happy as a frog on a fresh lily pad. He continues to chug along with his letters and numbers; having mastered them by sight, he's now progressed to printing them on Big Chief writing tablets. Once he finishes a page, Billy rips it out and pins it proudly in the guest room where he naps, since the far wall in my den is completely covered with his collages and artwork.

I wish Magnolia shared in Billy's excitement. After thoroughly inspecting my home every morning for the first month or so, Magnolia seldom enters anymore, acting troubled and distracted while she stands at the front door, rarely hugging Billy goodbye, or even acknowledging his existence.

He doesn't say it out loud, but there's no doubt in my mind it hurts Billy's heart to be neglected by his mother this way. I do what I can to brighten his spirits, but at the end of the day, I'm just his aunt and current caregiver. I pray Billy's young enough he can't recognize the difference; that he knows he's loved unconditionally, no matter the source.

To celebrate his scholastic successes and change our routine up a bit, I've been taking Billy over to Daddy's to teach him to swim in Daddy's gargantuan backyard pool.

"Can I go outside and play with my Nerf ball?" Billy asks while I stuff a change of clothes and towels into a bag.

"That's fine, as long as you stay on the lawn. If that ball of yours goes into the street, you wait for me to fetch it for you, you hear?" I instruct.

"Yes, ma'am," he nods.

"Okay, then. You can go on out. I'll be there in a minute," I reply.

I double-check the duffel, grab my car keys, and lock the door, something I'm loath to do but Daddy insists on, saying a single girl can't be too careful in this day and age.

I turn around to corral Billy into the car, when I'll be damned if he isn't in the middle of the road, chasing after that ball of his.

"William Theodore Brooks! You get back here this instant," I scream.

Billy scurries toward me, Nerf ball in hand, his expression contorted like he knows he's going to get a talking-to.

I hunch over and shake his shoulders. "Billy, I've told you time and again you cannot run into the street like that."

"I'm sorry, Maggie," he wails.

"Sorry won't cut it if you end up a heap of bones, Billy Brooks. There's a blind curve in the road. Cars can't see you until they're right on top of you. By then, it's too late," I remark forcefully.

"I know," Billy whispers as tears roll down his cheeks. He stares at his shoes, ashamed, then shoves his hands into the pockets of his swim trunks.

I exhale deeply. "I don't mean to be harsh, but it fills me with dread when you don't mind me." I pull him into my arms, "I do love you so, Billy boy."

"I love you, too, Maggie."

I brush Billy's tears away, then hold him awhile to help right the chilly air between us.

"Can I take my Nerf ball over to Papaw's house?" Billy asks, which somehow manages to break the ice.

"As long as you hold onto it real tight," I warn.

"With all my might," Billy nods.

Even though it's only been a couple of weeks, Billy's taken to swimming like a duck to water, no pun intended, with him mastering floating, kicking, and holding his breath while submerged in that short amount of time. This afternoon, I introduced the breaststroke to him, and he's been practicing across the short end of the pool to get the mechanics right.

"Okay, Billy. Once more then we'll call it a day," I say.

"Do we have to? I like playing in the pool," he fusses.

"We've been out here for an hour already and I don't want you to burn. Besides, Miss Clarice promised us lemonade and her famous chocolate chip cookies," I contend.

"Come to think of it, I *do* have a rumbly in my tumbly, just like Winnie the Pooh," he grins as he rubs his stomach.

"All right, Pooh bear. Last time," I chuckle.

Billy leans forward with his arms in front of him, pushes his feet against my hands, and away he goes to the other end.

"Well done, young man," Daddy praises from the covered porch.

"Hi, Papaw," Billy replies as he wipes water from his eyes.

I pull Billy out of the pool and help dry him off with a towel.

"It's a rare afternoon when you aren't at the dealership, Daddy," I remark.

"I had business here at the house. Besides, it's not every day I get to watch my only grandson in his athletic endeavors," Daddy responds and tousles Billy's wet head.

"Billy, why don't you go on into the kitchen? I believe Clarice has a fresh batch of cookies baked just for you. Aunt Margaret will join you in a minute," Daddy directs.

I towel dry my hair while Daddy takes a seat on a nearby lounge chair. He gestures for me to follow suit.

"It's mighty nice of you to teach Billy like you are, Maggie. Things have sure changed from when you were a child. Do you remember how I taught you to swim?" Daddy wonders.

"How could I forget? You threw me off the dock and into Lake Worthy at three years of age then hollered, "Swim, dammit! Swim!""

"In my view, that's still the best way to learn; your survival skills kick in," Daddy replies.

"What do you want to speak with me about, Daddy?" I ask.

"Hmm?"

"You've got that look on your face. What have I done this time?" I muse.

"I hope you haven't *done* anything," Daddy emphasizes.

"Are we going to talk in riddles, or are you going to cut to the chase?"

Daddy brushes some lint from his pant leg, stalling for time, while he formulates his thoughts.

"Families are fragile things, Margaret. They're difficult to create, yet so easily fractured."

"And?" I prod.

Daddy turns and stares me straight in the eye. "I've seen the way you and Ashby look at each other. I'm also aware he visits your home for lunch on occasion, ostensibly to spend time with Billy. But I'm a man; I know better."

I break away from his gaze, the truth prickling me.

"Need I remind you, Margaret, Ashby is your sister's husband. He is not available. I want you to keep that notion front and center in your mind. Do you understand me?"

I nod slowly, the hairs on the back of my neck standing on end from Daddy's astute revelation.

"Have you spoken to Ashby about this?"

"No, I haven't."

"Why not?"

"Because he's not my flesh and blood, Margaret. *You* are." Daddy gives me a knowing glance.

We sit in silence for a bit, and then he rises, pats my shoulder, and leaves me to wrestle with my conscience.

Mrs. Hadley

It's finally here: the day I've thought of and dreamed about for weeks now. In a matter of minutes, I will occupy the same space as my daughter, after sixty-one years of estrangement on this mortal plane. Granted, it will be in the virtual realm, but that's just a minor detail, at least to me anyway.

Cleo's got me all set up with a new avatar that resembles my current build and complexion but shaves several years off so I appear much younger than I really am. To my mind, I reasoned that a youthful version of myself would make me more approachable to Jane and her teammates. Deep down, though, I'm afraid vanity had something to do with my decision. It's hard to accept growing older sometimes, even when you're already old.

"Do you want me to refresh your memory on how the controls work, Mrs. Hadley?" Cleo asks as she snaps on my headset and hands me the joysticks.

"No, no. I think I'm good. Jane will be in there, right?" I wonder anxiously.

"She said she would be," Cleo answers patiently. "Remember, like before, I'm going to watch what happens. So, if you feel unsure about anything, I'll be there to help you. I can show up anywhere, anytime. You just call for me, all right?"

I nod, my heart racing a mile a minute.

"You ready, Mrs. Hadley?"

"Ready as I'll ever be," I reply.

As soon as I utter those words, I'm whisked away into the basketball arena space. I take a quick look around to get my bearings and notice several women at the other end of the court, a mixture of tall, short, black, white, and brown, passing and dribbling around the basket.

Then I spot her: my Jane. She's lithe and graceful running across the floor, her smile radiating enthusiasm and delight like a child opening gifts on Christmas day. I see that she's created an avatar to reflect her natural features: short, cropped hair, medium build, hazelnut complexion, with several years trimmed off, as I did. Perhaps pridefulness is an inherited trait.

A few of the ladies take notice of me gawking, so I hustle over to the rack and grab a basketball. Instead of a proper dribble, though, the ball glances off my foot and rolls in Jane's direction.

"Watch out!" I shout, before it tangles in Jane's stride.

She scoops up the errant ball and flashes me a smile. "Thanks for the heads up," she replies and tosses it back to me.

"Sorry about that. I'm a little rusty." My voice quivers anxiously.

"We all are," Jane remarks reassuringly. "Would you like to join us?"

"Oh, I don't know…" I hesitate.

"If you do, we'll have enough folks to play four-on-four," she points out.

In my mind's eye, I figured I could view Jane from afar for a while until I gathered my courage. But her friendliness and openness have caught me unaware, and I'm filled with dread. What if she suspects something right off the bat? What if I can't explain myself properly? What if it turns out she hates me?

"Well, uh…" I hem and haw as my real hands drench the controls.

"C'mon, it'll be fun," Jane coaxes.

"Okay," I nod weakly.

"What's your name so I can introduce you to everyone else?" Jane asks.

"Irene," I respond hesitantly, bracing for it to mean something to her. "But everybody called me 'Ree' back in the day," I add.

"Ree," Jane repeats. "I like it; it rolls off the tongue."

Jane turns her attention to her teammates. "Hey, y'all? This here is Ree. She's going to fill out our roster so we can do some scrimmaging."

After introductions are made, we divide up into two teams of four. Since I'm the tallest avatar out here, Jane selects me for her squad, and I quietly pray I don't embarrass myself too much.

But that's exactly what happens. See, I'm only acquainted with six-on-six basketball, where there are three players on the offensive end and three on the defensive side from each team, with no crossing the half-court line. Because of my height, I would camp out under the basket in high school and wait for my teammates to throw me the ball from the other side for an easy layup. Some games I never broke a sweat. So, full-court rules are a mystery to me.

Imagine my surprise after my team scored its first bucket. I stayed right where I was near the free throw line, while my teammates hustled down to the other end. It didn't take long for our opponent to figure out one of their own was unguarded, and an easy layup ensued.

"Hold on a minute," Jane says to the others. "Ree? What're you doing down there?" she hollers while jogging in my direction.

"I'm waiting for one of you to throw me the basketball," I reply innocently.

"But you've got to play defense, too," Jane remarks.

"Oh," I answer, befuddled.

"You've played ball before, right?" Jane asks.

"Six-on-six," I nod.

Jane stares at me, her mouth gaping. "Wait a minute. You've never played full-court basketball?"

"Not a lick."

"So, you've never guarded anyone?" Jane clarifies.

"No, ma'am."

"If you don't mind me asking, Ree, exactly how old *are* you, you know, out there?" Jane points her finger to the sky.

"I'll be eighty-one come January."

"You sure don't look it," Jane chuckles while she gazes at me from head to toe. "I guess we're going to have a bit of a learning curve with you. No matter, though. You ready to continue?"

"Let's go," I say, and take my spot under the basket.

The game progresses about how you would expect it to with someone who's a defensive novice. And, lord, it sure is ugly. For every basket my team makes, the player I'm supposed to guard winds up scoring at the other end with ease. To add insult to injury, my hand-eye coordination fails me, as more often than not I fumble passes or miss chip shot layups. Jane and the others encourage me, but as the game ends, I'm humiliated.

While her teammates leave the space, Jane approaches me, her expression sympathetic and understanding.

"Rough one, huh?" Jane wonders.

"You can say that again," I shrug.

"We all have games where nothing goes right," she replies, trying to cheer me up.

"I'm not usually this bad," I lament.

"It happens," Jane emphasizes. "I'm still getting used to the joysticks and how to move with them, myself. So, I've decided to work on my game in here every Monday evening. Would you like to join me, Ree? Maybe we could get better together."

My heart swells at her suggestion. Spending one-on-one time with my girl is a dream come true, even if it's virtually.

"I'd love to," I reply excitedly.

"Seven o'clock, eastern time?"

I nod eagerly. "I wouldn't miss it for the world."

Cleo

Now that the whirlwind of activity surrounding our metaverse improvements has finally let up, I've been able to take a breath and reflect on all that Jonathan and I have accomplished in the past weeks.

Not only have we devised a feasible option to keep the memory care residents of Worthy Community Home occupied and amused, but Jonathan and I have created an opportunity for Miss Margaret and Mrs. Hadley to revisit their memories.

From that, Mrs. Hadley was reminded of the birth of her daughter, something she had buried deep in her mind. But with our help and augmented reality, she's been reunited with Jane virtually, and, in time, may reveal to Jane her true identity.

As for Miss Margaret, she's reliving her first brush with love and all the tumult that accompanied it. Time will tell where that's headed, I guess. Regardless, Miss Margaret is calmer now and suffers fewer bouts of confusion while taking part in our project; that's a blessing any way you slice it.

Both Mama and Brian have warned me against getting into the thick of other people's business, but I just don't see the harm. If something positive comes out of it, what's wrong with a little, good old-fashioned meddling? Besides, it helps to satisfy my inner busybody, so everybody benefits.

"Earth to Cleo," Jonathan says, interrupting my thoughts.

"What?" I shake my head to return to the here and now.

"Are you with me, or do I need to repeat myself?" he asks annoyingly.

"Sorry. My mind was up around Pluto, but it's circling back down again. One more time for me, please?" I reply.

"What approach are we going to take with Ingram?" Jonathan reiterates.

He's referring to our "State of the Teams" meeting scheduled for a few minutes from now with our boss and the Bro Club.

"We'll explain how we've created a viable VR application with entertainment spaces that can produce sustainable revenue for Next Well, which will allow us to further explore the memory realm, thus enhancing the overall metaverse experience," I offer.

"That sounds a lot like a word salad," Jonathan remarks.

"You know as well as I do how much Ingram enjoys a good word salad, served with a large helping of BS on the side. It's his love language," I quip.

"True," Jonathan nods in agreement.

"It's early, but let's go down to the conference room and see if we can't snag a seat at the table," I suggest.

We hustle as fast as our legs will carry us, and much to our surprise, the room is empty.

"Would you look at that? We've got the whole place to ourselves. Hell must've frozen over," I marvel.

Jonathan and I take seats at the large oval table facing the wall of windows to the hallway, so we'll have a good view of who's coming and going.

"I've never sat at the table before," Jonathan remarks as he performs a 360 spin in his chair.

"Me neither," I respond, and prop my legs across the chairs on either side of me like I'm doing the splits. Good thing I'm wearing pants today.

Normally, Jonathan and I are relegated to the back forty, so sitting up here, with cushioned seats no less, is heaven.

While we revel in our newfound lounging status, Quinn, the ringleader of the Bro Club, saunters in, sipping a store-bought coffee and carrying an extra one in hand.

"Well, look who's here." Quinn checks his watch, "I figured you'd both be at IHOP for the early bird special. Isn't that what your clients prefer?"

"Where are the other bros, Quinn? Finishing up snack time with their juice and cookies?" I jab.

He sets the extra coffee at the head of the table—for Ingram no doubt—and settles in across from Jonathan and me.

"Unlike you two, my group doesn't require *all* of us to be in attendance to effectively communicate our project status," Quinn replies smugly.

"So, you drew the short straw?" I ask wryly.

"Shh," Quinn places his finger to his lips. "Quiet Cleo. I'm trying to imagine you with a personality."

"You know, Quinn, it's impossible to underestimate you."

Just as Quinn opens his mouth to deliver another salvo, Ingram breezes into the conference room.

"Thanks everyone for being here. Sorry I'm late," Ingram sits and takes a long draft from his coffee.

"Mmm, two sugars and a splash of cream, just the way I like it. Attentive as always, Quinn."

Quinn's lips curl with self-satisfaction. He's such a suck-up.

"I've only got a few, so let's get started," Ingram begins. "Cleo, where are we status-wise?"

"Well Ingram, we've had great success with the expansion of the enter-tainment areas..."

"I'm aware," Ingram interrupts with a wave of his hand. "I've reviewed the data and watched some of the footage. Have you secured a contract yet?"

"Um, no. We only rolled out Head in the Clouds eight weeks ago..."

"Wait a second," Ingram interjects. "I want to make sure I heard you correctly. Your project name is 'Head in the Clouds?'"

"Yes," I nod. "I think it captures..."

Ingram rolls his eyes as if he's never heard such an idiotic title, while Quinn snickers loudly.

"Whatever," Ingram says dismissively. "You need to start negotiations as soon as possible. I want no less than a two-year agreement, and I expect you to get it. Our division needs the cash flow."

Ingram turns to Quinn. "How are things going in the testing phase?"

"We've run into some problems," Quinn concedes.

Ingram swivels to Jonathan. "You're to pivot immediately and help Quinn's team sort out whatever issues they have. Both of you." Ingram stares me down for a hot minute.

"But..." I interject.

"We're done." And with that, Ingram grabs his drink and hustles out of the room.

Quinn leans in toward Jonathan and me, his smile smug and assured.

"See you soon," he goads.

Quinn and his boys may have gotten yet another lifeline from Ingram, but I'll be damned if I let Quinn get the last laugh.

Clementine

People are funny sometimes. You think you know them, then BAM, they do a 180 on you so fast it makes your head spin. Take my husband, Percy, for example.

During our forty-two years of marriage, Percy's always had an aversion to foods that are good for him, fruits and vegetables specifically, to where I've had to hide them in casseroles and such so he'll eat at least a little something that isn't soaked in grease. I think that's why he moans and complains so much about my ambrosia salad—it's too healthy for him.

Imagine my surprise, then, when I came home from work the other day to find Percy sitting in his recliner, watching the Fishing Channel, and munching on—wait for it—a salad. And not just any salad; a *green* salad with lettuce and tomatoes and cucumbers and a small dollop of dressing, but not a lick of meat.

At first, I thought I was in the wrong house, or the *Twilight Zone*, so I peeked out the window and double-checked the address on the mailbox, then had me a cold glass of water to clear any residual shock.

Finally, I gave Percy's head a good thump from behind to make doubly sure it was him.

"Ow! Damn woman!" Percy howled as he cowered from the blow, "What'd you go and do that for?"

"I was just checking to see if it's really you," I replied, eyeing him suspiciously.

"Who else would it be?" he cried.

"I don't know, *The Invasion of the Body Snatchers*? Cuz *my* Percy sure wouldn't be caught dead eating a salad."

"This ain't nothing, Clem. I thought I'd eat a little healthier is all."

"After forty years of me haranguing you about your diet, now you want to make a change?" I remarked dubiously.

"No time like the present," he said, then set his salad bowl down and pulled me into his lap.

"Percy! What's gotten into you?" I squealed with surprised delight.

"Be quiet now and give me some sugar," he demanded.

Percy kissed me with such eagerness it made my heart swoon like when we were young.

I thought Percy's dietary experiment would fade after a few days, but to my amazement, it's still going strong.

The usual suspects—me, Percy, Gabe, and Ella—are seated in Mama Pearl's family room for her customary Sunday feed, and Percy's attacking his fried chicken like they're locked in a battle for survival of the fittest.

"You're supposed to eat the thing, not scalp it, Percy," I remark while I watch him mutilate Ruth's delectable chicken.

"All the fat and calories are in the skin," he explains.

"Yeah, but when you take away the skin, you ain't got but a couple of bite-fulls left," I counter.

"Then I'll go get me another piece," he replies and continues to saw away.

"Say, Percy, did you take your boat out last week? The weather sure was beautiful," Gabe asks.

"Naw, I decided to do some walking around the neighborhood; get my heart rate up," Percy responds, then devours the few morsels of chicken to survive his assault.

"Hold up," I say. "You exercised?" I can't believe my ears.

Percy nods. "I also dug out my old weight set and pumped some iron." He curls his arms to show off his biceps.

"This from a man who keeps a cooler by his recliner so he don't have to get up to fetch another beer." I shake my head in disbelief.

"Not anymore. Meet the new and improving Percy," he grins.

"Wonders never cease," I roll my eyes, then turn to Ruth. "You got any macaroni and cheese left, Mama Pearl?"

"Let's go and see." Ruth rises and I follow her to the kitchen.

"Grab me another piece of chicken, Clem, preferably a breast," Percy calls after me.

"Where's Cleo and Brian today, Ruth?" I ask, while heaping my plate with pasta and fetching Percy the smallest bit of chicken I can find—a wing. That'll teach him not to say "please."

"They're both swamped with their jobs," Ruth answers.

"The last few times they were here, they looked pretty miserable. Things all right between them?" I ask gently.

"Fair to partly cloudy, according to Cleo, but she doesn't talk about it unless I bring it up," Ruth replies.

"They'll work it out. Cleo and Brian are one of those couples that are meant to be," I pat her arm reassuringly.

"I hear the VR experiment is going very well," Ruth remarks, changing the subject.

"It's a true blessing. I'm keeping my fingers crossed Hennessey Corp keeps it around when the testing is finished. When are you going to take a whirl in the metaverse, Ruth?"

"I have enough trouble keeping my life straight in the physical world. I can't imagine adding another dimension to the mix."

"It's fun and a nice diversion. I'm going to grab you some time and take you along with me. You'll be hooked after that," I tease.

Ruth leans in, "Ida Mae told me you have a male admirer."

"I don't, but Rebecca does." I smile and bat my eyelashes.

"You're a married woman," Ruth scolds.

"Not up there," I point to the heavens.

Ruth cocks her brow skeptically.

"It ain't real, Ruth. It's like a romance novel in 3D, and I'm the author."

"Mm-hmm," she answers, unconvinced.

"Trust me, Ruth. I know what I'm doing," nodding my head with certainty.

At least, I think I do.

Margaret

S*eptember 1970*

Since my come-to-Jesus talk with Daddy, I've been minding my p's and q's where Ashby's concerned, save for one, small slip-up.

I'd done everything I could think of to keep Ashby at bay, from extended swim lessons at Daddy's to long shopping sprees that dragged on through the lunch hour so Billy and I would miss his visits. That worked for a couple of weeks, but Billy started fussing about never seeing Ashby like he used to, so I was forced to devise a different strategy.

At first, I feigned migraines that would come on right after I put Billy down for his nap. I must've put on quite the performances because Ashby felt such sympathy for me that he brought me flowers—red carnations that smelled like cloves—and even made lunch for Billy and me the next time he came around. I was so touched by his thoughtfulness and concern, I decided I'd give in just that once and let him do as he pleased, imagined migraine or not.

But recently I came up with a foolproof way of discouraging Ashby: mysterious female troubles. All I have to do is clutch my abdomen and whisper "cramps," and Ashby no more wants to touch me than a hornet's nest. He must not have the faintest clue about a woman's monthly curse, since I've been milking the same excuse for five weeks now and it hasn't phased him. Ashby may get wise to me eventually; I guess I'll worry about that when the time comes.

Like clockwork, I hear Magnolia's car pull up in front of the house. When I open the door, Billy's face is swollen from tears.

"What's the matter, Billy boy?"

"

"I have something to discuss with you, Margaret," Magnolia says, her jaw firm and eyes ablaze.

She drags Billy by the hand into the foyer and my spine chills, bracing myself for what's next.

"Billy, go play in the guest room while I speak with your aunt," Magnolia directs sharply.

Billy snags his Nerf ball from the den floor and scurries away as if he can't bear to be near his mother another minute.

"What's on your mind, Magnolia?" I ask, struggling to keep my voice calm.

"I've signed Billy up for nursery school, Monday and Thursday mornings. It begins next week. He doesn't want to go, and I've met with much resistance from him. I expect you to help me convince Billy it's for his own good."

I let out a small sigh of relief, quietly thankful it's not an interrogation. Still, Magnolia's domineering attitude rubs me the wrong way.

"He's only four. That's a tad young, don't you think?"

"Billy's education must start early if he's to make something of himself. You wouldn't know anything about that, though," she sniffs disdainfully.

I bite my tongue and let her insult roll off me.

Magnolia turns to the family room wall covered in Billy's collages. "I assume this is your wayward attempt at teaching Billy his letters and numbers. What happened to the flashcards I gave you?"

"He didn't take to the cards very well. He's learned them *all* by doing it this way."

"Why didn't you tell me you changed his routine?" Magnolia snaps.

"I didn't think *how* Billy learned his letters and numbers was that big a deal. If you had bothered to ask Billy what we do around here, you would've found out sooner, I guess."

"Well, this simply won't do," she remarks, then proceeds to remove Billy's artwork from the wall.

"Magnolia! What are you doing?" I cry.

I grab her arm to stop her, but she yanks it away.

"Billy is *my* son, and he will be taught in the manner *I* choose," she shouts.

"Fine, I'll do whatever you want, just leave his pictures up there. Please?" I beg her.

Magnolia spins around to face me, her complexion red with rage.

"You don't tell me what to do, you hear me? You think you've got the world by the tail, don't you?" she scoffs.

"No, I don't," I answer defensively.

"I see you, Margaret. I see you. You think you can have anything you want, any man you desire, without any consequences, like that professor at your college. You thought nothing of having an affair with a married man and breaking up that marriage. And now, you think you've got Daddy wrapped around your finger, buying you this house, a car, and paying your bills, even after that scandal."

She inches closer to me. "But I've got news for you, *little sister*. Daddy didn't offer you all these airs and graces because he thinks you're special. No, ma'am. He did it to control you. You tarnished our family's good name Margaret Ann Worthington, and Daddy will move heaven and earth to make sure you don't turn into the town slut."

Instinctively, I slap Magnolia hard across her cheek, my anger seething.

"How dare you say such a thing to me. You think you're so smart, so clever, so superior. The fact is, *sister*, if it weren't for Daddy's money, you'd be just another spinster because you sure couldn't attract a man without it."

Magnolia returns the favor, striking me with all her might.

"Get out! Get out right now!" I scream.

"Gladly!" Magnolia shouts.

She rips Billy's collages in two and tosses them to the floor, before stomping out the door.

The sounds of sobbing come from behind me, and I turn to see Billy standing there, his face a puddle of tears.

"Mother... she... tore up... all my... art," he hiccups.

"I'm sorry, Billy. I don't think she meant to. Your mama and I had an argument. I think she was mad at me, but took it out on you."

"Can... we fix... them?" Billy asks.

"Sure we can. First things first, though. I think we could both use a hug. What do you say?"

Billy nods and wraps his arms around me. We hold each other, then, until all the bad thoughts drift away.

It takes the rest of the morning for Billy and me to tape his collages back together. We decided that what transpired earlier would be one of our little secrets since neither one of us wanted to bring Ashby into the matter.

I make Billy his new, favorite lunch, a peanut butter and honey sandwich with sliced bananas, just like the King, Elvis Presley.

As I nurse my Coca-Cola, I watch Billy and Ashby joke and horse around without a care in the world. All the while, my bitterness from Magnolia's scorn and judgment churns, roiling below the surface.

"It's time for your nap now, Billy," I say, and lead him to the guest room.

I find Ashby in his customary spot on the sofa, relaxed, his gaze hopeful.

I stand in front of him, meeting his eyes, considering my next move.

"What are you thinking about, baby?" he asks, his smile coy and alluring.

Without a word, I lean over and kiss him, fierce and demanding.

Ashby pulls away, panting with urgency. "You all right down there?" He gestures to my lower regions.

I nod slowly, then take his hand, lead him to my bedroom, and close the door behind us.

Mrs. Hadley

Even though it's been less than a week, it feels like forever and a day since I last saw Jane. Well, the virtual Jane, anyway. But Monday evening has finally arrived, thank the good Lord, and soon I'll be rubbing elbows, so to speak, with my girl once again.

Cleo is kind enough to work late tonight, so she'll be available to me in the metaverse should the need arise. I can't thank that young lady enough for all that she's done for me. Finding my daughter was a gift in and of itself, but Cleo's gone above and beyond anything I could ever dream of by creating a place where I can get to know Jane without revealing who I am, at least not until I'm ready.

It does grind on me in the back of my mind, though; my dishonesty. I know full well who Jane is, and how she came into this world, and there's no doubt I could fill in some of the missing pieces for her. But I'm not brave like that; not yet anyhow. So, I'll keep up this little charade for as long as it'll carry me, and when I finally admit the truth to Jane, I pray she'll understand.

"It's time, Mrs. Hadley. Are you ready to go?" Cleo asks.

"I'm nervous as all get out, but I'm as ready as I'll ever be."

Right when I utter those words, I'm transported into the basketball arena. I shake my head to orient myself, then feel a tap on my shoulder.

"Hey there, Ree. Glad you could make it." Jane greets me.

I twirl around and meet her gaze. The sight of her makes my heart leap with joy.

"I'm so happy to be here, Jane. You have no idea," I reply.

"Well, what do you say we get started? Why don't we jog up and down the court to get used to the joysticks?" she suggests.

"Sounds good," I nod.

We do a couple of laps, then Jane decides to kick it up a notch.

"Okay, Ree. This time I want you to glance behind you every so often, like you're coming down the floor to play defense."

We run to the other end of the floor, but my focus is on my joystick and not on Jane's instructions.

"Look back, Ree," Jane prompts.

Yet I continue forgetting. That's when Jane breaks into rhyme.

"*Watermelon, watermelon, watermelon rind. Take a look back and see who's behind. Uh-huh, uh-huh uh-huh,*" Jane chants, then repeats the phrase over and over again.

I chuckle at her poetry, but I'll be if it doesn't do the trick. It's not too long before I instinctively turn my head to spot what's coming.

"Great job, Ree," Jane encourages. "Let's work on our passing now. It'll help with our coordination."

Just like with my court awareness, Jane uses verse to get us into a rhythm.

"*Cinderella, dressed in yellow, went upstairs to kiss her fellow, made a mistake, and kissed a snake, how many doctors did it take? One, two, three, four...*"

We toss a basketball back and forth, singing her silly rhyme until one of us bobbles the ball—usually me. Then we begin counting again. To my surprise, it works, and my skill improves.

"Awesome, Ree. Like I've always said: 'Playing ball is like riding a bicycle; all it takes is practice.' Of course, I wouldn't know anything about riding a bike. I don't have any legs to speak of," she offers nonchalantly.

Her remark gives me a start, my heart-wrenching at the thought, and guilt overwhelms me.

"You okay, Ree?" Jane wonders gently. "Too much reality, huh?"

"No, no," I assure her. "I'm all right. I have to admit I'm not too agile in the real world, either."

"I was born with flippers for legs, so I've been wheelchair-bound my entire life," Jane explains. "I'm sorry if I upset you."

"It's me who should apologize for reacting the way I did. I can't imagine what you've been through," I respond.

"Bad things happen to all of us. It's what we make of it that counts," she replies with a smile.

My stomach clenches at her honesty and the truth I'm hiding from her. Suddenly, fatigue consumes me, all the way to my bones.

"I'm feeling pretty tired right about now," I say wearily.

"We've had quite a workout this evening. Why don't we call it a night?" Jane offers. "Can you join us on Thursday? Our team can always use another player for scrimmaging."

"I can't think of anything I'd rather do."

Cleo

My daddy taught me not to hate. Augustus Pearl was the kind of man who believed in making the best of any situation, turning the cheek for any person, no matter how unbearable the circumstances.

Daddy lived by example his entire life, forgiving those who wronged him, and making lemonade out of lemons, even when he was beaten down by daily hardships and challenges.

So, for my younger brother Moses and me, the phrase, "I hate," never flowed from our lips without a strong reprimand and stern glare from our daddy, Gus.

To stop our bellyaching, he would often say, "Nobody is guaranteed nothin' on this earth; the quicker you accept that, the faster you'll get to rightin' your ship." Those words of Daddy's roll around in my head like they were spoken yesterday, instead of six, long years ago when Daddy left us to be with Jesus.

You can imagine, then, my inner turmoil when it comes to Ingram, Quinn, and the rest of the Bro Club, because the term, "hate," now rears its ugly head at just the thought of them.

In our meeting the other day with Ingram, Quinn made it sound like he and the boys were having issues testing their new VR game, the same game—for all intents and purposes—Jonathan and I built, but when we dug into the particulars, we discovered the Bro Club hadn't begun testing at all. In fact, I'm not sure they know how to go about it, their skills are that rough.

Of course, complaining to Ingram would be a lost cause, so Jonathan and I put our heads down and went to work, devising a template for the bros that even a third-grader could follow.

During all this, I met with Ingram to get some ideas on how to formulate the proposal to Hennessy Corp for Worthy Community Home's metaverse contract. But all he said was, "Handle it," without breaking his gaze from his laptop.

And that's what I did. I collaborated with Legal to draw up the agreement, while Jonathan kept the home fires burning with Head in the Clouds. Then, I sidestepped Ingram entirely and got the seal of approval from Ingram's boss, just to cover Jonathan's and my behind should something go awry.

But my rage at the unfairness of it all churns just below the surface. I know Daddy would approve of how I've handled things thus far. Still, I pray my bitterness doesn't get the best of me someday.

This afternoon I'm meeting with Jillian Hennessey, the director of Worthy Community Home, to go over our contract and hammer out the details. To mark the occasion, I visited Auntie Ella's salon this past weekend to freshen my weave, and I'm wearing my best silk blouse and linen skirt, dressing the part of a corporate executive. There's no doubt about it: I look good.

Miss Clementine meets me at the nurses' station and we go on down to Jillian's office.

"Hey, Miss Jillian. Are you ready for us?" Miss Clementine asks as she taps lightly on the door.

"Come in. Come in. Have a seat. Have a seat," Jillian answers in her staccato cadence.

Miss Clementine and I do as we're instructed, then Jillian eschews the pleasantries and gets down to business.

"I've reviewed your proposal, Cleo, and everything looks to be in order except for one minor issue," she begins.

"What's that?"

"The length of the contract. I can't possibly agree to two years. I only have a few more months here before I join the Hennessey board, and I don't want to commit to more than a year when a new director will be taking over," Jillian replies.

"I can certainly understand that Jillian, but I'm not sure you're seeing the bigger picture," I counter.

"Bigger picture?"

"If you don't mind, Jillian, I'd like to get some feedback from Miss Clementine since she's on the front lines, so to speak," I reply.

"Miss Clementine, how many nursing openings do you have on the Memory Care floor?" I ask.

"We've had two positions unfilled for the better part of a year now," Miss Clementine responds.

"And the starting salaries are around, what? $40,000 a year?"

"About that," Miss Clementine agrees.

"Before the VR project, were you and the other staff members feeling overwhelmed because you were short-handed, Miss Clementine?"

"Lord, yes. We were near the breaking point," she nods her head.

"But now?"

"Things are much, much better. The residents are mentally stimulated in the metaverse and seem a great deal happier. And since my crew and I aren't chasing them around the halls any longer, we've got more time to devote to their needs," Miss Clementine explains.

"Do you think it's necessary to hire two more nurses now, Miss Clementine?" I ask.

She shakes her head. "As long as we've got access to your virtual reality program, I don't believe so."

I turn to Jillian. "Because of the success of our software, we've been able to improve your residents' daily lives and employee morale. And the cost of a two-year commitment is less than hiring two new nurses. Besides, who knows for sure, but the price of our services may very well increase in the next twelve months. It seems to me Jillian, agreeing to these terms is a win for everyone involved."

"Mm-hmm, mm-hmm, mm-hmm," Jillian answers stridently.

"What do you say, Jillian? Do we have a deal?"

Jillian swivels in her chair, clicking her pen repeatedly—clickety-clack, clickety-clack—as she mulls over her decision.

"I must admit, Cleo, your reasoning is sound. If you'll write up some talking points for me to bring to the board, I'll deliver your contract to them with my blessing," Jillian acquiesces.

Bingo. My work here is done.

Clementine

It's been about three weeks since our residents were introduced to the expanded VR spaces, and after a bit of a learning curve adapting to the new areas, they've acclimated beautifully.

As I mentioned to Miss Jillian the other day, the metaverse has reduced my workload by a country mile—or a third if you prefer standard math— now that I'm not rounding up wayward residents or keeping them amused. Virtual reality provides the entertainment all by itself.

As such, it allows me to check on the folks in my unit twice a day, so I'm able to monitor them closer than ever before. It's amazing the subtle changes I can pick up on just by spending ten minutes with a resident, instead of one or two: little aches and pains that might signal the beginning of something more serious; eating less or sleeping more than they used to; the way their minds drift when I speak to them for an extended period, indicating a medication change may be in order. These may be understated fluctuations, I'll concede, but profound in terms of their overall care. What's more, I feel like I'm making a difference, and all because I've been granted more of that precious commodity: time.

My afternoon rounds are much quieter than in the morning since most of our residents enjoy visiting the aforementioned metaverse during this part of the day. I breeze down the halls, poke my head in the rooms, and see VR goggles on each of them—happily engaged—then conclude my visiting hour at Miss Margaret's door.

She's seated at her table, pen in hand, hunched over a thick writing tablet.

I tap lightly on her door frame. "What are you up to, Miss Margaret?"

She peers over the rims of her bifocals. "I'm writing a letter."

"To an old friend?" I ask while I tidy up her bed covers.

"No," Miss Margaret answers stiffly. "To my sister Magnolia."

I stop in my tracks. Miss Margaret hasn't confused herself over her long-dead sister in weeks. She's been progressing, too, with better coherence and fewer outbursts since joining the virtual reality project. Hopefully, this is a minor slip-up, something we're all prone to on occasion.

The last thing I want to do is agitate her, so I decide to tread lightly and poke around a bit.

"Why do you need to write Miss Magnolia?" I wonder casually.

"Magnolia was insolent and just plain rude when she visited my home the other day. And she upset Billy something awful. I've decided to give her a piece of my mind. Billy and I deserve an apology," she says, nodding firmly.

The first thing that pops into my head is, "Who's Billy?" Maybe he's somebody from her past? Who knows. Miss Margaret doesn't discuss her memory travels with me.

"Well, Miss Margaret, I don't think your sister Magnolia is going to be able to apologize to you or read your letter, for that matter," I respond delicately.

"Why not? Is Magnolia being her usual, stubborn self?" she asks pointedly.

I take a seat next to Miss Margaret and place my hand on hers.

"It's nothing like that, Miss Margaret," I pause, gathering my courage. "Your sister's been gone for almost five years now. Don't you remember?"

Her eyes flash, a mixture of panic and confusion. She searches my gaze for answers, with one foot planted in the here and now, but the other one stuck in the past.

"I saw her yesterday," she remarks, bewildered.

"You've been spending a lot of time lately in the metaverse reliving your memories. I'd suspect Magnolia's been a part of that," I suggest.

"Oh," she mutters, her brow furrowed.

"It's all right, Miss Margaret. Jumping back and forth would be confusing for anybody," I soothe.

"I don't want to lose my mind," she whispers.

"You're okay, Miss Margaret. You're okay." I clasp her hand to calm her.

"Do you know who I am?" I ask gently.

She examines me for a moment, then her face brightens. "You're Clementine. You help me."

"That's right, Miss Margaret. I'm Clementine," I acknowledge with a smile. "Say, I've got a 100 Grand chocolate bar in my pocket. Would you care for half?"

"I don't know," she answers skeptically. "The doctor lady says I need to watch my sweets."

"Oh, Mama Pearl won't mind," I reassure her. "Besides, a little sugar never hurt nobody."

As we share the candy, I put on a cheerful exterior. Yet deep down, I can't help but worry if Miss Margaret's taking a turn for the worse, and if the circumstances she's reliving in the virtual world have something to do with it. Time will tell.

Margaret

I seem to be slipping lately—my mind that is. Like I'm standing on a steep slope, and little by little it gives way beneath me, sinking further into a deep, dark hole.

Ever since my tussle with Magnolia, I've been fixated, her words and recriminations on repeat, so much so that I can't be certain where the past ends and the present begins. It's unsettling, to say the least, and it causes me great angst, never knowing if and when the next shoe may drop.

They tell me I'm sick in the head, the doctors with their shiny stethoscopes and pristine lab coats. It's dementia, they say, with no cure on the horizon, but a chorus of treatments—pills and shots—nevertheless. I find my memories are fickle and peculiar now, so different than the younger version of myself. Back when I was a child, my brain was a steel trap with perfect recall, from school lessons to innocuous tidbits like what my mother served for Sunday supper six weeks prior; I could remember it all.

But as I've aged, and life has run roughshod over my dreams and desires, I find my mind plays delightful tricks on me, glorifying the happy times, and burying the painful ones so deep you forget they were even there. It's a blessing of sorts—selective recollection—because it keeps your heart from breaking all over again.

I know they're worried about me, Clementine and Georgina. I can see it in their faces: the concern, the doubt, even a little fear. I was doing so well, they tell me, so coherent, so together, almost like I was before the diagnosis. Then my battle with Magnolia happened, and I'm teetering on the edge again.

I suspect they'll try to persuade me to stop where I am and select a different set of photos to relive, in hopes it will end my downhill slide. I probably should, if I know what's good for me. But I can't. I just can't. There's something there I must see, something pulling me to finish what I've started. I'm certain of it. If I have nothing else, I have my certainty.

"Hi, Mother. How are you this afternoon?"

I glance up at Georgina, who's interrupted my thoughts. She breezes into my room sporting a different hair color; her natural flaxen shade instead of that god-awful flaming red she had been wearing.

"Weren't you here yesterday, Georgina?" I ask tartly.

"It's nice to see you, too. Can't I visit my mother two days in a row?" she wonders and kisses my cheek.

"Not unless you want something," I respond skeptically.

"You and your suspicious mind," Georgina scoffs.

"I see you went back to blonde. It's about time."

"Don't start, Mother," she warns.

"Hi there, Miss Margaret," Clementine interjects, smiling brightly as she knocks on my door frame.

"Another visitor, and at the same time. How about that? Why do I get the feeling this isn't a coincidence," I mutter. Even if I'm growing senile, I wasn't born yesterday. I can still spot a setup as clear as day.

"Now Mother, don't get defensive," Georgina replies gently. "Clementine told me about the confusion you've been having lately. We discussed it, and we think it might be due to the memories you're exploring."

I knew it. I just knew it. They're going to try and get me to quit where I am. Well, I'm not having it.

"If you think I'm going to change what I'm doing in that magic time machine gadget, you can put that notion right out of your mind. Both of you," I remark sternly. "I'm going to ride my recollections wherever they take me."

"Why do you have to be so stubborn? There's something in those memories that's affecting you; I would bet money on it. You don't want to get worse, do you?" Georgina argues.

"You're wasting your breath."

"Mother, look at all these photo albums," Georgina points to the stack on my bureau. "There has got to be some other time to go back and remember."

I fold my arms across my chest, resolute in my decision.

"I'm dug in."

"Dammit, Mother!" Georgina shouts.

"Let me tell you something else, both of you. I don't appreciate you two ganging up on me like this," I holler right back.

"Now, Miss Margaret. We ain't trying to upset you," Clementine chimes in calmly. "Georgina and I want what's best for you. That's all. We're coming to you out of love, nothing else."

"Well then, take your love walking, will you Clementine?" I sass, my eyes shooting daggers.

"Yes ma'am," Clementine replies quietly, then excuses herself.

"That was rude," Georgina scolds.

"She'll get over it. She's only the hired help," I mutter.

"Mother!"

"What?" I respond irritably.

"If you're not going to change what you're doing in the metaverse, will you at least tell me what goes on in there?"

"It's private," I sniff self-righteously.

"You never want to discuss it," Georgina shakes her head, fed up with my mood. "How about showing me some pictures so I have an idea of where you're starting from."

I think on it a minute, then decide to throw her a bone.

"Fetch me that blue scrapbook over there, will you?" I direct.

Georgina does as she's asked, then joins me at the table. I thumb through the pages until I find what I'm looking for.

"This was my first home, and my first car." I point to the small gingerbread house with my red Corvette parked in front.

Georgina leans over and inspects the photograph. "I didn't know you drove a Corvette."

"Mm-hmm. Your granddaddy owned the only Chevrolet dealership in Worthy at the time. He said that me driving around town in that car was the best advertising he could ask for."

"How long did you live in this house?"

"Not long. About a year, I think."

"It sure is cute," Georgina remarks. "Why did you move?"

"Huh, you know I don't remember," I reply, puzzled at the hole in my memory. "I loved that little house, but I can't for the life of me recall why I left it."

"Did you work for Grandaddy?"

"No," I shake my head. "I looked after Billy," I say, then flip the page to another set of prints.

"Who's Billy?"

"You know, Magnolia's son," I answer as I gaze at more pictures.

"I thought Magnolia had only one child, her daughter Chastity Lynn," Georgina responds.

I turn to Georgina, befuddled by her claim. "Billy was Magnolia's son by her first husband, Ashby. Chastity Lynn came along later when Magnolia married Charles."

"You've never mentioned Billy before. Or Ashby, for that matter."

"Of course, I have. You just never listen. Besides, you never met Magnolia, so you wouldn't know the first thing about her or her family," I snap.

"Mother, are Billy and Ashby part of the memories you're reliving?" Georgina asks carefully, her expression concerned.

I slam the album shut. "I've had about enough of this trip down memory lane. Go on, get out," I demand.

"Mother, come on. Don't be angry."

"I said, 'Get out!'" I roar.

"Okay, okay. I'm going. Calm down," Georgina pleads, and grabs her bag to leave.

"I'll be plenty calm when you're gone," I remark.

Georgina hightails it out the door and I breathe a sigh of relief.

Truth is, her questions about Billy and Ashby struck a nerve. Why, I'm not at all sure. But I aim to find out.

Mrs. Hadley

L ately, I've been dreaming a lot. That's nothing special, I know; a common occurrence for most people. But for me, it's altogether new, and a much-welcomed change.

For nearly all my life, I would lay my head down in the evening, only to wake up in the morning to stillness and emptiness. As if my mind didn't have much to relive or look forward to, so it had nothing better to do than to rest. Things are different now.

Take last night, for instance. My dream came on slowly at first, blurred around the edges like a kaleidoscope twisting into view until all the colors turned sharp and focused.

There we were, the three of us: me, my sweet husband James, and our daughter Jane, together holding hands in a field of wildflowers that swayed gently in the breeze, their petals kissed with sunlight.

Jane was laughing and singing, a child in my mind's eye; fully formed, legs and all.

She glanced at me, smiled, then said, "Look at me! See what I can do!"

Jane let go of our hands, James and mine, and ran through the flowers, spinning and dancing without a care in the world; free-floating through space and time.

Further and further, Jane drifted from us, all the while looking back before fading from our midst. As she reached the precipice between the field where we stood and what was beyond, Jane turned with a wave, and just like that, she was gone.

I awoke after that, at the point in slumber where your dreams feel as real as the day is long. Then the truth crept in, and I was reminded that Jane isn't a child, and she isn't complete; neither in physical terms nor in her knowledge of her past.

I've wrestled with these thoughts for a while now this morning, and then it occurred to me that getting a bit of fresh air would do me good.

I've gotten fairly proficient at walking with my cane, so much so that I can make the short journey outside to the courtyard with no help at all. There, I find a seat in the sun, hoping to bask in a bit of solitude. Instead, I get a visit from a most unlikely source: James.

I'm not much for daydreaming, mind you, but as sure as I'm breathing, my dead husband's voice pops into my head.

Why are you doing this, Irene? Why'd you have to go and bother Jane?

"She's our daughter, James," I say forcefully.

Why couldn't you leave well enough alone?

"That's mighty easy for you to say, now isn't it? You're dead and gone and six feet under. I'm the one left behind, rattling around this earth alone like a shriveled-up Milk Dud," I argue.

So, because you're lonely you decided to kick over a hornet's nest?

"That's as good a reason as any, in my view. Besides, we're the only kin we've got left, Jane and me. Family should be together," I reason.

That's if she don't turn tail and run, first. How exactly are you going to tell Jane you're her mama?

"I haven't figured that out yet," I admit.

Mm-hmm.

"Don't you dare doubt me, James Hadley. I'll let our daughter know about me and her history when I'm good and ready, and not a moment sooner."

Whatever you say, Irene. I'll believe it when I see it.

"I've had enough of your lip. It seems to me I wouldn't be in this predicament if you hadn't decided we should forget about Jane in the first place," I contend.

You can't put this on me, Irene. We both agreed. I didn't force you to do one, solitary thing. In the sixty years we were together, you didn't once ask about Jane. Not once.

"But I loved her," I cry. "I loved her all the same. I buried Jane in my mind, God help me I did. Shame on me as a mother. I've got a chance now to make it up to her. And come hell or high water I will. If you believe anything about me James, you can believe that."

"Mrs. Hadley?"

I turn to find Clementine standing beside me, her hand gently resting on my shoulder.

"You feeling all right? Some of the other residents told me you were out here. Said you were having some kinda argument with somebody they couldn't see," she explains delicately, her brow furrowed with concern.

"That would be my dead husband, James. We were having a scuffle over our daughter, Jane."

"I see," Clementine replies warily. "You know that's pretty unusual, don't you, Mrs. Hadley?"

"I reckon it is," I chuckle ruefully.

"I'm not going to have to start worrying about you, too, am I?" Clementine jests, with a hint of sincerity underneath.

"No, no," I remark, patting her hand. "I'm just a lonely old woman; nothing more."

"It's a beautiful day," Clementine observes, changing the subject. "Why don't we take a stroll around the grounds and stretch our legs a bit?"

Stiffly, I pull myself up with the help of my cane.

"I can't think of anything I'd like more, Clementine. Lead the way."

Cleo

There's nothing like being on the open road to clear your mind. Miss Sybil, my little Ford Festiva, and I have spent quite a bit of time these past weeks putt-putting between Dallas and Worthy for the Head in the Clouds project, and to a lesser extent, visiting Mama for Sunday supper, so there's been plenty of time for me to find my center.

But it's critical for Miss Sybil and me to make the trip this afternoon to Mama's house since I'm perilously low on her delectable food rations that keep Jonathan and me properly fueled at work.

Don't get me wrong; my journey today isn't all about food. I treasure Mama's and my extended family and friends' company as much as life itself. It's just my culinary skills leave much to be desired, to put it mildly.

As for Mama, her cooking is a source of pride and joy that she relishes sharing with others. So, everybody benefits. Of course, I always make sure to take care of the dishes before I leave, even though Mama tells me not to. It's the least I can do for all that she does for me; an implicit "Thank you" and "I love you" rolled into one.

I pull up in front of Mama's home and see that the gang's all here: Auntie Ella and her husband Gabe; Miss Clementine and Mr. Percy. My brother Moses is in there as well no doubt, trying to sneak a piece of Mama's fried chicken before grace is given.

"Lucy, I'm home," I call out in my best Ricky Ricardo impression. The family room is empty, so I make my way to the kitchen where I find everyone congregated. It's amusing how folks pack themselves into this tiny galley, the smallest room in the house, just to be around food. Or maybe it's to be near Mama. Perhaps it's some of both.

"Hi, baby. You're right on time for prayer," Mama says, then slaps Moses' hand away while he tries to snatch a loose piece of chicken skin.

"Grace first, Moses. You know the drill," she chides.

We join hands, bow our heads, and Mama thanks the good Lord for all our blessings. As soon as she finishes, Moses grabs two thighs and a handful of rolls before scooting out the door.

"Moses! Leave some for the rest of us," Mama cries after him. "I swear that young man will be the death of me."

"It's okay, Ruth. I'm not planning on eating anything but salad and collards today, anyway. So, there should be plenty for everybody," Mr. Percy chimes in.

"You're looking well, Mr. Percy," I remark. "Have you lost some weight?"

"I'm down about fifteen pounds and trying for five more," Mr. Percy nods. "I had to buy some new clothes cuz my old ones were hanging off me," he adds with a hint of pride.

"And draining our bank account dry in the process," Miss Clementine grumbles for everyone to hear.

"You don't want your husband looking like some bum on the streets, do you Clem?" Mr. Percy scoffs.

"Why change now?" Miss Clementine sasses.

"Cleo, where's Brian? I guess he couldn't make the trip?" Mama interjects to circumvent their war of words.

"He'll be by later. He has a presentation tomorrow and he's struggling to put on the finishing touches."

"Poor man. Burning the candle at both ends, I reckon. Will Brian feel up to the drive?" Mama wonders.

"I offered to bring him back leftovers, but he said it's been so long since he's been here, he's forgotten what y'all look like," I tease.

I grab a plate and begin heaping it full of macaroni and cheese and Mama's greens, when Miss Clementine sidles up beside me, her expression serious.

"Cleo, have you noticed anything peculiar lately about Miss Margaret?"

"You mean other than her having dementia and all?" I ask with a smirk.

Miss Clementine thumps my shoulder. "You know what I mean. In the metaverse. Miss Margaret's on the decline again. Is there something going on in there that's upsetting her?"

"I can't discuss what occurs in our study without Miss Margaret's permission. Next Well's contract with the community home stipulates privacy for the participants. Have you asked Miss Margaret about it?"

"Both me and her daughter Georgina," she nods. "Miss Margaret's as stubborn and tight-lipped as ever."

"If her condition worsens, I suppose I could speak to Jillian and see if there isn't a way around the agreement. Has Georgina thought about getting a health care power of attorney?"

"Miss Margaret refuses to sign one. Georgina said it took a judge to force Miss Margaret to hand over her assets to a conservatorship. She doesn't relish the thought of taking her mother to court again."

"What a mess," I reply, then lower my voice. "Between you and me, each metaverse visit is recorded, and there's a replay button on every VR headset. If someone wanted to, they could review Miss Margaret's sessions. Just saying," I shrug.

"I wondered what that button was for. So, you can rewatch anything that's gone on in there?"

"Yes ma'am," I reply.

I look over and catch Mama watching us anxiously. When our eyes meet, she quickly glances away, embarrassed by her eavesdropping.

"Hey, everyone! What's for dinner?" Brian cries from the foyer.

After a cascade of greetings in the family room, Brian joins us in the kitchen. "There she is," he says and pecks me on the lips.

"Good to see you, Brian. There's plenty of food. Please help yourself," Mama offers, and then she and Miss Clementine excuse themselves to give Brian and me some privacy.

Brian waits until the coast is clear, then leans in and dips me low, kissing me with gusto.

"Dang, Bri. What was that all about?" I giggle when we pull apart.

"Just in a good mood, baby," he responds, grinning from ear to ear.

"Any particular reason?" I wonder.

"Well, yes, actually. I heard back from Google earlier this afternoon."

"And?"

"They want me to go down to Austin for a second round of interviews. Can you believe it?" Brian answers, brimming with excitement. He folds me into his arms and hugs me tightly.

"That's fantastic, Bri. Really great," I respond, feigning enthusiasm.

I'm happy for Brian, truly I am. But what seemed like a hazy and uncertain opportunity before, has now become more real. And I'm not sure where I fit into all of that, or whether I want to.

Clementine

Percy has been driving me crazy lately. Wait a minute, let me rephrase that: Percy has been driving me *crazier than usual* lately.

It was bad enough when he retired and threw my routine into disarray. Then he had to go and buy that godforsaken boat which nearly put us in the poor house. And the kicker is Percy don't even use it that often. The boat just sits in the driveway with its dingy cover, an eyesore for all to see.

Now Percy's on this health craze, where not only does he restrict himself to vegetables with very little meat, he weighs his portions to watch his calorie intake. I'd thought I'd seen everything in our forty-two-year marriage, but when that man plopped his plate on that tiny kitchen scale the other night, I about keeled over from shock.

And his new diet is a major inconvenience, too. Before all this, I would prepare our meals and save some for Mr. Isaac, but anymore I have to put together Percy's rabbit food plus my own sensible dinner. A woman like me can't live on roughage alone, I'll tell you that. I've become something I never thought I would: a short-order cook.

All this, and not to mention how much Percy's spent on new clothes recently. It's enough to make your head spin, the sheer amount of change we've been going through. I don't like it. I don't like it one bit.

My morning rounds are finally done, and I make my way to the nurses' station to update some charts. Just as I open my Diet Dr. Pepper, my cell phone dings.

It's Percy:

Hey. For your budget book. Bought new jeans $126.58. Arugula $6.19.

Taking Gabe in the boat later. Hope that makes you happy.

Good lord. My jeans cost twenty dollars at Walmart and a head of lettuce is ninety-nine cents at Winco. I swear, it won't be long before that man drives me to drink.

I reach for my pocket notebook to record all these expenditures by my spendthrift husband when I notice it's not there. I pat my smock, the sides of my slacks, everywhere on my person, but it's nowhere to be found.

"Hello, Mrs. Babineaux," Mr. Isaac says, carrying an armful of Tupperware. "How are you this beautiful morning?"

"Fine, fine," I mutter offhandedly as I search my desk.

"I think that ambrosia salad you made was your best yet," he remarks.

"Glad you liked it," I mumble while I rifle through my trash can.

"Is everything all right, Mrs. Babineaux?" Mr. Isaac wonders delicately as he sets down the plastic containers.

"No, no sir it isn't. Nothing is going right," I reply anxiously, close to tears. "I can't find my budget book anywhere. It has all my purchases written in there. I'm lost without it."

"Do you remember where you were the last time you had it?" he asks.

I shake my head. "It's always in my shirt pocket. Always," I say forcefully as I point to my blouse.

"Small items like that are easy to misplace," Mr. Isaac commiserates.

"I sure don't want to spend my break hunting around for it, but I guess I have no choice," I shrug, feeling defeated.

"I don't know about that, Mrs. Babineaux."

I glance at him, completely confused.

"Hear me out. Let's get your phone set up with the budget app I use. It won't take but a moment to do, then you can go on and take a breather, maybe visit the metaverse for a spell to take your mind off things. In the meantime, I'll see if I can't find your notebook for you," Mr. Isaac offers.

"You'd do that for me?" I ask as my eyes mist up.

"It's the least I can do, what with all the kindness you've shown me since Lily passed," he replies. "Hand me your phone and I'll get you fixed up."

In a matter of minutes, Mr. Isaac downloads the software and shows me how it works. I record Percy's purchases and, according to Mr. Isaac, they go off to the cloud somewhere safe and sound.

"Thank you, Mr. Isaac," I say gratefully.

"You're very welcome. You best run along and take your break while you've got the chance," he suggests with a grin.

I snatch my VR goggles, then hustle down to my Happy Place for a much-needed distraction.

The weather is as perfect as ever here in the VR space, sunny and mild. I walk near the pond to see if Gregory is around and spot him in the distance, alone, without the usual gaggle of women surrounding him. I wave to get his attention. He notices me and gestures for me to join him.

"Hello there, Rebecca. How has your day been?" Gregory asks.

"So far it's been a handful, but it's better now," I reply.

"Follow me. I want to show you something," he says.

His arm falls behind me as he escorts us through a small thicket of trees until we reach a gentle stream dotted with lily pads, secluded from the rest of the park.

Gregory leads me to the stream bank, where a lovely bouquet is bundled together on the shoreline.

"For some reason, I got the feeling you might be having a bad day. I saw these and I thought of you," he smiles and hands me the posy.

I breathe in the blossoms' scent. "How thoughtful of you, Gregory. They're just beautiful."

"They're zinnias and daisies. I picked them myself. I found them across the way," he gestures to a small field several yards down from the stream. "I hope they help cheer you up some. That's what I was aiming for, anyway."

"I'm flattered. Thank you."

We stand in silence for a bit, watching frogs leap in and out of the water, the wind gently rustling the trees' leaves as if they were whispering sweet nothings to one another.

Gregory turns to me, "It's time for me to go."

"So soon?" I ask.

"I have things I've got to do," he points to the sky, "out there."

"When will I see you again?"

"Sometime soon. Maybe tomorrow. Look for me here. This will be our place," Gregory says and squeezes my arm.

Suddenly, he vanishes into thin air.

I place my hand on the spot where he touched me and my heart stirs. This is make-believe, I tell myself. There's nothing to worry about, I tell myself. These are the things I tell myself.

I remained in that lovely little cove for I don't know how long—too long probably—but I didn't care. I was living inside my very own romance novel.

When I finally returned to the nurses' station, I noticed something on my desk, small and rectangular: my budget book. Well, how about that? Mr. Isaac found it after all.

Margaret

October 1970

It's amazing the lies we tell ourselves in the cold light of day. How we rationalize the sins we commit, and blame others for the pain we cause, like they had it coming to them.

I say "we" as if everyone does this, as if everyone is complicit. But that's not entirely true. What I'm meant to say is "me," not "we." I'm the culpable one. The responsibility for my actions rests solely with me; no one else. I just can't admit it out loud, least of all to myself. So, I go on pretending I'm the injured party, when I know deep down that I'm no victim.

My affair with Ashby continues unabated. Since my skirmish with Magnolia, our fling has progressed to an intoxicating new level, full of fire and lust and passion. Where before I was timid with Ashby when he would take me in his arms, I'm now oftentimes the aggressor, leaving him to wonder on occasion, "What's gotten into you, girl?" Not that he's complaining. Our intimacy has unlocked a desire in me I never knew I had. And now that it's emerged, I can't get enough.

It's not just about the sex, either. I'm convinced Ashby genuinely cares for me; maybe he even loves me. Every now and again Ashby performs these little acts of kindness, like bringing me flowers or preparing lunch for me and Billy. And he was so understanding when I played those silly games to keep him at arm's length. That's love, isn't it? Those kind gestures surely can't be anything but expressions of love, can they? These are the questions I wrestle with inside my head.

Billy was caught in the crosshairs after my clash with Magnolia, torn between the two caretakers in his life, and grew moodier and more sullen as a result. He was dead set against attending nursery school, and the first few times I dropped him off, it took all that I had in me not to turn around and take him back home, his screaming and crying broke my heart so.

He's grown accustomed to it now, like all children do, and is even eager to go, thank God. But since then, a subtle shift has occurred between us, undetectable to the naked eye, yet apparent if you know where to look.

I tell myself this divide is because of school, that Magnolia coercing me into the role of enforcer also made me the scapegoat. In my heart of hearts, though, I'm not sure that's true.

One afternoon as Ashby was leaving, I gave him a long goodbye kiss, slow and deep and alluring. When I turned from the door, there stood Billy, gazing at me with suspicious eyes.

"You kissed my daddy," he said.

"It was just a friendly peck, Billy. All grownups do it," I replied, attempting to brush away his doubt.

"No, they don't." He shook his head slowly, his stare a mixture of sadness and reproach.

I leaned down so we were at eye level. "Let's just keep this between us, okay? It'll be our little secret."

Billy waited there without a word, quietly judging me.

"Look, Billy. We all do things we're not proud of. Take your bedwetting, for instance. How many licks do you think your mother would give you if she found out about your accidents, hmm?" I remarked cruelly.

He shrugged, then looked away as he stuffed his hands into his pockets.

"If you're a smart boy, you'll think twice before saying anything about this. You understand me, Billy?" I threatened. "Now run along to the guest room and let me be."

Billy did as he was told, but not before leaving me with the most heartbroken expression I've ever seen.

I tried to make it up to him after that, cooking his favorite lunches, creating mud pies with him in the rain, teaching him new dance steps to "impress the ladies." Billy's forgiven me I think, but the light in his eyes that was just for me faded on that day, and its brightness hasn't returned since.

The doorbell rings, interrupting my thoughts. I glance at the clock—ten thirty—wondering who could be calling at this hour of the night. I peer out the window and see Magnolia's car parked in front. Suddenly, what little energy I have drains away. I stay where I am, frozen, waiting to see if Magnolia will change her mind.

Two quick knocks follow, letting me know she's determined. How typical. I take a deep breath before I open the door, bracing myself for another battle in our dirty little war.

I'm shocked by Magnolia's appearance. I can't remember a time when her hair wasn't perfectly arranged, and her makeup flawlessly applied. But even in the dark, I can see how disheveled Magnolia is, her clothes badly creased and deep bags drooping around her eyes like she hasn't slept in days.

"May I come in?" she asks.

Silently, I turn and step into the family room, leaving her to follow behind.

Defensively, I fold my arms in front of me. "What is it, Magnolia?" I wonder curtly.

"I'm not here to argue, Margaret, and I won't take much of your time. I know it's late," she begins.

"Things between me and Ashby have been a mess lately. And with Billy giving me grief about nursery school, it was just too much, so the other day I snapped," Magnolia explains wearily.

"Be that as it may, I want to apologize for what I said before. I had no right, and I'm truly sorry." Magnolia exhales deeply. "I feel as if my world is spinning in the wrong direction. I was so sure about everything: Ashby; my marriage; my position. My life was going along as it should, all very nice and orderly and pleasant."

Magnolia's gaze wanders as her mind drifts somewhere else. "But I guess nice and orderly and pleasant isn't good enough for Ashby. You see, something is happening that I never thought possible."

Magnolia swallows hard, struggling to choke out the words. "My husband is having an affair. There it is. I've said it out loud."

She continues, her voice quivering. "I don't know who she is, but as sure as I'm standing here, Ashby is being unfaithful."

Magnolia peers straight at me, her eyes unwavering. "For the first time in my life, I have no control, with no idea what to do about it. And it's driving me insane, Margaret. Just so you know, your sister is going mad," she says with a peculiar, crazed smile.

With that, Magnolia turns on her heel and careens swiftly out the door. I'm rendered speechless by her verbal tsunami, so all I can do is watch her go.

Mrs. Hadley

The good Lord sure does work in mysterious ways. After James passed, I didn't think my life held much hope for me. I was resigned to living the rest of my days lonely and isolated, with only my memories to keep me company. But no longer. Now, I wake each day with excitement and optimism, all because of Jane. We've become fast friends in the few weeks since we met, and she's folded me into her virtual world as if we've known each other for years.

Our Monday evening training sessions have become a regular fixture in my routine, as have her team's Wednesday night practices. Much to my surprised delight, my joystick skills have really improved, enough so I can keep up with the others, and I've even turned into a decent ball handler. All this and I'm nearly eighty-one years of age. Wonders never cease.

My rapport with Jane has been easy and fun. We joke and tease one another, the mood light and airy between us, without much talk of who we are beyond our virtual walls.

That is, until this evening.

There we were, playing a four-on-four, full-court game, with me, Jane, and two of her teammates scrimmaging the other ladies. My crew needed a bucket to win. Jane directed our squad on offense, passing the ball around until one of us got open for a shot.

I rolled away from my defender and cut to the basket, waving my arms to show I was in the clear. Jane saw me and lobbed the ball near the goal, where I tipped it in off the glass for an easy score.

"Great job, Ree! Way to go," Jane shouted excitedly.

I was offered congratulations and high-fives from the rest of the players, and then they dispersed just as quickly as they had appeared, returning to their lives in the physical world.

As has become our custom, Jane and I lingered for a bit in the empty gym, exchanging small talk before we left.

"I tell you what, Ree, I sure do love winning," Jane said with a grin. "I don't care if it's a silly game of Tiddlywinks, I want to win."

"I'm the same way," I agreed. "James and I used to play checkers all the time. And lordy I hated it when he beat me. Losing put me in a foul mood for the rest of the day," I chuckled.

"I hear you. Is James your brother? Your husband?" she asked innocently.

My breath hitched at her inquiry, as I searched my mind for how to respond.

"I understand if you don't want to talk about him," Jane quickly interjected. "I figured since you and I have become friends, we could share a little more about ourselves."

"No, no, it's fine. You caught me unawares is all," I stammered.

"So, who's James, then?"

"James was my husband. He passed a few months ago," I replied with quiet caution.

"I'm sorry to hear it, Ree. That must be awfully difficult. Did you two have any children?"

I slowly nodded my head, my anxiety stirring. "One child; a daughter."

"That's nice. Are you two close?"

I swallowed hard and glanced away, unable to continue her gaze. "We're estranged. But I hope to do something about that soon," I responded, my heart racing.

"I see. Well, I'll pray for you, like I always do. But now I'll add your husband and daughter to the mix," she smiled thoughtfully.

"Thank you," I answered gratefully. "What about you, Jane? What's your world like?" I asked, full well knowing some of the answers, but desperate to deflect the conversation away from me.

"Me?" Jane thinks for a moment. "To tell you the truth, I love my life. Every night I thank the good Lord for my blessings, then wake up the next morning grateful my eyes have opened to another day."

"That's a wonderful attitude. I wish some of that would rub off on me. I can get down in the dumps sometimes," I replied.

"Don't get me wrong. My outlook wasn't always sunshine and rainbows. For a long time growing up, I was angry and bitter. But Sister Agnes helped me through all that, and I came out the other side a better person."

"If you don't mind me asking, what happened to change your perspective?" I wondered.

"Love. Sister Agnes showed me how it felt to be loved," she explained. "I think I've mentioned this to you before, but I was born with stubs for legs, flippers really. My mother took a drug called Thalidomide when she was pregnant with me which causes birth defects. And I don't know if that had anything to do with it, but I was placed in an orphanage after I was born. My parents abandoned me there."

"Oh, Jane," I said, a lump forming in my throat.

"Well, I say they abandoned me, but I don't know that for a fact. My parents could've died or something. I never bothered looking for them, and they never found me, so..." Jane's voice trailed off for a moment.

"The sisters at St. Joseph's said at that time in the early sixties, children with disabilities were often left with them because they could provide better care. But as a little kid, I felt deserted," Jane continued.

"Tell her, Irene. Tell her." My thoughts whispered to me.

"That must have been so hard for you." Shamefully, these were the only words I could muster.

"It was in the beginning. Before Sister Agnes joined St. Joseph's I was miserable. I would watch the other children run around and play games, while I was stuck in my wheelchair. There was many a time I got so fed up, I'd tumble out of my chair on purpose so I could join them. Mother Superior put a stop to that by wrapping a sheet around me to keep me hemmed in."

"That's awful," I responded in horror.

"It *was* awful. Then when I was eight—almost nine—Sister Agnes joined St. Joseph's from a convent in Illinois, and my life turned on a dime. She was born with a clubfoot, so Sister Agnes understood what it was like to be different. She took all of us handicapped kids under her wing and taught us how to make the best out of what we had."

Jane nodded with a smile. "Sister Agnes is the one who turned me on to basketball. She'd lower the goal for me in the old gym so I could make baskets and not get discouraged."

"Sister Agnes sounds like a wonderful person," I remarked.

"She was the closest thing I had to family. When I turned eighteen and was about to leave for college, Sister Agnes gave me nearly nine hundred dollars—all the money she had in the world—to help with my expenses. We kept in touch over the years and spent holidays together. She passed three years ago. That was the hardest day of my life," Jane shook her head sadly. "Her kindness opened my heart, and for that, I am forever grateful."

She grew quiet after that, as if repeating her story knocked the wind out of her sails.

"Thank you for sharing," I said; such pitifully sparse words that didn't do her history justice.

Unbeknownst to Jane, we stood together on the edge of a precipice, where I could change her world forever with just the tiniest shred of detail. But my cowardice got the best of me, as it had so many times before. Jane excused herself, and silently, I watched her go.

Clementine

I'm a little embarrassed to admit this to myself, but I believe I've become hooked on technology. Between my weekday strolls in the metaverse to the new budget app Mr. Isaac fixed me up with, I can't get enough of the high-tech experience.

As such, I've recently added a new arrow in my computerized quiver: Candy Crush. Now I realize that I'm late to the party and this computer game has been around for years, but that don't minimize how truly addictive it is, even to older folks like me.

I can play that sucker for hours on end, to the point where my phone battery's gone dead a time or two since I was too engrossed swapping different colored candies to notice. And don't think for one minute my husband Percy hasn't noticed my new obsession and hasn't teased me unmercifully because of it.

Oftentimes while we're watching television in the evenings, I'll wait until Percy falls asleep in his recliner, then whip out my cell phone and do battle with my multi-hued opponents.

"Careful, Clem. You're gonna sprain your fingers," he'll say with one eye open and a sly grin.

Or I'll be in bed playing quietly, minding my own business while Percy's brushing his teeth. Then when I least expect it, he'll poke his head around the bathroom door and shout, "Focus, Clem, focus!" Which of course spoils my game in all sorts of ways.

Interestingly enough, it appears the tech bug has bitten most everybody at Worthy Community Home, up to and including Miss Margaret. Truth be told, things between Miss Margaret and me were kind of awkward after she hollered at me to get out of her room the other day. Her daughter Georgina and I were only trying to convince Miss Margaret to select some new memories to relive, but she wouldn't hear of it. As a result, I became her scapegoat and the object of her anger. And believe you me, Miss Margaret can hold a grudge.

Thankfully, it didn't last long. The following day while I was making my morning rounds, Miss Margaret grabbed my hand before I left her room and said, "You know I didn't mean what I said yesterday, don't you?"

That was Miss Margaret's way of apologizing, and I gratefully accepted it, full well knowing how difficult it was for her to admit she had been wrong.

But our reconciliation hasn't deterred me from investigating what goes on with Miss Margaret in the metaverse. I'm convinced there's a connection between her recent downward spiral and her memories.

So, I took Cleo's suggestion to heart and tried on several occasions to sneak off with Miss Margaret's VR headset. Because she's part of Cleo's memory testing, Miss Margaret has a charging station in her room, unlike the other residents who have to share their goggles, which makes it more difficult for me to get ahold of.

A few times I've moseyed over to her chest of drawers and attempted to walk away with her headgear, but she's caught me red-handed on every try.

"Clementine, what are you doing with my bug-eyed binoculars?" Miss Margaret would ask.

"Oh, nothing, Miss Margaret. I don't know what got into me," I'd reply with a chuckle.

"Bring those over here, will you?" she'd command.

I think Miss Margaret got wise to my intentions because she don't let those goggles out of her sight now; she even sleeps with them under her blanket.

It appears my detective skills could use some work. But I'll keep trying to do what's best for Miss Margaret, even if she gives me grief. I just need to come up with a more creative way to get my hands on her headset. Knowing me, that shouldn't be too hard.

Cleo

As the saying goes, it's the little things in life that make it worth living. For instance, a heaping wedge of double Dutch apple pie—made with two layers of crumbly goodness instead of one—warmed in the break room toaster oven, topped with a thick slice of sharp cheddar cheese, and served with a hefty scoop of vanilla bean ice cream on the side, is as close to Heaven as you can get here on Earth. Auntie Ella worked her culinary magic again over the weekend, and Jonathan and I are currently enjoying the fruits of her labor; pun intended.

"I think your aunt should audition for the *Great British Baking Show*," Jonathan remarks as he polishes off the last of his dessert. "She would be unbeatable."

"I'm pretty sure you have to be a British resident to compete," I reply.

"Then Netflix should film a show here in the States because it's a shame Ella's talents are going unrecognized. Her skill set is a national treasure," he adds.

"Let's not go overboard, Jonathan," I chuckle. "But I'll tell her how much you enjoyed the pie."

I stare at my empty plate and fantasize about licking it clean. Would Jonathan judge me or join in the fun? Either way, I opt to resist, deciding that discretion is the better part of valor when it comes to cubicle mate etiquette.

As I gather our dishes, Quinn, the pinheaded leader of the Bro Club, barges into our cubbyhole, looking flustered and agitated.

"Are you two done with the double-blind testing data yet? Ingram's breathing down my neck."

"Aww, Quinn, it's so cute when you try to talk about things you don't understand," I say dryly.

"I don't know what your problem is, Cleo, but I'm guessing it's hard to pronounce," he retorts, not to be outdone.

"It's hilarious watching you try to fit your entire vocabulary into one sentence," I razz.

"I envy people who've never met you, Cleo."

"All right, both of you, that's enough," Jonathan interjects. "I sent the file over yesterday, Quinn."

"Well, I didn't get it," he snaps.

"Did you look under the subfolder labeled, 'Testing'?" Jonathan asks.

Quinn's smug expression craters. "I didn't know there was one."

"Your team *created* that folder," Jonathan emphasizes matter-of-factly. "Regardless, the file is there. All the information has been properly evaluated. Ingram should be pleased. Is there anything else?"

Quinn averts his gaze. "No, that'll do it," he mutters.

"Dang, Quinn. You got owned bro," I wisecrack.

For once, Quinn keeps his insults to himself and leaves our cubby as quickly as he came.

"Thanks for stopping by. Let's not make it a habit," I call after him.

Jonathan shakes his head and rolls his eyes at me.

"What? I didn't say anything you weren't already thinking, partner."

I stifle a yawn, and momentarily entertain the notion of taking a quick nap in the empty office down the hall; my food coma is that strong. But deadlines await, so I return my nose to the grindstone, open my laptop, and scroll through my messages.

"Hey, Jonathan. Jane Smith sent me an email," I announce.

I scan her missive, then give him the rundown.

"Jane wonders if it's possible to open the arena space to other participants when her team is there on Wednesday nights. She says her group appreciates the exclusivity they've had so they could get up to speed on the VR controls, but they're ready for the challenge of playing new people."

"That's a good idea. Since the objective was for Mrs. Hadley to meet Jane, and that's been accomplished, why not expand their horizons? It couldn't hurt," Jonathan opines.

"I wholeheartedly agree," I nod. "I'll let Jane know. Isn't it beautiful when great minds think alike?"

"Don't get ahead of yourself," Jonathan says impassively, but with a teasing smirk.

"Watch out now. It's not smart to bite the hand that feeds you," I warn with a wink.

"Touché, Cleo. Touché. By the way, is there any pie left?"

Margaret

They're at it again. They being Georgina and Clementine, I mean. They're still trying to convince me that reliving a different set of memories would be better for me; that what I'm doing now is destructive to my health. The same old song and dance.

They're both chomping at the bit to find out what I'm experiencing in the way out yonder. Clementine's even tried running off with my bug-eyed binoculars a time or two, I guess to see for herself what I'm remembering in there. Now, I may be old and senile, but I'm not dumb, so I don't let those goggles out of my sight anymore.

I know Clementine means well. But I'm not up to sharing my recollections with anyone. They are for me and me alone. Even that little gal Cleo joined the fray after my last session, wondering if perhaps it wasn't time for a change.

"You sure you don't want to visit some other memories, Miss Margaret?" Cleo asked, her face etched with concern.

"Why would I do that for?"

"Well, your mind's been wandering into some pretty intense situations lately, and we've only got a few weeks left on this project. Wouldn't it be nicer to recollect some happier times?" Cleo said.

"My mind's leading me to those memories for a reason, and I aim to see it through," I replied firmly.

Cleo sighed. "All right then. But you can always reconsider."

"This is all just between us, isn't it, Cleo? No one else knows?"

"Yes, ma'am. Everything is confidential. I won't discuss what goes on in there with anyone," she assured me.

I figured that was the case. Yet ever since my brain's been on the fritz, I need reassurance every now and again. Otherwise, it makes me anxious.

Be that as it may, I'm getting so close to what I've been searching for; I can feel it. And I don't want or need any interference from folks who think they know better.

"Mother?"

"Hmm?" I turn my attention from the window to see Georgina at my door.

"Are you all right?"

"I'm fine," I respond and fix my gaze outside again.

"Where were you just now?" Georgina asks as she retrieves a stack of papers from her shoulder bag.

"Nowhere special."

She kisses my forehead and hands me the bundle. "Here are your bank statements. I've got to run. If you have any concerns, which no doubt you will, we can discuss them tomorrow."

A sense of foreboding wafts through me, a warning that my time is short and there are things I need to ask; things that require my attention.

I take her hand. "Can't you stay a minute, Georgina?"

"You want me to stay? Usually, you shoo me out the door as soon as I get here," she says, bewildered by my request.

"Yes. Yes, I do. It seems like every time you visit, we only talk about me, or fuss at each other, or both. I'd like to hear what's going on with you. I don't ask you nearly enough," I reply, and point for her to take a seat.

"Okay," she responds skeptically.

"How are my grandchildren?"

"They're good."

"Your job?"

"Dull as ever."

"How are you and that husband of yours getting along?"

"He has a name, Mother," Georgina responds tersely.

"I know," I raise my hands in surrender, "I'm sorry. How are you and Kevin doing?"

She folds her arms and glances at the floor. "I'm fine. Kevin's fine. I mean, he seems to be fine. He's been busy with work, and the roof's leaking again so he's spending all his free time repairing that, plus he's going to coach the girls' soccer team again…"

"I hear a whole lot of words coming out of your mouth, Georgina, but you're not saying anything," I interrupt. "I think you know what I'm getting at. How's your marriage? Is it any better?"

"You've never been one to beat around the bush, Mother, I'll give you that," she observes with a sigh. "Kevin and I have been seeing a therapist for the past six weeks."

"And?"

"And he's trying to work through his feelings for me."

"English, please."

"Kevin's not sure if he's in love with me anymore," Georgina spits out the truth, her expression shattered.

A moment passes, then I ask her delicately, "Do you still love Kevin?"

"Yes, I do," she responds, her eyes misty with tears.

"Then you listen to me. You do everything in your power to make him fall for you again, you understand? If that means stroking his ego, buying him a new car, or wrapping yourself naked in Saran wrap to get his attention, you do it. Whatever it takes."

"What happened to cutting my losses and letting him go? That was your advice before," she says stiffly.

"Yeah, well, I was wrong," I admit. "I've come to that realization a lot lately. Don't be like me, Georgina. Don't tear your family apart. Family is the most sacred thing we've got in this world, and it's so easy to destroy. I'm not sure why it took me so long to understand that. But I do now."

I wake with a start. It's dark outside and I'm not sure where I am, but I know who I have to see: Magnolia.

I throw on my coat, slip on my shoes, and head into the hallway, trying to decipher where the exit is located. I walk past a bank of desks, hoping I'm going the right way.

"Miss Margaret? Where are you off to?" I hear behind me.

I don't stop, my mission still in front of me.

"Miss Margaret, hold up!"

I turn and see the plump lady who takes care of me hustling in my direction.

"I haven't the time. I must go," I say.

"But Miss Margaret, it's the middle of the night. Whatever you've got to go do can surely wait until the morning," the woman replies as she catches up to me.

"It *can't* wait," I shake my head vigorously. "I have to see Magnolia right away. I have to explain to her what I did. I have to make her understand."

"Now, Miss Margaret. You know as well as I do your sister's no longer with us," the nice lady answers, her brow furrowed with concern.

"She's not?" I ask as confusion wafts over me.

"No, ma'am. Magnolia's been gone five years now. Remember?"

I explore the depths of my mind, sifting through the cobwebs, discovering that it's true.

"Do you know who I am?" she wonders kindly.

I search her face but I can't seem to place her.

"I'm Clementine. I've been looking after you for eighteen months here at Worthy Community Home. Why don't we go on back to your room, and I'll tuck you in with a nice, hot water bottle? It'll make you feel better. What do you say?"

"I'd like that," I remark, suddenly weary. "Can you stay with me awhile? I'm feeling a bit out of sorts."

"You bet I will. Come along now," Clementine smiles warmly, takes my hand, then leads me slowly down the hallway.

Mrs. Hadley

Well, it's the moment of truth. Mama Pearl is putting me through my paces this afternoon, testing my strength to see whether I can kick my walker to the curb for good, and rely solely on my cane for transport.

"Push against my hand, Mrs. Hadley," Mama Pearl directs.

I'm flat on my back, my right leg raised off the bed, and give her palm a good shove with my foot.

"Wonderful. Your limb strength is greatly improved on that side," she remarks. "Now, let's try the left."

Another strong leg thrust and I pass this part of the exam with flying colors.

"Why don't you grab your cane and get out of bed?" Mama Pearl suggests.

I do as I'm asked and slide easily onto the floor, my feet firm and steady.

"Go on and walk into the hallway and I'll watch your gait," she requests.

I mosey into the corridor, my stride fluid and even. Where before I would lean on my cane for support, now it mostly serves as a safeguard since my muscle tone has developed so well.

"All right, Mrs. Hadley. I believe we're done. No more walkers for you," Mama Pearl announces.

"Can I ask Mr. Isaac to tear it up into little pieces and throw it in the dumpster out back?" I wonder.

"That might be a little extreme," she chuckles. "But he can fold it up and stow it in your closet for you. How does that sound?"

"That'll do I guess," I say with a shrug. "At least it'll be out of my sight."

"You should be proud of yourself, Mrs. Hadley. The progress you've made is nothing short of remarkable," Mama Pearl observes.

"Why thank you, Mama Pearl. It's amazing what you can accomplish with the right motivation," I respond with a smile.

"Afternoon everybody," Cleo calls from my doorway.

"Hey there, Cleo. You're the first person to hear the good news: I am now strictly a cane user. No more clunky walkers for me, thank you very much," I declare, grinning from ear to ear.

"Congratulations, Mrs. Hadley," Cleo replies cheerfully.

"And I owe a lot of my success to you and your mama here. With her wonderful doctoring and your metaverse experiment keeping my spirits up, it's made the transition so much easier," I pronounce.

"Speaking of doctoring, I've got more patients to see so I'd best be running along. Now Mrs. Hadley, even though you're cleared to use a cane, that doesn't mean you can let your guard down. No speed walking down the halls or anything like that. And make sure to watch your step. A broken hip never did anyone any good," Mama Pearl warns.

"I'll be careful. I promise," nodding my head in agreement.

"You take care, Mrs. Hadley," Mama Pearl pats my shoulder. "Cleo, give me some sugar," she leans in for a peck on the cheek from her daughter. "All right, I'm off."

I turn to Cleo. "What are you doing in my neck of the woods? You got a session with somebody this afternoon?"

"No, not today. I was in with Jillian finalizing my company's contract with Worthy Community Home. A two-year deal, signed, sealed, and delivered by yours truly," Cleo beams.

"Look at you, Cleo. A mover and shaker and you ain't but twenty-three years old. Watch out, it won't be long before you're running that tech firm all by yourself."

"Well, we'll see about that," Cleo grins. "Anyway, I wanted to let you know that we have a firm end date for our project: three weeks from tomorrow," Cleo emphasizes.

"Oh?"

"Yeah, so if you were thinking of letting Jane know who you really are, Mrs. Hadley, you have a deadline," she clarifies.

"Oh, I see," I reply, then let the news linger in the air.

"You *are* going to tell Jane you're her mother, aren't you, Mrs. Hadley?" Cleo's brow furrows.

I look away, wringing my hands.

"Mrs. Hadley?"

"I don't know, Cleo. Jane and I are friends now. I don't want to mess all that up with the truth. We can just go along like we have been. What's the harm?" I rationalize.

"For one thing, I won't be able to let Jane and her team use the basketball space like they do now once the new contract begins. You may not see Jane as much then, or at all, for that matter," Cleo points out.

"Surely Jane would want to keep in touch," I counter.

Cleo exhales, irritated with my waffling. "Mrs. Hadley, I know it's not my place to tell you what you should do. But I wonder how you would feel if you were in Jane's shoes? Wouldn't it make a difference?" She smiles ruefully, then squeezes my arm. "I'll see you soon."

Cleo leaves me to wrestle with my conscience. How about that? She's just as wise as her mama.

Clementine

I don't need to glance at my watch. My internal clock confirms what I already know: five more minutes until my break and another rendezvous with Gregory, my virtual paramour. My pulse quickens at the thought of it.

Ever since Gregory found that tiny, secluded area on the other side of the pond, Our Spot as he so aptly named it, my workdays revolve around the metaverse. I'm perpetually plotting when I can sneak away for a visit with him, even if I don't know if he'll be there or not.

He's coy about when we can meet, always vague about which days and how long he can join me; that darn, pesky reality interfering with our dream world. I feel like I'm in high school again chasing after a boy, something I haven't done since my courting days with Percy.

Finally, it's four o'clock on the dot. I grab my headset and hustle down to my Happy Place to jump heart-first into my awaiting Shangri-la.

The weather is perfect as usual, sunny and mild, and I stroll over a little hill to enter Our Spot. Gregory is already there clutching a bouquet, glancing over the stream as frogs play hopscotch on their lily pads.

"Gregory," I call.

He turns to me and his face brightens, full of warmth and possibility.

"There she is. Hello, Rebecca. How are you this fine afternoon?"

"Much better now that I'm here," I reply with a smile.

"I picked these for you," Gregory hands me the nosegay. "I'm not sure what kind of blossoms they are, but I saw them, and I thought of you."

I breathe in their glorious scent. "They smell heavenly. Thank you, Gregory."

"I never thought the weekend would end. Those couple of days were sure lonesome without you," he muses.

"Time can hang heavy sometimes, that's true. But I don't see that as a bad thing. How does the saying go, 'Absence makes the heart grow fonder?'"

"That's all well and good for some folks. I prefer for things to hurry up and get here," Gregory confesses with a roguish grin.

"They do say patience is a virtue," I tease.

"I don't see anything virtuous about being away from you," Gregory remarks as his hand falls behind me and reaches around my shoulder.

He pulls me closer, and I nestle into his arms. The feel of him makes my head swoon.

We stand there in easy, comfortable silence, our beating hearts the only detectable motion between us, admiring the calmness of the water and the gentle rustle of marsh grasses as they sway in the breeze: bliss, sheer bliss.

After a bit, Gregory turns to me, his expression somber.

"It's time for me to go, Rebecca. But standing here with you in my arms, I know what will tide me over until we meet again."

Before I can respond, Gregory cups my face with his hands, stares deeply into my eyes, and brushes his lips against mine, softly yet firmly, like this is meant to be.

I sigh against his mouth as he lets go, wishing it could go on longer, the feeling so new and so familiar all at once.

"Until next time," Gregory whispers.

And before I know it, he disappears, returning to wherever he came from.

I linger for a moment more in Our Spot, filled with joy and wonder. There's no denying it: I'm in love. That's right. I'm in love with a fantasy I can see and touch. Ain't that something?

As I lock the door to my Happy Place and return to the here and now, I hum absentmindedly, my mind still flushed with the metaverse afterglow.

"You all right, Mrs. Babineaux?"

I spin around to see Mr. Isaac behind me, VR goggles in one hand and a mop in the other.

"I'm fine, Mr. Isaac. Just preoccupied is all," I reply.

"It's easy to happen in that virtual reality machine," Mr. Isaac points to my headset. "It's amazing the folks you can meet in there. I can't get enough."

"Me neither, Mr. Isaac. Me neither."

Margaret

October 1970

It's not what I thought it would be when we first began this, Ashby and me. The truth is, I can't remember now what I was searching for, other than the hunt, the chase, and taking something meaningful away from my older sister. The repercussions didn't occur to me, the collateral damage of a marriage teetering on the brink of ruin was of no consequence. I just coveted winning; that was all.

I got what I wanted, I guess; Ashby wound tightly around my finger and at my beck and call, but I can hardly stand the thought of him anymore. Seeing Magnolia the other night, so frail and fragile, the scales fell from my eyes, and I finally understood the sheer agony this was causing her. And I must put a stop to it. Now. Today.

I will sit Ashby down while Billy naps and tell him that it's over. No more lunchtime visits, no more shenanigans. If Ashby wants to see Billy, we can meet at Daddy's house. But not here. Not ever again.

It'll all go back to the way it was before. Ashby and Magnolia can heal their marriage and start anew. I'll continue to look after Billy and sign up for a class or two at the junior college until I figure out what I want to do with my life. Maybe I'll even meet a cute college boy and get hitched. Who knows?

I'm betting a year from now this whole affair business will be a blurry memory, something akin to a bad dream. That's what I tell myself, anyway. That's what I'm praying for.

Since Magnolia's confession, she hasn't set foot near my home. Instead, Ashby drops off and picks up Billy, telling that little four-year-old he's a big boy now, and big boys don't need their daddies to walk them inside. So, I wait for Billy's knock to begin our day, since he still can't reach the doorbell.

Soon enough, I hear a light tap-tap-tap, fainter than usual, and open my door to a most curious sight to behold.

"What in God's name are you wearing, Billy?"

He peers down at his bright orange and royal blue Hot Wheels pajamas, then shrugs.

"My jammies," he replies nonchalantly.

"Who dressed you this morning?"

"I did. Daddy said to wear what I wanted to school, so I figured why change when I already had clothes on," Billy remarks matter-of-factly.

"Of course your daddy would say that," I mutter, shaking my head. "What did your mother think about your outfit?"

"She was still asleep. She's been doing that a lot lately."

"You can't go to school in your pj's. Come on in and let's get you into more suitable attire," I reply.

Billy follows me into the guest room while I grab a fresh T-shirt and jeans from the dresser—our stash as we refer to it—in case Billy has an accident.

"Arms up," I direct.

As I pull off his nightshirt, a feverish heat rises from his chest.

"Oh, Billy. You feel awfully warm." I check his forehead, too.

"Do you hurt anywhere?" I ask.

"My throat's a little sore," he confesses.

"Let me see. Open wide," I command.

Sure enough, his mouth is scarlet red.

"Well, there'll be no school for you today. You've come down with a bug," I opine.

"Do I have to stay home?" Billy whines. "Teacher's having show-and-tell this morning and Tommy Madison said he would bring his old toad. It's got warts and everything."

"You don't want to get Tommy or your other friends sick, do you? It's best to stay here and rest," I reason.

Billy's sour expression tells me he's going to put up a fight, so I come up with a more favorable alternative.

"Say, do you know what my mama would give me when my throat was sore? Chocolate ice cream with lots of sprinkles on top. Is that something I can interest you in?"

"You bet you can," Billy exclaims. "Ice cream beats a toad any day."

"Come into the kitchen with me and I'll give you some baby aspirin for that fever of yours, then you can have a scoop or two."

While I make sure Billy chews his pills, the front door bursts open, then slams shut with a sharp thump.

I race to the entryway to see Ashby standing there, breathing heavily, his suit jacket off and tie undone.

"Ashby, what on earth are you doing here, and why did you bust into my house like that?" I shout.

"It's Magnolia. She knows about us," Ashby replies, his face ashen white.

"How?" I wonder, speechless.

"She was sorting the laundry before work and found a handkerchief with your lipstick on it," he confesses.

"So?" I shrug. "That doesn't mean anything. It could've gotten on there lots of ways," I reason coolly, but my heart thumps a mile a minute.

"That's what I told Magnolia. But she doesn't believe me. She's on her way here now. I think we should just tell her the truth and be done with it," Ashby suggests, his eyes wild and desperate.

Before I can respond, Ashby points behind me.

"Why is Billy not at school?" Ashby demands.

Billy's head peeks around the kitchen wall, no doubt eavesdropping.

"He's sick with a fever and sore throat. You would've known that if you had bothered to ask him how he was this morning," I retort.

"I don't need little ears listening to our discussion. Billy, come here boy," Ashby orders.

Billy approaches timidly, cowering from his father.

"Go outside and play. Maggie and I have grown-up things to discuss," Ashby says sternly.

"He's ill, Ashby. Billy can go to the guest room and shut the door," I argue.

"No. Billy's going outdoors," Ashby thunders.

He grabs Billy by the scruff of the neck.

"Be careful with him, Ashby. He's not a rag doll," I plead.

"Can I have a toy to play with?" Billy asks quietly, bracing for a blow.

Ashby grabs Billy's Nerf ball and throws it into the yard.

"Go fetch," Ashby responds gruffly, shoving Billy out the door.

Ashby turns to me, his expression manic.

"You listen to me, Margaret. We are coming clean to Magnolia. We are going to tell her that we're a couple and that I want a divorce," he threatens.

"We are doing no such thing, Ashby. There is no us. We are not a couple," I contend.

"Like hell we aren't. You belong to me," Ashby roars.

"It's over, Ashby. We're done," I explain firmly and without apology.

Suddenly, a deep sense of foreboding overwhelms me, making my neck hairs stand on end, and I reach for the front door handle.

"Where do you think you're going?" Ashby grabs my arm.

"Billy can't be outside," I yank away from his grip.

As I step onto the porch, Billy's halfway across the street, chasing his Nerf ball that's blown away.

"Billy! Stop!" I scream.

Yet my cries are for naught.

A late-model Cadillac rounds the blind curve and barrels into Billy, throwing his body several feet down the road.

"Billy!" I shriek.

I rush to Billy's side and stare at his lifeless body, such a tangled mess of bones and flesh that I can't tell where he begins and ends, the orange ball he clutches in his tiny hand the only semblance of normalcy remaining.

"Look at what you made me do!" I turn to see Magnolia standing beside the car.

"This is your fault, Margaret! This is your fault! Look at what you made me do!" she wails repeatedly.

Ashby wraps his arms around Magnolia to steady her as she breaks down in front of us, shattered by the realization she has run down her only child.

Then everything fades to black.

Cleo

Oh, no. Oh, no. Oh, no.

"Miss Margaret?" I cry as I yank the VR goggles from my face.

She's slumped over in the chair, her headset dangling from her forehead. I gently remove it and check for a pulse. It's weak and thready.

I race into the hallway, looking up and down the corridor for help. Mr. Isaac is in the room next door, waxing the floor.

"Mr. Isaac, I need help," I shout. "It's Miss Margaret. Something's happened. Get my mama or Miss Clementine. Somebody," I plead.

Calmly yet urgently, Mr. Isaac grabs a walkie-talkie from his belt and calls a Code Red.

"It'll be all right, Miss Cleo," Mr. Isaac says, composed and decisive. "Help is on the way."

Almost instantaneously, a bevy of blue-scrubbed personnel rushes past us, including Mama and Miss Clementine. I follow to join them in Miss Margaret's room.

"She's got a pulse," Miss Clementine assesses.

"Let's get her out of this chair," Mama directs.

Miss Ida Mae and Miss Clementine lower Miss Margaret's limp body onto the floor.

Mama begins checking Miss Margaret's vitals.

"Has 911 been contacted?" Mama wonders.

"Yes, ma'am," Miss Ida Mae nods.

"It happened all of a sudden," I explain frantically. "One minute Miss Margaret was in the metaverse, then the next she was hunched over."

"It appears she's had a stroke," Mama determines.

As I step closer to Miss Margaret, I notice the telltale drooping on the left side of her face, and her left hand clenched into an awkward fist.

"Did anything unusual occur while she was revisiting her memories, Cleo?" Mama asks without judgment.

"Well, she *did* remember something traumatic," I acknowledge uneasily.

I swallow hard and take a deep breath, silently considering whether I'm the cause of Miss Margaret's suffering.

Before Mama can respond, two paramedics hustle into the room. Mama and Miss Clementine give them the rundown on Miss Margaret's condition, then they attach her to an IV, strap her into a gurney, and whisk Miss Margaret away.

"There's nothing more we can do but keep Miss Margaret in our prayers," Mama says quietly.

The clickety-clack of high heels echoes from the hallway, which can only mean one thing: Jillian, the Home's director, is on her way.

"Okay, okay, okay. What happened here?" Jillian wonders in her typical rapid-fire delivery.

"It looks like Miss Margaret had a stroke. We'll know more once she's admitted to the hospital," Mama replies.

"Mm-hmm, mm-hmm, mm-hmm," Jillian responds with her arms folded and an index finger tapping nervously against her elbow.

"Did your virtual reality testing cause this, Cleo?" Jillian stares at me with an unwavering gaze. Apparently, she's not one to beat around the bush.

I feel everyone's eyes on me and I freeze. "I... I... don't..." I stammer.

"Miss Jillian, there ain't no way of telling what might've prompted Miss Margaret's condition," Miss Clementine interjects.

"She's old and has dementia; that's two big strikes right there," Miss Clementine reasons.

Jillian nods slowly, mulling over Miss Clementine's rationale.

"There aren't any other residents participating in this memory project of yours, are there, Cleo?" Jillian asks matter-of-factly.

"No, ma'am. Miss Margaret was the only one," I confirm.

"That's reassuring. Good thing she signed a release form," Jillian remarks bluntly. "I have four weeks left here before I join corporate," she emphasizes while glancing severely at each of us. "I'm warning you: don't rock the boat. Keep everything on an even keel. Got it?"

Mama, Miss Clementine, and I nod in agreement.

"Good. I'll contact the family. And Clementine, keep me posted on Margaret's status," Jillian commands.

"Yes, ma'am, I surely will," Miss Clementine replies as Jillian leaves us and takes her stilettos walking.

Miss Clementine shakes her head in disgust. "Four more weeks of that woman just might be the death of me."

"Ain't that the truth," Mama commiserates with a sigh.

Clementine

Just as Mama Pearl suspected, Miss Margaret did indeed suffer a stroke, paralyzing her entire left side as near as the doctors could tell. She has yet to wake up, her brain suffering from such a lack of oxygen that bleeding occurred, leaving her in a deep coma. For how long, no one knows.

Since Miss Margaret is stable now, her daughter Georgina fought tooth and nail to have her mama transferred back to the Home to be cared for here. The hoops Miss Georgina had to jump through weren't from the hospital; their administrators were as accommodating as can be.

No sir, the obstacle in Miss Georgina's path was the one and only Miss Jillian Hennessey, Worthy Community Home's esteemed director. I use the term "esteemed" in the pejorative, mind you.

Miss Georgina argued that since her mama was in a steady state, she should be allowed to return and be attended to by the staff she was familiar with. Miss Georgina reasoned that when her mama woke up from her coma, it would be a terrible shock to Miss Margaret to arouse in a strange place and not recognize where she was.

Miss Jillian responded with just a single word to Miss Georgina's heartfelt plea: liability.

So, I went in and cajoled and sweet-talked Miss Jillian, promising I would take responsibility for Miss Margaret's care, which isn't much but monitoring vital signs and changing out IV bags.

Miss Jillian hemmed and hawed, flip-flopping back to front and upside down, yet she finally relented, most likely due to the pages and pages of waiver forms she required Miss Georgina to sign.

After wading through all that nonsense, Miss Margaret was delivered back to her old room this morning, albeit with more medical equipment and paraphernalia than before.

I must say, it sure is good to see her again, even if she can't sass me yet. I'm hoping she recovers to that point, though. Miss Margaret has been a handful, there's no denying it. Still, I love her like she's family, the bond between us as strong and complicated as if we were blood.

While things are looking up on the work front, my love life has been less than fulfilling recently. Gregory has been absent from Our Spot, and with the weekends interfering, I haven't been held by him in days. When we were together last, and he kissed me for the first time, I knew in my heart of hearts I was falling for him. But how can you love with certainty a feeling or idea? In the end, that's all Gregory is. Although the metaverse allows for physical sensations between us, it's not genuine; it's fiction. I just need to remind myself of that. Easier said than done.

Now you'd think since I've been feeling more romantic lately, Percy would be all too eager to join in the fun. My telltale moves to let Percy know I'm in the mood are to shove my hands into his back pockets, pull him close to me, and nuzzle my nose against his chest. Strange, I'll concede, but it gets the job done.

Normally, Percy will smile that naughty grin of his and respond, "Give me some sugar," and then we're off to the races. That ain't what's been happening, however.

The past few overtures I've made to him, Percy's complained of being too tired or feeling under the weather; well-worn excuses to let me down gently. Then he'll offer to rub my feet or scratch my back instead to compensate for my disappointment. It's not the same, though, and no doubt Percy's aware. I try not to dwell on it, telling myself that maybe Percy really *is* tired from all that walking he does and the time he spends in virtual reality. Still, something's off; I can sense it in my bones.

Mrs. Hadley

It's funny how you can so easily forget the experiences that once brought you joy. How those memories fade into the distance as the years pile new ones on top of them, and they get lost in the shuffle of life.

But what a delight when those old recollections bubble to the surface. Like buried treasure from long ago that washes to shore, those memories gleam again as if they were freshly made, and are even more satisfying the second time around.

If someone had told me three months ago when I began this experiment with Cleo that I would be playing pickup basketball games with random folks in the metaverse, I would've thought they had gone off their head. Yet here I am, running up and down the court with strangers as if I were a teenager.

Jane requested our arena time be opened to everyone now that the team's up to speed using our VR controls. Jane figured some outside competition would be fun, and boy was she right. While scrimmaging against Jane's teammates was helpful to polish my skills, after a bit, it was pretty easy to guess everyone's moves and tendencies on the court. Our progress plateaued as a result.

Now, with the influx of fresh people, every game is a new adventure. Since I'm not a part of her team, Jane plays the other ladies first, which I totally understand, but she makes certain I get plenty of minutes. Besides, even though my avatar appears much younger, I have to remind myself I'm nearly eighty-one years of age, and my reflexes ain't what they used to be.

That doesn't mean I don't get in a few good licks here and there. This evening's final game was a close battle between us and five other fellas. The score was tied with only a few seconds remaining. I was in the game because one of our other tall girls had fouled out.

So, there I was, guarding this hefty, young man under the basket, when his teammate broke free from his defender and dribbled unfettered toward the rim. Just as he launched what was sure to be the winning shot, I sidestepped my guy and swatted the ball away from the net, rejecting that sucker into the waiting arms of Jane, who took off down the court for an easy layup.

Congratulations rained in from the other players, which never gets old. Even the youngster whose basket I denied muttered, "Nice block," a little mortified that an older woman could perform such a feat.

"Dang, Ree, you smacked that ball into next week," Jane said as we slapped our hands over our heads for a double high-five.

"It was second nature. I'd forgotten what that feeling was like," I replied with a satisfied grin.

"And I'll bet you're going to try it again soon, huh?" she joked.

"You got that right," I chuckled.

"Anything new happen this week?" Jane asked.

"Why yes, as a matter of fact, something did," I nodded my head. "That old clunky walker of mine got shown the door. Well, the closet anyway."

"Say it ain't so, Ree."

"From now on, I'm strictly a cane user, so help me God," I shouted happily.

"*Fan... tas... tic.* And it only took you what, three months of rehab, to accomplish? Impressive, girl, truly impressive," Jane shook her head in amazement. "You know, I've been meaning to tell you. I got fitted with leg prosthetics late last year, but I didn't see much point in trying to walk like regular folks. It's *so* hard, and it hurts my stumps *so* bad. I got discouraged and gave up."

"After meeting you, Ree, and hearing you describe how hard you've worked to get stable with a cane, it motivated me to begin again," Jane explained. "The past few weeks, I've been seeing a physical therapist, and I'm learning with crutches right now. I tell you what, though, I think I'm going to graduate to walking sticks soon, just like you."

Jane reached out and squeezed my hand. "You're my inspiration, Ree."

My heart melted at the thought of inspiring my daughter to do anything, let alone mastering how to walk.

It was the perfect opportunity to tell her. We were alone, the two of us, with no one there to interrupt. Yet like with so many chances before, I squandered the moment, allowing Jane to leave without the truth, once again letting my cowardice rule the day. And I hated myself for it. I truly hated myself.

Margaret

There are people around me. I can hear them. In and out. In and out. The nice lady who cares for me, Clementine? And the doctor woman that warns me not to eat sweets. Their voices buzz with my name. They talk at me, and about me, but not to me.

My body isn't right. One side, the left? It's rigid and twisted, like a knot that's been wound too tight. Try as I might, I can't move anything. I'm so, so tired.

I must be in a helluva shape, something my daddy used to say when someone was on a downhill slide. I suppose that's what happens to us unlucky ones as we approach the end; we don't go quickly; we linger.

My mind drifts, too, between now and that horrible, wretched day. Images flash before me as if they're color photographs in a slide show. There's Magnolia, screaming. There's Ashby, struggling to hold her. Then there's Billy, or what's left of him.

Urgent voices break into my thoughts.

"Her blood pressure's spiking," the doctor lady warns.

"Miss Margaret, stay with us," Clementine orders.

All at once, I float away to somewhere else.

I'm standing near the cemetery in Worthy, just over a small hill where I can't be spotted. It's frigid out here, like mid-January instead of October, the sun's warmth shrouded by thick clouds.

A priest draped in robes says some things in front of a small casket. I can't make out the words.

Ashby's alone, separated from the others, his hands jammed into his pants pockets like Billy used to do, his expression shattered and drawn. Daddy's across the way, his arms clutched tightly around a woman with hair as white as snow, hunched over with grief.

I scrutinize her closer, and my breath hitches. My God, it's Margaret.

I'd heard tell of this before. Mama shared stories about folks, usually women, who'd suffered a terrible shock one day, then the next they'd wake up to not a drop of color on their head. Like they aged an eternity overnight. The stress did it, Mama said.

And I've done it to Magnolia.

She loved her hair, my sister, as red as a sunset and always perfectly styled. Not anymore.

I wait for the service to finish, for everyone to get into their cars and go back to the house for food and drink. I've never understood why they throw a party on the one day they know the deceased can't attend. I remember when I was a child dressing up in my Sunday best to attend the funeral of some distant relative, and wondering out loud why they served cake afterward. "It's for the living," Mama told me when I inquired. It made no sense then, and it surely makes no sense now.

Daddy leads Magnolia to a waiting black limousine and folds her into the backseat like a ragdoll, her nerves spent. I linger where I am while Daddy watches the car drive away, and then I call to him since we're the last of the attendees remaining.

"Daddy?"

He turns with a start, recognizes me, then lets out a deep sigh, as if he's exhaling the weight of the world from his shoulders.

"What are you doing here?" he asks. "I told you not to come."

"I couldn't stay away. I wanted to pay my respects," I explain.

Daddy doesn't answer me. He just removes his glasses and rubs his bloodshot eyes.

"No one saw me. I didn't think it would matter."

"You didn't *think*? You didn't *think* it would *matter*? That's your problem, girl, *you don't think*," Daddy shouts.

I flinch, startled by his outburst.

"I warned you, Margaret. I warned you about Ashby. But you did it anyway. The consequences be damned," he shakes his head ruefully.

"I'm sorry, Daddy," I cry.

"Sorry? No, little girl. You say you're sorry when you wear your sister's shoes without her say-so. You say you're sorry when you eat the last piece of her wedding cake so there's nothing left to save for her first anniversary. Sorry doesn't cut it when you ruin her marriage." Daddy spits out the words like they're poison.

"I don't know what to do. What can I do to make it better, Daddy?" I plead.

"You still don't get it, Margaret. There is *no* way to make it better. There is *no* turning back from this."

He grabs my arms and shakes me. "You broke your sister, Margaret. You and Ashby. She used to be so strong, so brave. And now, Magnolia's just a shell, with nothing left on the inside. She'll never be the same."

"Time will help, won't it, Daddy? Things always seem brighter once enough time has passed," I rationalize.

"*You've ruined our family, child.* You've *ruined* it. Get that through that thick head of yours. No amount of time or regret can put our family back together again."

The words that he has spoken, jagged and sharp, hang frozen in the air. I try to look around them, through them, as if they were never there. Yet they hover between us, no matter how much I wish for them to disappear.

"Oh, Daddy," are the only words I can muster.

He pulls me into an embrace. "I'll always love you, Margaret. You're my baby girl. And you'll never want for anything as long as I'm alive. But there are some things you can't get over. And this is one of them."

Daddy kisses my forehead and walks to his car, his shoulders slumped, weary and defeated. With my gaze, I follow his Cadillac as it rounds the corner and disappears from view, knowing full well this is the last time I will ever lay eyes on him.

Clementine

Up and down. Up and down. Miss Margaret's pulse has been fickle today, like her heart can't make up its mind. One minute it's beating along all fine and dandy, then the next it's off to the races. Mama Pearl tried various elixirs and potions throughout the afternoon, struggling to find the winning combination to keep Miss Margaret's rhythm steady. Finally, Ruth landed on some medicine, a beta blocker, that seemed to keep Miss Margaret's vitals in check.

I admire Mama Pearl's tenacity. Most doctors would've shipped Miss Margaret back to the hospital and been done with her, but not Ruth. Although she's of the opinion Miss Margaret's malady is clinical in nature, I happen to believe there's something more going on with our patient. Miss Margaret's spent a lot of time mulling over her memories, and it's hard to shut those off on a dime, even in a coma. Maybe Miss Margaret is struggling with her thoughts, or maybe she's near the end like Mama Pearl imagines. Either way, Miss Margaret's unsettled, and that ain't good for nobody.

As such, Mama Pearl asked me to stay later than usual until the evening shift took over, so I could keep an eye on Miss Margaret and get the night crew up to speed on her condition. Ruth is stretched too thin as it is, and I'm happy to do anything I can to lessen my dear friend's burden.

"Text me if Margaret takes a turn for the worse, will you, Clementine?" Mama Pearl said while she was leaving.

"I will, Ruth. You can count on it. Now, go on and get you something to eat. I've got an extra bowl of gumbo in the lounge refrigerator. It's yours if you want it," I offered.

"I need to do rounds," she insisted.

"You're not going to be any help to us if you're laid out flat from low blood sugar," I countered.

"Yes, ma'am," Ruth nodded with a chuckle. "Oh, and make sure the night staff has my phone number. I don't want their first call to be 911."

"I *understand*, Mama Pearl. This ain't my first rodeo." I pointed to the hallway. "Go. Food. Pronto." I ordered.

By the time I get everything squared away for the evening, darkness has already fallen. The air is warm, humid, and still, what some folks call a weather breeder.

I load my car and make the quick trip home, weary from the eventful day and hoping for a bit of peace.

"Percy?" I call.

"Percy? Where you at?"

No reply. Typical.

I wander the hallway to find Percy in his study, sitting at his desk with a VR headset fixed on his forehead while he stares off into space.

I tuck my index finger under the strap of Percy's goggles, pull it back, and let it snap against the side of his head with a resounding thwap.

Percy jumps from his chair, whipping off his headset.

"I didn't hear you come in," he says sheepishly.

Hmm. That's an odd response.

"Where's the 'Damn, Clem. What'd you do that for?' Didn't that sting you?" I wonder.

"Not really," Percy answers nervously, like he's been caught with his hand in the cookie jar before supper.

I narrow my eyes skeptically. "You're acting mighty strange, husband. You have been for a while now. What's going on with you?"

"Nothing, Clem." Percy shakes his head, avoiding my gaze.

Seeing how fidgety and anxious he's become, an ominous prospect hits me like lightning.

"If I didn't know better, Percy, I'd suspect you're having an affair," I utter calmly while goosebumps prickle my spine.

Percy peers down and rubs his forehead. His silence is deafening.

"What do you have to say for yourself, Percy? Are you stepping out on me?" My voice rises.

"I don't know," he eventually mumbles, meek and hesitant.

"What kind of answer is that? It seems to me it's a pretty simple question; either yes or no," I shout. "Let's try this again: Are you, or are you not, having an affair?"

Percy shrugs his shoulders.

"We've been married a lot of years, Percy Blaine Babineaux. You owe me the truth."

"It's complicated, Clem," is all he sees fit to say.

"But you've met someone?" I clarify.

"Yes," Percy replies weakly.

"Do you care for her?" I ask, just above a whisper.

"I think maybe I do," he responds, finally meeting my eyes.

My breath catches as my world suddenly spins out of control. Hurt, confusion, and betrayal course through me, all mixed up and back to front. Instead of tears, anger rises from within, spilling out and over toward Percy.

"Nuh-uh. I ain't playing this game with you," I wag my finger at him. "Don't nobody deserve to be treated second best. You go get your things and find somewhere else to sleep tonight. Because you're sure not going to under this roof."

"Clementine, it's late. Be reasonable," Percy objects. "Let me stay in the guest room."

"No, sir. You should've thought about that before you took up with somebody else. Now, get out," I holler.

Percy sighs, knowing he's waging a losing battle. Slowly, he wanders around the house, gathers some of his stuff, and shoves it into a duffle bag. After a bit, the garage door opens and closes, signaling that he's left me. And for the first time in forty-two years, I'm alone.

Cleo

I've never done this in front of anyone before. If Mama knew what I was engaged in at the moment, she'd be mortified, embarrassed, and give me a stern talking-to all in one fell swoop. We can't help it, though, Jonathan and me.

Our offense? Devouring Mama's scrumptious macaroni and cheese right out of the eight-by-ten casserole pan it was prepared in. No plates, nothing. Just two tablespoons, one for each of us, and that's it. Oh, and napkins. We're not barbarians after all.

Now, Mama's mac and cheese isn't something out of a blue box. No sir. Mama's concoction is made from scratch and has all sorts of extras in it like nutmeg, smoked paprika, and red pepper flakes for some kick. But there's one component that sends it over the top and straight to nirvana; not one, not two, but *five* cheeses: American, Gouda, fontina, Gruyere, and last but definitely not least, cheddar.

Take all that yumminess, combine it with enough butter in the roux to make a dairy cow jealous, and you've got the creamiest, most blessed creation to ever grace a utensil.

Naturally, Mama being Mama, she's aware I don't eat enough vegetables, so she stuffs her dish with tiny broccoli florets and carrots, plus small chunks of ham so I'll partake of the roughage. It's a meat-and-three all in one bite.

And it's glorious.

"I can't eat anymore, or I'll explode," I sigh.

"Do you mind if I finish it off?" Jonathan asks.

I stare down at the almost empty Pyrex container and figure there are maybe six to seven bites left.

Even though my stomach tells me to stop, my taste buds say otherwise.

I scoop one more hefty spoonful and shove it into my mouth as fast as possible before sanity intervenes.

"Mm, mm, mm," I swoon. "Okay, the rest is yours."

Jonathan inhales the remainder in under ten seconds. Impressive.

I lean back in my chair, the eventual food coma already beginning to swarm.

"Jane emailed me. She wondered if her team could play a real game against somebody, with a running clock, uniforms, the whole nine yards. Sort of a last blast in the metaverse before their time is up," I apprise Jonathan.

"How would we organize an opposing team?" Jonathan asks. "Everyone they scrimmage against now are random people."

I close my eyes, torn between dozing off and brainstorming a solution.

"It'd be nice if we knew a group who's familiar with VR and also reliable as a control sample," he continues.

I sit up quickly in my chair as an idea strikes me from out of the blue.

"We have the perfect gang for this right around the corner: The Bro Club," I grin.

Jonathan looks skeptical. "Do you think they'd want to participate?"

"Sure, they would. Quinn and his posse would love nothing better than to show us up. And there's no greater arena than the metaverse," I reason.

"It's worth a try," Jonathan shrugs. "When do you want to approach them about it?"

I hop to my feet, revitalized by this new challenge. "There's no time like the present."

"Remember, Quinn moved to the empty space down the hall," Jonathan calls after me.

How could I forget? In yet another epic brown-nosing feat, Quinn somehow coaxed Ingram into letting him take over the old storage room, theorizing that he could get more work done if he wasn't in a cubicle. Of course, Ingram wholeheartedly agreed.

I turn the corner to see Quinn's feet propped up on his desk and a gaming console splayed across his lap, furiously engaged in destroying a fictitious, two-dimensional foe on his computer screen.

"Is this what you do all day? Play other companies' software?" I needle. "No wonder you never get anything accomplished."

"You know, I thought there might be an eclipse coming. But I see it's just you invading my space," Quinn remarks, still glued to his game. "It's important to keep tabs on what the competition is doing."

I walk around to the side and unplug his desktop from the wall.

"What the hell, Cleo?" Quinn shouts.

"I've got a proposition for you, and I want your full attention."

"Are you selling Girl Scout cookies or something?" he asks drolly.

"That's cute." I roll my eyes. "There's a group of older ladies who play basketball in the entertainment area Jonathan and I created. They'd like to compete against another team before the project is over, and I thought you and your boys might be interested."

"It sounds like we'd be doing you a favor. No thanks," Quinn replies.

"Kind of," I nod in agreement. "Visualize, though, how you and your gang could humiliate Jonathan and me in our own space."

"Why are you trying to help these people, anyway? We're not social services; we're a tech firm," he chides.

"Because it doesn't cost us anything to make them happy, so why not do something nice for someone else?" I argue.

"I'm not sure," Quinn says dubiously.

"Look, Quinn. I don't have the time nor the crayons available to explain the benefits to you. So, stop your dawdling and give me an answer."

He rubs his chin, contemplating his decision. "There needs to be more in it for me. If my guys win, you and Jonathan have to do all our designs and testing for six months. Take it or leave it."

I curl my lip at the prospect, yet grudgingly give in. "Fine. Six months. And if the ladies win, Jonathan and I get your swanky new office here."

"You're not in a position to negotiate, Cleo."

"It isn't any fun if you don't have some skin in the game," I reason.

Quinn squints at me, considering my offer. "Okay."

"I'll get back to you with the particulars," I respond.

"You and Jonathan better get ready for a lot of late nights," Quinn remarks with a smirk.

Back at our cubicle, Jonathan is hunched over his laptop, intently reading something on the screen.

"I've got good news and bad news. Which do you want first?" I ask.

"The good," he responds without breaking his gaze.

"Quinn and the boys are in," I answer.

"And the bad?" Jonathan wonders.

"If they beat Jane's team, you and I have to complete all their designs and testing for six months," I utter quickly, bracing for his response.

"It may not matter," Jonathan replies. "Check your LinkedIn messages."

Intrigued, I sign onto my account. As I scan my inbox, the word 'Meta' jumps out at me from the address bar. Meta, the largest virtual reality platform company in the world, has reached out to both Jonathan and me. I quickly open the missive and my eyes about pop out of my head.

"Oh, my Lord," I gasp. "Meta wants an interview."

I turn to Jonathan and he's grinning from ear to ear.

"Cleo, we may have hit the jackpot."

Mrs. Hadley

My mind has always been restless, constantly fretting about this, that, or the other thing for as long as I can remember. Yet as the hours tick by and my time with Jane grows shorter, my thoughts have been working overtime.

My dreams, too, have changed these past days. Not long ago, they were occupied by a younger Jane, with James and me within reach; a family of sorts, however fragmented we appeared. Now, they've turned from bittersweet longings for what might have been to horrific nightmares, full of seething anger, recrimination, and regret. The visions that haunt me are identical, and follow the same, treacherous pattern of heartache and misery.

They begin with Jane's face—wholly perfect, lovely, and assured—suddenly fracturing, with large chasms veining in every direction, until it shatters into a million pieces.

I drop to my knees, struggling to pick up the shards and rearrange them into some kind of order, as if putting the fragments back together again would right the wrongs I committed in the past, and since then. My hands bleed from my labor, the jagged slivers shredding my skin while leaving permanent scars.

She laughs at me, pointing her finger at the pitiful sight that I am, splayed there on the ground while I grope desperately to mend the chaos that Jane has become.

All at once, Jane's laughter turns to screams, powerful and full-throated, her voice a mixture of contempt and despair.

"*You did this*," she shrieks.

"Look at me. Look at what you've done to me. I'm broken," Jane wails.

I wake up at that point, drenched in sweat, fearful of closing my eyes again.

As I lay here at present, waiting for the sun to rise and a new day to begin, I hear him call to me.

"Irene, you know what has to be done."

"James?" I ask the sound in my head.

"You don't have much time left, Irene. Our daughter is waiting for you," he replies.

"I'm so scared, James. These dreams I've been having; Jane hates me. She crumbles into bits like I've crushed her with the truth," I answer ruefully.

"That's just a notion you've conjured up, Irene. That won't happen."

"How can you be so sure? You don't know how she'll react. Nobody does," I argue.

"You have to make a plan and see it through," James counsels.

"I'm still of the mind that Jane would be better off if she never knew I was her mama. Things are going along fine as they are. Why should I upset the apple cart?"

"Now, Irene. Figure it out now," he commands.

"All right, all right. Hold your horses. You always were as impatient as the day is long. Let me think," I say, scratching my forehead. "Her team and I have one more practice, then there's a final game Jane was telling me about the other night. We get to wear uniforms and everything, like it's a real competition."

"Good. Do it then," James responds.

"Well, I can't tell her *before* the game," I contend.

"I understand that Irene," he replies testily. "Afterward is the perfect opportunity. Wait until the two of you are alone. Jane and you linger after scrimmages and the like, anyway. This will be no different."

"But how can I explain it so she'll understand?"

"Take her by the hand, admit to her who you really are, tell her you're sorry for the hurt you've caused, then let the chips fall where they may," James advises.

"Okay," I nod in agreement, "that's a good suggestion. I like it. But what if Jane ends up hating me? What'll I do then?" I ask, as my old, familiar doubts settle in.

"You'll go on, Irene. That's all you can do. Look at it this way," James reasons, "a few months ago you didn't even remember you *had* a daughter. Cleo comes in with her memory machine and helps you find her. You've been given a gift. Now it's time you returned the favor to Jane."

"I'm sorry you're having to do this all by yourself, Irene," he continues. "I shouldn't have asked you not to speak of her. I shouldn't have buried Jane in our past. I was wrong. I hope you can see fit to forgive me."

"Oh, my sweet James. There ain't nothing to forgive. We both made mistakes, whether we meant to or not. One thing I know for sure. I miss you, husband, every hour of every day," I whisper, tears pricking my eyes.

"As do I, Irene. As do I," he murmurs wistfully.

Clementine

It's been just three days since Percy left, but it feels more like an eternity, what with the size of the hole in my heart. Forty-two years is a long time to spend with someone. After a while, you ain't yourself anymore. You're a part of something bigger, like an enormous tapestry woven together, fastened and stitched by love and time.

I used to think there wasn't anything that could tear me and Percy apart. Sure, we've had our tussles and squabbles over these many decades, yet nothing so severe that could chafe our connection, or weaken our bond. Then, the unthinkable happened: Percy pulled a thread from our fabric and let it fray.

I'm of the mind that loyalty and trust are the seams that bind a marriage, making it sturdy enough to weather any kind of turbulence. Without them, the framework is shoddy and easily unraveled, often tattering to pieces, leaving only heartbreak in its wake.

So, when Percy couldn't tell me what lives in his heart, whether there's another he's grown fond of, or even—God help me—loves, I was shaken to my core. I felt our sturdy cloth, over forty years in the making, rip in two, the shredding sound still echoing in my head.

With his tail between his legs, Percy slept over at Gabe and Ella's place that night, no doubt fearful of what I might do if he spent money on a motel, given how mad I was when I kicked him to the curb. He's been over there ever since.

As for me, I was able to keep it together at the Home the next day, thankful for the many distractions. But when the weekend came, I couldn't bring myself to attend the Hen Brigade, the Saturday gathering of my small circle of friends at Ella's hair salon, The Weave Queen. The first one I've missed in over three years. Instead, I stayed here at the house and licked my wounds, not even rousing from my bed to go to church this morning.

Being the good friend that she is, Ruth has been texting and calling me nonstop since that evening. I figured as soon as Percy showed up at Gabe and Ella's home, Ella would beat down Ruth's door and give her the 411 on my situation. Ella never can keep things to herself. It's just as well, though, since I didn't have it in me to tell Ruth myself.

In an unprecedented move, Ruth canceled her usual Sunday after-church feed, coaxing me into coming over for a proper dinner and a shoulder to lean on, with no other folks around and their wondering minds. It took her the better part of an hour to convince me, but I finally gave in when she threatened to send the police over to my house for a welfare check. Ruth ain't the type to take no for an answer.

"Come here, baby," Ruth says as she opens her front door to me.

She folds me into an embrace, compassionate and strong and brimming with love, then leads me to the hub of her abode where most of the arguing and crying and living takes place: her tiny, galley kitchen.

Ruth pours a couple of large brandies into snifters and sets them in front of us at the table. Now, Ruth ain't usually one to imbibe; in fact, she never touches the stuff socially. But in dire circumstances such as this, Ruth is of the opinion that a stiff, brown alcohol such as brandy is medicinal in nature and mighty effective in calming your nerves.

I take a long pull on my glass and feel instantly better, almost human.

"How're you holding up, Clem?"

"I think I'm in shock," I say and drain the rest of my drink.

"Do you want to tell me what happened?" Ruth asks gently.

"There isn't much to tell. I get home from work like I always do, thinking I'm going to have a nice, quiet evening, and it turns into anything but. I find Percy on his headset, off in the metaverse doing God knows what, so I surprise him. And the look on his face, Ruth; I just knew something was going on. I asked him, straight up: 'Are you having an affair?' Then, get what he says next," I tap her on the arm for emphasis, "'I don't know.'"

"He don't know?" Ruth repeats with a side-eye.

"He don't know," I duplicate irritably. "I tell that man it ain't no multiple-choice question, and I deserve some truth out of him after all these years. You know what his reply was?"

I wait for a beat. "It's complicated."

"Mm. Mm. Mm," Ruth shakes her head in disgust.

"Well, that didn't sit too well with me, so I suggested he find some other accommodations till he figured himself out," I contend with a nod.

"This is where we are now, I guess," I sigh with a shrug. "Percy can't make up his mind and I'm in limbo."

"Percy's had a lot of change in his life here recently, Clem. Retirement is a hard thing for some men to tackle. They struggle to find a new purpose," Ruth responds.

"That don't excuse him taking up with somebody else," I reply bitterly.

"You're right," Ruth agrees softly.

"We should've had a family, Percy and me," I say ruefully.

"Clementine," Ruth scolds lightly, "one thing ain't got nothing to do with the other."

"Oh, yes it does," I argue. "When I found out I was barren, we should've done what Percy wanted and adopted. I was just too damn tightfisted and cheap. If we had us some kids and maybe some grandkids, Percy would have more of a reason to stay with me. As it is, I'm the only family he's got."

"And I'm not enough for him." I choke out the words and bury my face in my hands.

Ruth takes me gently into her arms and comforts me as I shed the first of many tears to follow.

Cleo

I f I've learned anything in my relatively short time here on this planet it's that life is unpredictable. One minute, you're as sure of your path as the back of your hand; where you're going, and who you're going with. Then, out of the blue, life throws you a curveball or two, low and inside, and you have to adjust so you don't strike out.

Now, I'm not normally one to use sports metaphors. Truth is, I avoid physical activity at all costs, preferring instead to engage in the "sedentary arts"—eating and sleeping. But my daddy used to make me watch baseball with him when I was a kid, and try as he might to get me interested, I never took to the game, usually dozing off after the first couple of innings.

I'll never forget how Daddy would yell at the TV when the score was close. "Keep your eye on that pitcher. He's going with the curve," he'd say. And more often than not, the batter would swing and miss, or stand there as the ball sailed past him for strike three.

Daddy would jump out of his chair, puff out his chest, and holler, "I told you so, you big dummy. That bender done caught you looking," he'd scold like he was a coach or something.

Then Daddy would turn to me and caution, "Cleo, always keep your eyes open. You never know when a bender is coming at you, and they're mighty hard to handle."

It took me years to understand he wasn't referring to baseball.

I wish I had paid more attention to those times with my father and committed to memory all the little exchanges we had. As I age, my recollections of him are harder to summon and duller around the edges.

I pray they don't fade entirely; his wisdom is hard to replace.

But I digress.

I've got a couple of "benders" I'm contending with at present, the first being the considerable interest from Meta I've received—the leader in virtual reality technology—and what that might mean for my career.

Somehow the folks at Meta learned of Jonathan's and my memory research and are conspicuously intrigued. For the life of me, I don't know how they discovered our testing protocol since it's proprietary. I guess Big Brother really is a thing; nobody can keep a secret anymore.

Yesterday evening, Jonathan and I had our first round of interviews, online of course since Meta is a tech firm after all. We Zoomed afterward like giddy schoolgirls and compared notes.

Our verdict? The job sounds like a dream. Jonathan and I would partner together and have our own budget, so we wouldn't have to beg for funding like we do now.

We'd also share a large office, just the two of us, to "foster meaningful collaboration," according to the HR rep. I don't get what that means exactly, except that I won't have to be quite as creative with my napping as I am currently in our cubicle.

Since Next Well "owns" our memory data, Jonathan and I would need to start fresh, but with the development money Meta would provide, the possibilities are endless.

And Ingram isn't making it difficult for Jonathan and me to leave. In fact, when we sat down with our dear leader to discuss goals for the new quarter, Ingram informed us that "Next Well is exiting the memory space and pivoting to gaming exclusively."

"Who made that decision?" I asked curtly, not even *trying* to hide my anger.

"I did," Ingram replied. "Furthermore, once your project is completed, you two will join Quinn's team and report to him. I'm adding another layer of management between us."

Jonathan and I sat there, stunned.

"Quinn's getting promoted?" I marveled after I picked my jaw off the floor.

"Yes," Ingram responded curtly. "We're done." And with a wave of his hand, Jonathan and I were dismissed.

So, it would seem that Meta is the perfect fit, and I should drop to my knees and pray to the good Lord for them to hire me as soon as possible and rid myself of the mess at Next Well. There's one problem, though. Meta's new position is in Austin, which leads me to my other "bender:" Brian.

He stopped by last night after my interview, a dozen roses and a bottle of bubbly in his hands.

"Hey baby," he said, handed me the flowers, and kissed me soundly.

"Hey yourself. To what do I owe the pleasure of this beautiful bouquet?" I asked while I rummaged around for a vase and some glasses.

"I don't need a reason to bring my girl some roses," he countered.

"And the hooch?" I pointed to the liquor.

Brian stretched out his arms and grinned. "You're looking at the new internet security manager for Google," he proudly announced.

"Well, how about that?" are all the good wishes I could summon.

I pulled Brian into an embrace and hugged the daylights out of him, struggling to hide my apprehension.

"How did your interview go with Meta?" he asked, changing the subject.

"Good, good. It seems like we could be a good fit," I answered uneasily.

"And the job is at their Austin office, right?"

"That it is," I nodded.

"This is all working out perfectly," Brian continued and pecked me on the lips. "What do you say we get married?" he offered eagerly.

"Hold up. Wait a minute there, Bri," I said warily. "Are you asking me for real, or is this a hypothetical?"

"Maybe a little of both?" he replied.

"I don't have the job yet," I cautioned.

"But you will," he responded. "Then we can be together forever. I'm telling you, it's fate, baby."

I patted his chest to slow him down a bit. "Maybe so. We'll have to see how this Meta thing works out, though. Let's take a breath and enjoy your success. Why don't you open the wine, and we'll toast to your new job?"

"You got it, beautiful," Brian answered and busied himself with the task at hand.

Whew, I thought to myself. It looks like I've bought myself some time. Daddy was right on the nose with circumstances like this: curveballs sure are hard to manage.

Margaret

Georgina's sitting beside me. Holding my hand. Speaking to me.

"Wake up, Mother. Come on now. Wake up," she says.

Just like she did when she was a child. I used to call Georgina my Little Alarm Clock back then. Always the dependable one. On-time for everything. School. Work. Life.

She's been visiting me a lot, my Georgina. Whenever I return to the here and now from wherever it is I go; my thoughts? Heaven? Hell? I don't know. Georgina is next to me, keeping me company.

If not her, then Clementine is around. Clementine and that doctor lady; Mama Pearl? They massage my limbs. Lather lotion on my dry, shriveled skin. Roll me over so I don't get bed sores. Clementine sings to me on occasion. Hymns. Soft and low. I do appreciate it. All of it. Even if I can't tell them.

Why do they care for me? I haven't a clue. I've been awful to every one of them. I don't deserve their grace. Yet they give it to me anyway. Such kindness shown to the likes of me.

Lacey, my youngest, is the smart one. As near as I can tell, she hasn't set foot inside this place. It's just as well. I've treated her the worst of all.

Lacey was my difficult child. Never good enough for me. Never a kind word between us. A liar extraordinaire. Could look you straight in the eye and swear to you what was up was down. What was false was true. The same as me. How does the saying go? The apple doesn't fall far from the tree? A chip off the old block? Lacey and me in a nutshell.

I never saw Daddy or Magnolia again. After Billy's funeral, I packed up and went to Dallas. Met a man in a bar my first night in town. Married him the next. The day after he beat me silly. On the fourth afternoon, I stole all the money he had in his wallet. Went back to Worthy. Got the marriage annulled.

Even though Worthy was a small town, it wasn't hard to lay low. Blend in. I was gossip fodder for a while, till the next big thing came along. That's how life works.

Six months later, Daddy died. A heart attack. I didn't attend the funeral. I didn't want to face all those people. The looks they would give me. The judgment they would render. So, I kept my distance, thinking that's what Daddy would've wanted. Truth be told, I was just plain chicken.

Magnolia contested the will. Said Daddy wasn't in his right mind and I shouldn't see a penny. The lawyers argued. I got my money in the end; for all the good it did me.

Magnolia kept to herself in Daddy's big old house. Stayed there the remainder of her life. She remarried. Had a daughter I never met. Her husband swindled some investors and went to jail. They divorced. Word is she was never the same after Billy. Her heart never mended. All that damage caused by my one stupid mistake.

After a little, I spread my wings and met a man. My second husband, Harold. He bought Daddy's Chevy dealership from the family. Harold was kind. Serviceable. Safe. And as dull as a box of rocks. Security was what I craved most at the time, so he sat well with me. For a bit. Then my eyes wandered elsewhere. I did get Georgina out of the deal. That was a blessing.

My last marriage was to Chuck. How that man lit a fire in me. Burned so bright I couldn't see straight. But Chuck liked to spread his love far and wide. Said he couldn't help himself. I put up with it. When I got pregnant with Lacey, Chuck packed up one day and was gone. Heard there was oil to be found in West Texas. He never came back. I think Lacey blamed me for never knowing her daddy. Maybe it was my fault. Truth is, I never tried to find him.

Lacey's like her father, too. Always running toward grass she thinks is greener. Turns out, it's the same shade wherever she goes. Then she's left wondering why she's so disappointed. Shame on me. I never taught her the difference. Should have; didn't. I deserve what I get. A long, miserable slog. I'm reaping what I've sown.

"I'll be going now, Mother," Georgina says, squeezing my hand. "Rest well. I want to see those big, beautiful eyes of yours open for me tomorrow."

There's the brush of Georgina's lips on my forehead. The pitter-patter of her shoes.

Oh, child. I'm so sorry. I'm going to disappoint you once again.

You see, my sweet, sweet Georgina, I'm minded to die.

Mrs. Hadley

Well, tonight's the night: The team's big game, and then afterward, having a heart-to-heart with Jane so she'll finally learn the truth about us.

I'm excited and nervous all at the same time, like a long-tailed cat in a room full of rocking chairs. On the one hand, the idea of fresh competition in a game day atmosphere is exhilarating, just like the thrill a feline senses when she sees those chairs swaying to and fro. On the other, I haven't a clue what Jane's reaction will be, like that same cat who wonders how she'll ever make it across with those rocker legs in the way. It's full of danger, with disappointment and regret lying in wait ready to pounce, but we've got to go through it to get to the other side.

As always, Jane was upfront with me about my playing time for this evening, explaining that her teammates would get the majority of minutes since her squad has been together so long. But if one of the bigger girls gets into foul trouble, she assured me I would be the first one off the bench. She's such a thoughtful person, my Jane.

To help me feel a part of things, Jane asked for my input on our uniforms and right away I suggested burnt orange and white, the colors of the University of Texas down there in Austin. Ever since I was knee-high to a grasshopper, I've followed their sporting achievements and am one of their biggest fans.

Thankfully Jane agreed, so we settled on white shorts and tops outlined with burnt orange piping, the word 'Texas' in bold letters across the chest. Even though I'm a longtime Longhorn fan, I understand that a little orange can go a long way, so we didn't make the uniforms a solid color. And let me say, the final product looks sharp.

While the day crept along, James popped into my mind on a few occasions, offering words of encouragement.

"You've got this, Irene. You've got this," he'd whisper to me.

I sure hope so, James. Fingers crossed.

"It's about time, Mrs. Hadley. Are you ready?" Cleo asks as she hands me my VR goggles.

I let out an anxious sigh. "Ready as I'll ever be," I reply.

"Good luck," Cleo says, then takes me away to the metaverse.

I shake my head to get my bearings and see that the stands are full of noisy fans, their cheers ringing in my ears. I have no idea whether they're real or conjured, but it's a nice addition, nonetheless.

I take a quick look around and notice all the little extras Cleo and her partner included to make the experience as authentic as possible: there's a large, orange Longhorn emblem painted in the middle of the floor with burnt orange outlining the court; banners suspend from the rafters revealing previous school milestones like league championships and notable players; and a huge Jumbotron hangs over the arena displaying images of each of the players, with advertisers shopping their wares to boot. The atmosphere is electrifying, sending chills down my spine. I guess Cleo must've been listening in when I told Jane about my love for this college, what with the small touches here and there. Miss Cleo did good, real good.

Jane and the rest of the team are warming up on one end of the court, while our challengers do the same on the other side.

"Ree, over here," Jane calls and waves me over.

At our last practice, Jane filled us in on our opponent, who is apparently a group of young men from Cleo's work. Cleo made sure their avatars and likenesses were as close as possible to what they are in the real world. She didn't want us to have to play against seven-foot giants with the skills of Michael Jordan. I know my teammates and I are mighty thankful for that.

I take a closer look at the other team's jerseys and chuckle to myself. They call themselves the Stealth Bombers. Cute. But goodness those boys have terrible taste in clothes; their uniforms are much too long and baggy, in a hideous purple with lime green accents. Bless their hearts, maybe they're color-blind. As I watch them laugh and cut up, it's plenty apparent they aren't taking this competition seriously, not like my team which is laser-focused during pregame drills.

The horn blares, letting us know it's time for the game to start. Three referees go to the middle of the court for tipoff, while Jane groups our team.

"All right, y'all, this is it: our last dance in the metaverse. And by the looks of things, it appears the gentlemen we're playing against think they've already won." Jane nods toward our opponents who are finishing up a dunking contest and paying no mind to the officials ordering them to stop.

"Let's give 'em hell, ladies," Jane continues. She places her hand in the center of our circle. "Together on three: 'Team.'" Our players take their positions on the floor, and with the opening jump ball, the game begins.

And things don't go well.

The Stealth Bombers are so much more athletic than we are, running the floor, cutting to the basket, and shooting the ball as if they play in virtual reality all day, every day. My team looks lost most of the time, and before long, we're behind by twenty points with five minutes left until halftime. To stop their momentum, Jane calls a timeout to regroup.

"We're getting our butts handed to us. It's time to shake things up. Ree, sub in for Donna. I want you on that big guy, Quinn," Jane orders.

I enter the game and right away we are on offense. I set a screen for Jane, then roll towards the basket as she passes the ball to me. I get my shot off before Quinn can block it and the ball banks off the glass for two points; only our fifth bucket on the night.

I hustle back on defense and Quinn tries to dribble to the hoop, but I poke the basketball away from him and take it down the court for an easy layup. He doesn't take too kindly to that, so he decides to taunt me.

"Think you're all that, huh lady? I wouldn't get too cocky," he warns.

"I'm just getting warmed up," I reply with a grin.

The jawing between Quinn and I continues until halftime, and I'm pretty sure I'm getting under his skin; we've cut their lead to ten.

There's just one problem, though; I'm pooped. Those few minutes on the floor, moving the controls around at warp speed has about worn this eighty-one-year-old down to a nub.

"Ree, I want you to start the second half," Jane directs.

"I can't, Jane. I've got to rest," I respond wearily.

"Okay then," Jane nods. "Let me know when you're ready."

Jane coaches Donna, my replacement, on Quinn's tendencies and Donna does a good job scoring around him, but Quinn's size dominates on the other end, giving her trouble when it's her turn to defend him. With fifty seconds left and our team losing by one, Donna commits her last foul and is out of the game.

"Ree? Are you good?" Jane asks, looking my way.

I nod and rise from the bench at a snail's pace, trying to conserve my last ounces of energy. The Stealth Bombers have possession of the basketball and slowly bring it down the court, trying to run out the game clock. I watch closely and anticipate a pass to Quinn, stepping in front of the ball and intercepting it. I dribble furiously toward our basket while time expires and launch a shot from half-court, with Quinn bumping into me as I let it go. His attempt to stop me is all for naught: the basketball hits the net with a perfect swish.

"We won! We won!" Jane shouts.

Sure enough, our team wins by two.

The other ladies dogpile on top of me, cheering and celebrating our unexpected victory.

"That was a great shot, Ree," Jane remarks while hugging the daylights out of me. "We did it. We really did it," she exclaims.

While Quinn saunters by me, his head down muttering to himself, I reach out to shake his hand, but he shoos it away and instead kicks the basketball across the floor in disgust. Hmm. I guess he ain't one to show much sportsmanship, or more to the point, he's a mighty sore loser.

As the revelry dies down, Jane's teammates and I say our goodbyes, promising to keep in touch, yet knowing in our heart of hearts we'll probably never see each other again. One by one, the other women leave, returning to their real lives, until it's just Jane and me remaining in the big, empty gym.

"It's time, Irene," James whispers in my head.

Jane approaches, a huge grin crossing her lips. I swallow hard, take a deep breath, and begin my speech.

"Jane, I have something to tell you." The words tumble out fast and furious.

"Me, too. You go first," she replies kindly.

I inhale, then exhale sharply. "I'm your mama."

"Oh, Ree," Jane chuckles. "You're so funny and sweet. I feel like a daughter to you, too."

"You don't understand, Jane. Listen to me now." I place my hands on her arms and stare straight into her eyes so there's no mistaking what I'm saying to her. "I'm your mama," I repeat slower and more deliberately.

Jane searches my face, rolling over in her mind if what I'm saying could possibly be true.

"No, no," she shakes her head, "that can't be. You live in Texas."

"I lived in Ohio for a bit, a long time ago. James, your daddy, was in the Air Force stationed in Dayton," I explain. "After a little, I got pregnant. My morning sickness was so bad I couldn't keep anything down. I worked for a lady, a general's wife, and she gave me some pills that were supposed to cure it."

I sigh ruefully. "They did the trick all right, but they came with some terrible side effects."

"You took Thalidomide?"

I nod slowly.

"Did you know? Did you know I'd turn out the way I did?" she wonders, her brow furrowing with shock and confusion.

"No, baby, no. It was a new drug. The doctor didn't have a clue something was wrong till you came out of me."

"So, you abandoned me there? To what, to die?" Jane asks, her voice rising.

"The doctor didn't think you would survive. He said it would be better for everybody if your father and I left you with him. And that's what we did," I answer, hanging my head in shame.

"Why now? Why did you look for me now, over sixty years later?"

"It was Cleo and that project of hers," I confess. "I had some old pictures from when James and I were first married, and all those memories of you came rushing back to me."

"You'd forgotten about me?" Jane wonders indignantly.

"I buried you, yes. Way down deep. Lord help me, I shouldn't have but I did. I thought if I didn't remember, then I could live with myself. I regret that as much as anything else," I respond sadly.

"This whole thing was Cleo's doing," Jane shakes her head, the truth broadsiding her as she puts the pieces together. "Did Cleo concoct this entire scenario so that we could meet?"

Silence is my only response.

"Why couldn't you leave well enough alone, Ree?" she shouts. "Why did you have to go and blow up my life? To make yourself feel better?"

"Don't you think I've asked myself those questions? The last thing I would ever want to do is hurt you. But we're kin, Jane. At the end of the day, we're the only ones we got left, you and me. I figured that could be something to build on."

Jane stands there without a word, quietly judging me.

"Come on now, Jane. Please. Ain't we got enough to start with?" I beg.

"To think I trusted you. To think you were my inspiration to walk on my own. What a sucker I've been. It was all a lie. One, gigantic lie." Jane spits out the words, full of contempt, yet tinged with disappointment and sorrow.

She leaves me then, my Jane, and I'm all alone again. My worst fear coming to pass.

Clementine

There's been lots going on with me these past days. For starters, Percy's back home. After a week of taking advantage of Gabe and Ella's generosity, he came around to the house, hat in hand, and begged forgiveness, swearing to me that he was on the straight and narrow. No more wandering eyes for him, Percy assured me. All he felt was love and tenderness, he said, and would make it his mission to win my trust again, no matter how long it took.

The skeptic in me wondered aloud whether his about-face had more to do with him wearing out his welcome at Gabe's than a renewed affection for me. But Percy swore to me that wasn't the case. So, I let my guard down and allowed him to stay, with the understanding that he was to sleep in the guest room and cook and clean up after himself; maid duty would not be part of the deal, thank you very much.

Since then, the last few evenings I've returned from work to find the house spotless and dinner ready, with all my greasy favorites on the menu from fried pork chops to collards with fatback. Nothing remotely healthy would touch my plate for the time being, Percy promised.

"I thought you were turning vegan on me what with all those salads you were eating before," I mused to Percy one night.

"What's that phrase you like to say to me? Moderation in all things? Well, I've taken it to heart and turned over a new leaf. Besides, vegetables are overrated. A little fat never hurt anybody, anyway," he chuckled.

The ice began to slowly thaw between us, until yesterday morning when Percy tried to kick our relationship up a notch.

"Give me a little sugar before you leave," Percy said as he placed his arms around my waist and pulled me closer.

"Nuh-uh, no sir," I replied and stopped him with a stiff-arm to his chest.

"Come on now, Clem. I miss you. How long is this gonna last?" he pouted.

"Until I say so and not a second before," I scolded. "You ain't been back very long, Mr. Babineaux, and we got some work to do, you and me, before I can settle in with you again," I pointed out. "You damn near blew up our lives. I think that deserves a pout or two."

"You're right, Clem. As usual," he sighed and shook his head.

When Percy left, I didn't feel much like cooking, so the meals I would prepare for Mr. Isaac fell by the wayside. One early afternoon, Mr. Isaac approached me at my desk with the last of his empty Tupperware.

"Everything all right, Mrs. Babineaux?" he said uneasily.

"I've been better," I replied, preoccupied. "Why do you ask?"

"Well, I noticed there haven't been any new containers for me in the break room," Mr. Isaac answered awkwardly.

"Oh, Mr. Isaac," I snapped to attention, "I'm so sorry about that. Things are out of joint at my house right now, and to tell you the God's honest truth, I plum forgot."

"There's no need to apologize Mrs. Babineaux. I understand, truly I do," he soothed. "I've taken advantage of your generosity for far too long, anyway. Just so you know, when you're hungry, I left you a little something in the fridge. It ain't much, but it'll do in a pinch. And you'll find it there every morning until you get back on your feet."

Sure enough, each day since, I've been spoiled by Mr. Isaac with a peanut butter and honey sandwich, the crusts cut off exactly the way I like it, and a Diet Dr Pepper. I don't know how Mr. Isaac knew my preferences, but his kindness is a welcome comfort to me.

As for the metaverse, I stuck my toe in every so often after I turned Percy out of the house, hoping deep down to find Gregory at Our Spot. But I've not seen hide nor hair of that man since our kiss, and as time goes on, I wonder if I ever will again.

The cynic in me tells me it was just a crush, a fantasy stirred up to pass the time and add a little spice to my otherwise stale existence. Besides, none of it is real.

Yet the romantic in me wants to believe Gregory somehow knows of my troubles and is giving me the space I need to confront them without distraction. Then, he'll return to me when my mind isn't so conflicted.

I prefer to think the latter is true. There's something about Gregory, his ease and familiarity, that stays with me. And sometimes, I wonder to myself if I might not know him out here in the physical world. That notion is too much for me to wrap my head around most days, so I let it lie fallow. Still, it lingers, poking at me now and then.

Margaret

It's almost time. I can feel it. Whatever strength I have is ebbing away. Like water swirling at the bottom of a drain before it's gone.

Georgina's left for the evening. I held on for her visit. I wouldn't let myself go under. Not until we had one, last sojourn.

Seeing as how I'm in a coma, she did all the talking. Told me she loved me. Said it was okay if I wanted to leave. She understood. Everybody has their time, she whispered. If it was mine, then that was all right with her.

Such a good girl, Georgina. She did the best she could with the hand she was dealt. I pray she'll be happy. Hope I didn't scar her too badly. She deserved a better mother than me. I loved her. Even though my actions said otherwise. She and Lacey both. I didn't say it enough. Or take the time to show it. After what happened to Billy, I guess I forgot how.

Regrets. Too many to count.

The biggest? Magnolia. I should've told her how sorry I was. I should've begged forgiveness.

Maybe I'll see her where I'm going. Maybe I won't. I'm departing this earth with a tortured soul. Of my own doing.

Just now, as I lie here, a gentle wisp of wind touches my face. Like an angel's kiss.

Something compels me to open my eyes. I do so, heavy-lidded and blurry.

An image comes into focus, sharper and more distinct. Standing right in front of me.

I'll be damned. It's Magnolia.

Clementine

There are times in my life when I've chosen to stop for a beat and thank the good Lord Jesus for His many blessings. This is one of those times.

Without Cleo and the metaverse keeping our memory care residents occupied here at the Home, I wouldn't have the space available in my schedule to keep a closer eye on things. Some patients need more help than others on occasion. Take Miss Margaret for instance: She ain't a bit well.

Mama Pearl and I held out hope those first few weeks after her stroke, praying Miss Margaret would turn the corner and open her eyes. But she hasn't yet, and with how weak she is now, I don't suppose she ever will. So, I spend any extra minutes I have with Miss Margaret, monitoring her vitals, speaking to her, letting her know she's loved.

Her daughter Georgina just left, and I'm on my way home for the evening as well. Yet something calls me to check on Miss Margaret one last time before I go.

I smooth her bed covers, make sure her IV bags are plenty full, then make a note in her chart. As I turn to leave, I hear a low rumbling sound, like a moan. I spin around to see Miss Margaret's eyes are open and she's struggling to move her mouth.

"Miss Margaret, you're awake," I cry. "It's so good to see you."

"M... M," she responds.

"Would you like some water?" I ask.

She shakes her head slightly.

"M... Mag," Miss Margaret repeats, her face drooping badly to one side.

"Don't push yourself. Your speech will come back in due time."

"M... Mag... Magno... a," she stammers.

This go-around, I don't try to stop her. I let Miss Margaret continue, as it finally dawns on me, she's got something to get off her chest.

"P... ple... s," she murmurs, "fo... give... me."

"Now, Miss Margaret," I soothe. "You're sister ain't with us anymore. Remember?" I take her good hand in mine. "I'm Clementine. I keep care of you every day."

"Mag... Magno... a."

Miss Margaret grips my fingers with all the strength she's got left.

"Fo... give... me. P... please. P... please."

She stares at me, clear-eyed and determined. Miss Margaret needs me one last time.

I lean in closer, stroke Miss Margaret's fine, flaxen hair, then whisper softly, "You are forgiven, Margaret. Rest easy now. You are forgiven."

Miss Margaret releases a gush of air like she's been holding her breath, tethered to her past, waiting for mercy.

And tonight, Miss Margaret is free.

A faint, peaceful smile crosses her lips, then she leaves me. I close her eyelids, gently kiss her forehead, and note the time of her passing.

Goodbye, Miss Margaret.

Some might say I had no right to do what I did. That judgment and forgiveness are for God and God alone to parcel out; no mortal should mess with that.

But I disagree. I happen to believe that spreading love and granting grace is why we were put on this silly little planet. Otherwise, what's the point of it all?

I wander into the hallway where Mr. Isaac is mopping the floor.

"Mr. Isaac, would you be so kind and fetch Miss Jillian for me, please?"

He straightens and leans against the mop handle, his gaze narrowing with concern. "Everything all right, Mrs. Babineaux?"

I shake my head and sigh.

"It's Miss Margaret. She's gone home."

Mrs. Hadley

I was unsure what would happen the day after I confessed to Jane. But that next morning, the sun rose in the east, and true to form, it set in the west. Life went on. The world kept on turning. Nothing stopped. That's not to say my heart wasn't shattered to pieces. When Jane left me in that big arena all by my lonesome, I stood there and cried a flood of tears. For how long, I can't recall. What I do remember is Cleo appearing before me, coming to the rescue, gently folding me in her arms, and holding me tight as if she was never going to let me go.

Somehow, Cleo led us back from the virtual realm to my room. She put me to bed, exhaustion hitting me like a hammer, and I fell into a deep slumber.

In the days following, Cleo would come to visit, sitting with me in silence while I continued my waterworks. She held my hand, stroked my back, handed me tissues, until I had no tears left to shed.

When I was finally up to it, Cleo let me do the talking. I took stock of what occurred between us, Jane and me, thinking long and hard about whether I made the right choice; whether I should have kept my secret to myself and avoided all this misery.

"Have you heard from her?" I asked.

"All I've received from Jane is a package with her team's VR headsets. That's it," Cleo answered ruefully.

"No note? No email?" I wondered.

Cleo slowly shook her head. "I'm so sorry for what happened."

"Oh, child," I sigh, "you don't need to say you're sorry. Not one bit. You, James, Clementine; all of you were right. I had to tell Jane. No matter how much it must've hurt her, she deserved the truth."

I placed my hand over hers. "Cleo, you finding Jane was like plugging a hole in my heart I didn't know I had. Getting to spend time with her, learning who Jane is as a person; oh my, what joy you've brought me. You reunited me with a part of myself. I can't thank you enough for those gifts."

"No regrets?" Cleo asked tentatively.

"Not a one," I said.

"I wish it would've ended differently for you," Cleo lamented.

"Who knows," I shrugged wistfully, "maybe it will."

"Would you like to jump back into the metaverse? There are plenty more areas you could enjoy that have nothing to do with basketball," she offered.

"I think I'm done with my time in the virtual world. I'll leave it for others to explore," I said with a smile.

"What are you going to do for fun?" Cleo asked.

"Well," I pointed to a large stack of books on my night table, "there's always reading."

"That old pastime?" Cleo teased.

"It'll do in a pinch," I replied and winked at her.

Since our talk, Cleo doesn't stop by as often anymore. I suppose we said everything that needed to be said, at least for the time being. I'm guessing if she hears from Jane, Cleo will let me know, and the same goes for me. As of now, I've resolved to stiffen my lip and get on with what's left of my life. No more feeling sorry for myself.

Still, each night I ask the good Lord a few simple requests: For my Jane to find it in her heart to forgive me, and for Him to grant us both some tender mercy. All this I pray, Amen.

Cleo

Seeing as though I've only attended a handful of funerals in my relatively short time on this earth, I wasn't sure what to expect as Miss Margaret's burial drew near. Would there be plenty of Worthy townsfolk on hand to pay their respects since the Worthingtons were such long-standing pillars of the community? After all, the county *is* named for them. Or would most people stay away and find better things to do with their time, given that Miss Margaret was such a tough nut to crack?

When the day arrived, Miss Clementine and I decided to go together. Mama wanted to accompany us, but the Home was overrun by a flu bug, and her hands were full of sick residents needing her care. As Miss Sybil, my trusty Ford Festiva, crested the hill near Worthy Cemetery, I didn't have to wonder about attendance any longer; it was packed. So much so, I had to park on a side street a few blocks down.

I dropped Miss Clementine off at the grounds. She wasn't used to wearing heels and her corns were acting up, she said. I think some of it had to do, too, with her desire to people gaze for as long as possible. Miss Clementine is just as nosey as I am. And, she's extremely reliable at letting me in on all her juicy observations which is a plus.

I caught up with her, seated at the very back of the crowd.

"I was able to snag the last two chairs," Miss Clementine marveled.

I looked around and noticed a few familiar faces, but most of them were strangers to me.

"I grew up in Worthy, but I don't recognize half the people here," I remarked, shaking my head.

"Most of these folks run in well-heeled circles," Miss Clementine said with a knowing glance. "They don't cross the tracks much into our neck of the woods."

"Who's that sitting next to Georgina?" I nodded across the way.

Miss Clementine grabbed the eyeglasses dangling from a chain around her neck and nestled them on top of her nose for a better view.

"Well, I'll be. She came after all." Miss Clementine clucked her tongue.

"Who?" I asked.

"Lacey, Miss Margaret's wayward daughter," she whispered.

On closer inspection, I could see Lacey's resemblance to Miss Margaret: the same, strong jawline, clenched and stiff; the bleached hair perfectly styled, if not a tad longer than her mother's; and the identical gaze, sharp and spoiling for a fight.

"Lacey's the spitting image of Miss Margaret," I observed. "Is that her husband sitting beside her?"

"Number four," Miss Clementine muttered.

"How old is Lacey now?" I wondered.

"Thirty-nine," Miss Clementine said, shaking her head.

Oh, my. If you had asked me, I would've sworn Lacey was northwards of sixty. Mm, mm, mm. My daddy used to say that folks such as Lacey were rode hard and put up wet. Mama would always scold him, preferring instead to remark that some people liked a good time but didn't know when to stop. Either way, life has been unkind to Lacey. I know how that weighed on Miss Margaret so.

The preacher began the service, said a few words about God and death, then Georgina stood up and spoke of her fond remembrances and love for her mother. Nothing out of the ordinary.

But I was caught off-guard by what happened next. One by one, people rose from their seats and regaled us with stories about Miss Margaret: how benevolent she was with her money, paying folks' grocery bills when they fell behind at the Piggly Wiggly; sending Christmas cards to complete strangers down on their luck with a little cash tucked inside; settling accounts at Worthy General Hospital for those less fortunate than her; to name a few.

The last lady to speak had the most surprising anecdote of all; a woman named Katherine. She told us of her daughter, Grace, who contracted leukemia at age seven. Much like those who spoke before her, Katherine said Miss Margaret covered Grace's medical expenses, even ensuring that a morphine pump be delivered to their home when Grace was near the end and insurance wouldn't cover the cost.

What was special about this tale was what Katherine described after. Katherine came to Miss Margaret with an idea following Grace's passing. Katherine noticed how many in Worthy needed a meal and a helping hand every now and then, and she wanted to create a space where folks could grow some of their own food and gather for dinner, no questions asked. Miss Margaret listened quietly, then fished her checkbook out of her purse and asked, "How much do you need?" Katherine said Miss Margaret's only request was that her donations remain anonymous.

And out of that meeting, Grace's Garden Kitchen was conceived. Wonders never cease.

As Miss Clementine and I walked to my car later, I tried to square in my mind the Miss Margaret I came to know at the Home and the one described by all those who benefited from her generosity.

"I never knew Miss Margaret was so charitable," I said.

"I'd heard rumors of her kindness over the years, but I had no idea how many lives she touched. You think you know somebody," Miss Clementine replied, as much to herself as to me.

"I must confess, Miss Clementine, I feel guilty six ways to Sunday with how Miss Margaret passed."

"Why is that?"

"If she hadn't been a part of my memory testing, maybe she wouldn't have suffered a stroke. Maybe she'd still be alive," I answered regretfully.

"Well, you can stop that foolish talk right now. Listen here: Miss Margaret knew exactly what she was doing. Remember all those photo albums she had? How me and Georgina begged her to relive a different part of her life? She could've picked a new memory whenever she wanted to. Nope," she shook her head, "something in her mind needed to be reconciled. You gave her a gift, Cleo. Can't nobody change my mind on that."

"You think?" I wondered doubtfully.

"I know," she said with a determined nod.

Miss Clementine grabbed hold of my elbow to steady herself as she plucked off her high heels. "Ah, that's better."

"Do you want me to fetch the car for you?" I asked.

"I don't believe that's necessary," she replied and weaved her arm through mine. "A stroll in the fresh air will do me good."

We continued in companionable silence, thinking about all that had occurred, and what Miss Margaret meant to us and to so many others.

Clementine

I t used to be, early on in our marriage, that I'd come home from Worthy General Hospital where I worked back then, and Percy would finish his route at the post office soon after. We'd cook together, taking turns chopping, slicing, stirring, and frying until our dinner was prepared. It seemed like we had much to talk about in those days, keeping each other abreast of all the little events that took place during our time apart: who we saw, what we did, with bits of gossip sprinkled in here and there to keep things lively.

As the years rolled by our routine changed. Not all at once, but subtly, gradually, until it shifted into something altogether different; almost unrecognizable to the younger Clementine and Percy if they had the means to look into the future and inspect it.

Our drifting began innocently enough. I'd take on an extra shift paying time and a half; Percy would stay after for poker night with the boys or meet them down at the bar for a drink. What started as an occasional evening hiccup became more frequent, and before long, the new normal.

Eventually, Percy and I didn't speak but a few sentences to one another over the course of an evening, instead eating the meals I prepared alone on trays in front of the TV. Percy would fall asleep in his recliner, and I would doze off on the couch until I stirred, threw a blanket over him, and shuffled off to bed.

Then Percy retired and things fluctuated again. He didn't know what to do with himself. He strayed, or thought long and hard about it at least, but decided he'd better not. And here we are today.

It wasn't anybody's fault, the staleness that developed between us. It's what happens over forty years with the same person, I guess. Your relationship grows old and dull right along with you.

We're awkward still, him and me. Percy remains in the guest room, but he lets me know at every opportunity how much he wishes we were man and wife again in every way imaginable.

His groveling *does* have its benefits. I return home to a warm dinner every night and spotless surroundings. I even get to watch whatever I want, up to and including *The Bachelor*, a show he couldn't stomach before, yet now he's so engrossed he'll discuss the merits of each potential couple with me. Percy's spending more time with Gabe, too, going out in the boat on nice days to fish, although with winter approaching, those days are dwindling. All this in an effort to win me back.

Percy is trying hard; I can see that. It's all very nice between us, very polite, but in the end, not very good. The problem is me. I don't know how to get back to the way we were before. That's what Percy wants. Maybe that's the problem; I don't want that. I need something different.

Take this morning, for instance. I woke up to the mouthwatering smells of coffee brewing and bacon frying. Two of the best aromas in the world, at least in my book. I went on out to the kitchen and there was Percy, wearing one of my aprons, dishing up two plates of food.

"Hey there, beautiful," he grinned.

On the table was a lovely bouquet of yellow and white daisies; my favorite.

"Where did these come from?" I remarked with delight.

"We needed more eggs, so I went down to Piggly Wiggly when they opened, saw those pretty things near the cash register, and thought of you," he answered and winked.

"Why thank you, Percy. That was very thoughtful of you," I replied and arranged the nosegay in a mason jar full of water.

"You said this afternoon was gonna be kind of rough at the Home, what with Miss Margaret's daughter coming to clear out her mother's things. Maybe if it gets tough to handle, you can think of those flowers and it'll brighten your day," he shrugged.

"Percy Blaine Babineaux, you actually paid attention to what I said? There's a first time for everything," I teased.

"Of course, I did. I always try to, Clem, even when I don't act like it," Percy replied earnestly, then cleared his throat. "Say, I forgot to mention, me and Gabe are going fishing on the lake later."

"Ain't it supposed to be awfully windy today?" I asked.

"That's the best time for catching bass. The breeze stirs up the water so they can't see your line too well," he said.

"You still got your life jacket, don't you?" I pressed.

"*Yes*, Clem, I have it," Percy said with a bite. "Let's not get off on that subject again."

"Okay," I raised my hands in surrender.

"It's nice to know you care." He strolled over to me and leaned in close. "How about a tiny bit of sugar? On the cheek, maybe?"

I turned my face toward him, and Percy left a quick peck. We exchanged small smiles, and then, emboldened, he went for my lips. I pulled my head away with a jerk.

"Too much?" he sighed.

"I'm still not there yet," I patted his chest. "I best be leaving. Got lots going on."

I scurried away as fast as my legs would carry me, the silence so uncomfortably thick you could cut it with a knife.

After the early morning tension with Percy, the hustle and bustle around the Home is a welcome diversion. I enter the break room and see that Mr. Isaac has left me lunch in the fridge, as has been his custom for weeks since my dustup with Percy.

I've told Mr. Isaac repeatedly he doesn't need to continue, that the turbulence at home has passed and I'm more than capable of preparing something myself. But he won't hear of it.

"It's part of my routine now, Mrs. Babineaux. I'm getting too old to change it again," he tells me with a grin.

Recently, too, Mr. Isaac's been bringing me peonies from his garden and placing them on my desk at the nurses' station. The unusual warm spell we've been having has stirred his plants to bloom once more, even though it's the middle of November. Mr. Isaac says it's a pity to allow the blossoms to wither on the stems, so like today, he creates a lovely posy for me to enjoy.

I lean in and inhale the flowers' glorious scent. Two floral arrangements in the span of twenty-four hours? It must be my lucky day.

As usual, time flies by, and during the late afternoon, Miss Georgina appears with boxes in tow, ready to clear out her mama's belongings. I offer to help, yet she politely refuses.

"No, no, Clementine. I can handle this. There's not much here, anyway," Miss Georgina says.

Looking around, I see that she's right. There's a small assortment of clothes, Miss Margaret's records and stereo, her photo albums, and a smattering of odds and ends. Not much in the way of worldly goods that would do justice to the whirling dervish that was Miss Margaret. I guess that's what memories are for.

"If you change your mind and want me to pitch in, Miss Georgina, just let me know," I reply and turn to go.

"Clementine, wait," she responds. "There's a question I wanted to ask you. Mother was searching for something near the end." Miss Georgina's eyes well with tears. "Do you...," she clears her throat, "do you think she found what she was looking for?"

I take Miss Georgina's hand in mine and meet her earnest gaze. "Yes, ma'am. I believe she did."

She lets out a gush of air, much like Miss Margaret did before she passed. I guess both mother and daughter were holding their breath, waiting for the right time to exhale.

A gust of wind rattles the window, shaking it forcefully.

"The weatherman said it would be breezy, but goodness, that was mighty fierce," I marvel.

"The winds of change?" Miss Georgina wonders.

"Maybe so," I respond hopefully. "You can't carry these boxes out by yourself while it's blowing like this. When you're ready, I'll help you take them to your car."

"Thank you, Clementine. For everything," she says.

Her shoulders slump, and Miss Georgina buries her face in her hands, deep sobs consuming her. I wrap her in my arms and hold her tight until she's done. Sometimes, a good cry makes everything a bit better.

An hour or so later, Miss Georgina emerges from her mama's room with a cart full of boxes. If anything, the wind has picked up, and the gales push against us as we make our way to her sedan. We unload quickly, exchange a swift hug, then I pull the cart back inside.

There in the lobby, Gabe is standing next to a police officer.

"Gabe? What are you doing here in my neck of the woods?"

Gabe's clothes are soaked, his expression grim.

"You were supposed to be on the lake with Percy," I continue.

Suddenly, it hits me like a two-by-four. He *was* with Percy.

Cleo

Mama hasn't been like this since Daddy died: nervous and agitated; calling and texting me at all hours of the day and night, making sure I'm alive and not roadkill on the side of the highway somewhere. It's understandable, of course, because our family hasn't lost anyone close to us *since* Daddy; not until Mr. Percy.

Thankfully, Mama was at the Home when Miss Clementine learned the news. She said the screams Miss Clementine let out made her heart skip a beat, the sheer sorrow and agony that punctuated each wail was unlike anything Mama had ever heard before.

Right away, Mama knew it was Miss Clementine—Mama'd recognize that voice anywhere—and ran out into the lobby in the direction of her cries. There was Miss Clementine, curled into a ball on the floor, her body trembling from the shock of it all.

Mama said Mr. Gabe was hunched down beside her, struggling to soothe Miss Clementine, but she shoved him away, like an animal who wanted to lick their wounds alone in a bit of peace. Mama pushed through the crowd and picked Miss Clementine off the ground, whisking her away to a private room so she could grieve without curious eyes watching.

Mr. Percy drowned. He and Mr. Gabe went out on the lake to fish, the wind a tad blustery, but nothing they couldn't handle, Mr. Gabe said. The bass were really biting, with Mr. Percy catching six in the span of an hour. It seemed like every time Mr. Percy cast his line, another fish was hooked on the other end, Mr. Gabe marveled. He'd never seen anything like it.

The breeze picked up. Mr. Gabe suggested they go back to shore, but Mr. Percy wanted to snag one more for dinner. All of a sudden, a gust so strong Mr. Gabe thought it was a waterspout toppled their little boat over. Mr. Gabe grabbed the side and held onto the boat for dear life, the current leading him back to the shoreline. He hollered and shouted for Mr. Percy, but Mr. Percy never answered.

Once Mr. Gabe reached the bank, he asked some folks to call the authorities, explaining that there was a man overboard and missing in the lake. By the time the police arrived some minutes later, Mr. Percy's body had already washed ashore, right alongside a life jacket.

Mama took Miss Clementine into our home, fixing up my old bedroom with some of Miss Clementine's things so she could be as comfortable as possible. Mama helped her with the burial arrangements and called people Mr. Percy knew so Miss Clementine would be spared reliving such a painful event. That's Mama for you; always a pillar of strength in times of crisis.

The funeral earlier this afternoon was a somber, yet beautiful affair. Mr. Percy was well-loved, as evidenced by all the folks who attended; standing-room-only at Worthy Covenant Church, where scores of men shared stories about their escapades with Mr. Percy that took well over an hour.

Throughout the liturgy, Miss Clementine kept peering into the aisle next to her, like she recognized someone, or was waiting for somebody to arrive, I'm not sure which. Maybe all of it was too much for her and she needed to daydream a bit to take her mind off things. Regardless, Miss Clementine was exhausted after, and asked Mama if we couldn't leave early and skip the reception; she didn't have it in her to chitchat with another person. Mama, usually a stickler for etiquette, didn't bat an eye, led Miss Clementine to the car, and away we went.

Mama's tucking Miss Clementine in for a nap, and I can hear Mama humming "To God Be the Glory" to soothe Miss Clementine's heart. They have such a beautiful friendship.

As for me, I've been checking my phone all day for the long-anticipated email from Meta containing my job offer. It was all I could do not to take a quick peek during the service, but I successfully fought the temptation. Sure enough, while I'm relaxing here on the couch, the missive arrives. Oh, my. Things just got real.

"All right, Cleo, what's the news?" Mama wonders, disrupting the imagined happy dance in my head.

"Why do you ask?" I reply, struggling to contain my excitement.

"Because you look like the cat who ate the canary. So, out with it."

"Meta offered me a job," I shout with delight.

"Shh now," Mama places her finger to her lips, "Clem's trying to sleep. What's a Meta?"

I wonder to myself whether Mama lives under a rock, but instead of asking, I do the mature thing and merely roll my eyes. "It's only the largest, most prolific virtual reality company on the planet. And they want yours truly to pioneer their memory research."

"Well, how about that? My girl is going to be the next big thing," Mama says proudly.

"The pay is great, and the benefits are fantastic, plus I get free breakfast, lunch, and dinner every day. There's just one thing, though...," I pause, "the job is located in Austin."

The grin that was affixed to Mama's mouth turns South in a hurry.

"I see," she replies quietly.

"This is huge, Mama. Opportunities like this don't come along very often. Besides, Austin is only three hours away," I reason.

"I understand," she nods slowly, letting the news sink in. "Does this have something to do with Brian's new job? Is that what this is about? Are you two planning on getting married?"

"It has nothing to do with Brian," I snap. "This is about me. I didn't go looking for Meta; Meta came looking for me." I huff and puff.

"Okay, don't get all worked up. Does Brian know, at least?"

"You're the first person I've told. Sorry for biting your head off," I mumble, my words tinged with guilt.

"I guess you'll have some decisions to make soon. Would you like to talk them through? I've always been a good listener," she replies mildly.

"No thanks," I answer a bit too dismissively.

"You know, Cleo, it's times like these when I sure do miss your father. Gus always knew the right thing to say; at just the right moment. Sometimes, I wish we could see him again, if only for a little while."

Mrs. Hadley

It occurred to me not long ago that the human spirit is more malleable than we give it credit for. As we age, folks will sometimes say, "I'm too old for that," or "I'm set in my ways," and let their lives stagnate and wither. By then, their routines are hard-wired, making change a scary, nerve-wracking prospect, and trying something new easy to resist.

I'll admit I'm guilty of this. James and I were together for so long, we often finished each other's sentences and rarely ventured from the little cocoon we built for ourselves. After James passed, the loneliness hit me like an anvil, heavy and thick, and I thought, well, this is how my life is going to be until the end.

Then Cleo came along and corrected all that foolish thinking of mine. For once, I took a chance, putting myself out there with Jane, at the risk of being let down. It didn't work out like I wanted, but I hold out hope that one day she'll forgive me. That's what's different now: I have hope.

As such, I've spread my wings here at the Home and strived to become part of the community. The old Irene would've hung her head in despair for the rest of her days. The new and improved Irene has put in the effort and made some friends in the past few weeks; I've even started a book club with a few of the women I've met. And since Thanksgiving is only a week away, I've already fixed on what time to meet my new companions for supper that afternoon. These folks help to fill the void in my heart left there by James and Jane. We all need that from time to time: the human touch.

Now that I'm ambulatory, albeit with a cane, I take walks around the grounds, sometimes with others, but mostly alone, to listen to my thoughts.

I like to sit outside in the sun, too, although there's been a chill in the air lately, signaling the changing seasons.

I still speak to James. During a stroll, he'll pop in for a chat every once in a while, to reminisce about funny moments from our past, quarrel over current events shaping the world, or think back on the love we shared. They're not sad or dreary, my visits from James. They're memories of what was, the depths of our feelings brought to the forefront to inspect, and I treasure each of them dearly.

It's about four o'clock. I can tell from the angle of the sun hanging low in the west, caressing my cheeks, warming my skin. I'd best be going in to wash up for dinner, but I decide to linger outside for a few minutes more. The Vitamin D will do me good.

Just as I feel myself drifting off for a catnap, the sound of metal tapping the sidewalk, click-click, click-click, followed by the thud of heavy shoes, jars me from my slumber. I shield my eyes from the sunlight to catch a glimpse of what's making all that racket.

I recognize the silhouette, the shape of their face, even in all the glare.

It's Jane.

I pull myself up with my cane and walk toward her as fast as these eighty-one-year-old legs will carry me. Jane stops abruptly and waits. Unsure of our next move, I do the same. We're separated by only a few feet.

"Jane, you're walking," I marvel.

"I'm walking," she nods and glances down at her prosthetic lower limbs and forearm crutches. "It took me months of practice, but I'm standing on my own two feet now. And it feels glorious."

"It's a miracle," I say in amazement. "How did you know where to find me? I never gave you my address."

"Cleo. I asked her not to mention it. I didn't want to make you nervous or let your mind wander. I thought it best to come see you in person unannounced, so I can say all the things I need to say, face-to-face," she remarks solemnly.

"Okay," I reply anxiously, bracing myself. "What would you like to say?"

She sighs deeply as she leans on her crutches. "I had a whole plane ride to figure out the right words. They never came to me. Except that, you being my mother was the furthest thing from my mind when we first met. I felt a connection to you, sure, an inkling there was something deeper, but I brushed it off as a silly notion. I've been wrestling with your revelation for weeks, struggling to understand why you and my father made the choices you did. You told me you had your reasons. I'd sure like to hear them."

"It would be easy for me to scream at you; to empty all my anger until I see fit you've had enough," Jane shakes her head. "All this time, though, the one thing that kept circling around in my head was something you said right before I left you that evening."

"What was that, Jane?"

"We're kin, you and me. We're all we've got left. And you wondered if that wasn't a foundation to build on. I've given it a lot of thought, Ree. I believe it is. I think it's a place to start. I've got two weeks' vacation and a room booked at the Holiday Inn down the road. I'd like to get to know you better; to find out everything there is about you and my father. What do you say, Ree? Would that be all right with you?"

"Oh, Jane," I reply through happy tears, "I can't think of anything I would love more."

Clementine

It used to be that time was a commodity I could rely on. I had this internal clock where I sensed what hour it was from a feeling in my gut, nothing more. It was a gift, helpful in all kinds of ways, and kept me from having to check my watch as often during my shifts.

All that changed, though, on November tenth, at five thirty-seven in the evening, when Percy left this earth.

Time, once as dependable as the beating of my heart, passes now in a blur, so much so that I have to consult my calendar to remind myself what day of the week it is. I go through the motions, rising in the morning, caring for my residents at the Home, then after, returning to Ruth's place, all the while not remembering a single thing I did, as if I'm in a never-ending daydream that I can't shake.

The fact is, I don't know what to do with myself now that Percy's gone. Forty-two years of marriage felt like a lifetime. It was, I guess, when you think about it, since most of it was spent with the same person. Being Percy's wife was the longest habit I've ever had, and I'm at a loss as to how I'm ever going to break it.

Thank the sweet Lord Jesus for Ruth. She's been my rock through all of this, taking me into her home, making funeral arrangements, insisting that I eat at least a little something to keep my strength up and not taking no for an answer. Above all, she offers me her shoulder to cry on when grief washes over, when I can't hold it in another minute—which it does on the regular. Good old Mama Pearl, her strength is priceless.

When it comes to thinking on Percy, all the things he meant to me—the good and the bad—the mistakes we made, the regrets I have, well, I ain't got the strength to examine all that quite yet. My mind's still too crowded with sorrow to do it proper. One of these days, I hope the noise will die down enough for me to roll my thoughts around and give Percy his due. Until then, I pray he can find it in his heart to forgive me for this weakness.

As I said, I don't remember much of what occurs at the Home, except for this one thing: the exchange I had with Mr. Isaac yesterday afternoon. I suppose it's easier to call it to mind than other, more mundane events since our encounter still sticks in my craw, twenty-four hours later.

I was returning a VR headset to the nurses' station, when I happened upon Mr. Isaac in the hallway, with a big old grin plastered across his face.

"It's wonderful to see you escaping into the virtual world again, Mrs. Babineaux. What with all that's taken place lately, it must feel good for you to get away for a bit," he said good-naturedly.

I don't know what it was exactly, but that assumption he made rubbed me the wrong way.

"Well, Mr. Isaac, for your information, I've not *been* in the metaverse, and I don't *plan* to be ever again," I replied tartly.

"I apologize, Mrs. Babineaux. I just assumed...," he remarked, a tad flustered by my reaction.

"You know the old saying about assuming, don't you?" I interjected.

It seemed Mr. Isaac didn't get the hint, or he thought I was joking, because the next sentence that came out of his mouth chapped my behind like nobody's business.

"I was thinking Mrs. Babineaux, that maybe you'd like to go out for a cup of coffee with me sometime. I've found a little companionship does me a lot of good. Perhaps it could do the same for you."

That did it. My top done blew off and I let that man have an earful.

"Shame on you, Mr. Isaac. My Percy ain't been in the ground long enough for him to get cold and you're asking me out on a date?" I scolded.

"No ma'am. That wasn't what...," he stammered.

"You listen here, Mr. Isaac. I don't plan on being with nobody else for the rest of my days, do you understand? My Percy was *it* for me. So, you can put any notions you got about courting me right out of your head. While you're at it, you can pass that message along to Gregory, too."

"Who?" Mr. Isaac asked.

"Gregory," I snapped, "your metaverse alter ego. You give him the 411 that Rebecca won't be coming around no more. You got that?"

Mr. Isaac nodded slowly, his jaw hitting the floor.

I turned on my heel, then pivoted back for one more swing. "And another thing. From now on, you and I will be strictly professional. No more lunches. No more flowers. We will speak on an as-needed basis. We clear?"

He cleared his throat. "Yes, ma'am," he replied weakly.

"Good," I said, then trotted off to the nurses' station, feeling high and mighty for putting Mr. Isaac in his place.

The nerve of that man.

Cleo

Mama planted the seed in my head. I don't know why it didn't occur to me sooner. After Mr. Percy's funeral, Mama mentioned how she wished we could see Daddy again, if only for a bit. The thing is, we can, at least in the virtual world. It just hadn't dawned on me until now.

So much has happened since Daddy passed, and so much change is waiting in the wings. The curve balls he warned me to watch out for, benders as he liked to call them, are coming at me; there's no stopping them. Decisions need to be made, but, as usual, I've been postponing the inevitable. I've always held the view that it's a good deal easier to put off until tomorrow what could be accomplished today. I'm a procrastinator through and through, although Mama prefers the term "lollygagger." To each their own. We are divided by a common language, I suppose. But I digress.

One item *is* settled: my future career plans. Once Jonathan and I received the formal offer from Meta, we accepted immediately. Neither of us had to think twice. Our new jobs don't begin until after the first of the year, so we put our heads together to decide when it would be best to give notice to Ingram and Next Well. Since we're a team, we thought it was important to present a united front. We fixed on early December, a mere week away.

It's been hard for me to contain my excitement and not tell Ingram to go suck an egg. So, Jonathan's been watching me like a hawk to make sure I don't pop off before it's time. He's even taken over most of our work assignments because I can't seem to force myself to get anything done. We're short-timers here, after all. To compensate, I've brought him two of Auntie Ella's vanilla bean cheesecakes covered in chocolate ganache, and a whole slab of ribs Mama grilled just for him. Jonathan seems to think this was a fair trade. I do, too; it gives me a chance to catch up on my napping.

Oh, and about our cubicle situation: Jonathan and I decided not to make good on our bet and force Quinn to vacate his office to us after he and his crew lost the metaverse basketball game to Mrs. Hadley's team. We figured the humiliation of losing to a bunch of women old enough to be his mother was embarrassing enough. I *have* enjoyed rubbing his face in it, though. Quinn's perpetual smirk has all but disappeared and he now avoids me in the hallways, turning on his heel whenever he sees me coming. I sure hope Quinn likes his humble pie. I find it delicious.

The other detail that needs ironing out has to do with Brian. I haven't told him yet that I accepted the position with Meta. Whenever he asks, I tell him I'm still waiting on the particulars, or some such nonsense, with my fingers crossed of course, so God will know it's a little white lie. According to Mama, they don't hurt anybody.

I don't know what to do when it comes to Brian. My love for him is thick, and he'll have a hold over me until the day I leave this mortal plane. I believe that to my core. But is that enough? There's an uneasiness that hits me when I think about Brian and forever; a voice that screams "independence."

I need to mull this over with a proper sounding board, someone who knows me like the back of their hand. And there's no doubt in my mind, that person is Daddy.

Emboldened, I sneak into the storage room at work and snag a VR headset. I turn off the video feed so our encounter can't be watched live or recorded for prying eyes to view later. I fish out a picture of Daddy, one where he's repairing a car in our garage, and I scan it in. I snap on my goggles, and with a deep breath, I jump right in.

Everything is the same: the tools hanging above Daddy's workbench; the creeper he uses to roll underneath a vehicle; various shop towels draped over hooks on the wall; the smell of grease and sweat and Old Spice blended into a unique fragrance all his own.

Our old Ford truck sits in the bay, candy cane red and in mint condition. Daddy named it Gertrude after an auntie who wore the same-colored lipstick to church on Sundays. If we couldn't find Daddy in the house, we knew to look for him out here, working on his beloved pickup.

The Ford's hood is open, and the clank of a socket wrench fills the air.

"Daddy?" I ask tentatively.

His head pops up over the hood ornament. "Who's that?" He squints, then recognizes me, a wide smile crossing his lips. "Cleovantra? Well, I'll be. Come closer so I can get a good look at you."

Daddy meets me halfway, wiping his hands with a rag, gazing at me for a long minute, taking me in.

"Ain't you a sight for sore eyes. All grown up I see, and as beautiful as ever. Your hair's different," he observes.

"Do you like it?" I wonder as I rub a few strands idly between my fingertips.

"It suits you," he replies.

"I wanted to look older, for folks to take me seriously at work."

"It does the trick," Daddy remarks. "Well now, sweet girl, what did you want to talk to me about?"

"Why do you ask?" I frown.

"Because you wouldn't have conjured me out of thin air if you didn't have something to say," he answers, tossing the grease-soaked rag aside.

"Well Daddy, you're right." I bite my lip, stalling for time. "There is something; something to do with Brian. You see, Daddy, lots is going on in my life at the moment. I got a new job, in Austin, for really good money. Brian's got a new gig down there, too. He wants to get serious; move in together, get married—the whole nine yards. Our relationship is coming to a head, and I'm not sure what to do. I need your help."

"No, you don't baby," he shakes his head.

"What? Yes, I do," I counter.

"You don't, Cleo. You know what you want. The problem is, you've always used this," Daddy taps my forehead, "when you should be using this," he points to my chest.

"It's so difficult, Daddy. Can't you decide for me?" I beg.

"I've told you, Cleo. You don't need me to. Take a hold of that heart of yours and listen to it. It'll set you straight," he reasons.

"You think?" I ask, searching his face.

"I know," Daddy nods decisively, then sighs. "You best be going now."

"I'm not ready to leave just yet," I wrap my arms around his waist and snuggle in close. "I'm scared, Daddy. Change is hard," I whisper.

"One thing you need to learn, my headstrong girl, is that change don't ever stop. The sooner you accept that fact, the easier it'll be to take life as it comes. Because we ain't got much of a choice," he replies. "Do you remember who said that to you?"

"You, Daddy?" I ask meekly.

"Your mama. She's got a whole lot of wisdom to share, and she's always right; I can't recall a time when she wasn't." Daddy steps out of our embrace and takes my hands in his. "Your mama is also a part of the living. I'm not."

"But I miss you, Daddy."

"I know you do. I'm a figment of your imagination, though. No matter what kind of contraption you create, I'm still just a memory. That's all I'm ever going to be from here on out." He kisses my forehead, "It's time for you to go, Cleo."

"This is goodbye, then," I mutter as sobs come over me.

"I prefer 'So long,' myself."

"Can I see you again?"

"Someday. Only not like this. Watch out for those benders now. And swing for the fences every chance you get," he says with a wink.

"One more hug for the road?" I ask.

Daddy draws me in, and I linger a moment more, memorizing the feel of his stubble, the warmth of his breath, the beating of his heart.

"I love you, Daddy."

"I love you, too. Go on now. Git," he says.

I remove my headset then, brush away my tears, and return to the land of the living.

Mrs. Hadley

All my life I've been terrible at goodbyes. The trouble began way back when, I must've been three or four I think, when my cousins, Jeffrey and Jocelyn, would come over for a visit every Sunday after church. My how we loved playing together—hopscotch, tag, hide-and-seek—you name it. Since I was an only child, they were like a brother and sister to me.

As the sun fell and evening gave way to darkness, my auntie would call from the back porch, "Jeffrey, Jocelyn, come on in and say goodbye to Auntie Louise and Uncle John, please."

That's when my waterworks would begin. I'd wail and sob, begging my auntie to take me home with them so us cousins could continue our socializing. This always rubbed my mama the wrong way.

At first, Mama would attempt to soothe me. "There, there, Irene. Don't you cry. Jeffrey and Jocelyn will be back next week." Try as she might, her overtures never worked on me, my howls so strong they dissolved into hiccups, deep and throaty, where it was all I could do not to gag.

My antics forced Mama's hand, literally and figuratively, and she'd pop my behind with a firm tap, then give me a stern talking-to. "That's quite enough, Irene. You stop this foolishness right now, you hear?"

In my teenage years, my goodbyes were just as precarious, but more internalized, so I wouldn't embarrass myself like when I was a child. I'd hug a friend a tick longer, or hold onto a beau's hand a smidgen more, my heart performing backflips at the prospect of leaving them.

When my mama and daddy passed, it was a slow, difficult crawl. I nursed both of them, which gave us plenty of time for farewells; too much time, in fact, that made it all the more agonizing when they did finally go.

Thank God for James. He died in his sleep with no warning. That was a blessing for each of us: he didn't linger, and I was spared another prolonged departure by someone I loved.

You can imagine, then, how difficult it was for me when Jane's visit came to an end. The fifteen days we spent together were some of the best of my life. We talked, we laughed, we cried. I told Jane about her father and the little quirks that made James so special to me: his kindness, his humor, all the things that made him my truest love.

Clementine dug around the Home's storage rooms and found more photos of mine that were mistakenly stowed away somewhere. Jane got to see what her daddy looked like in all the glory of his youth, and how he aged into a fine, handsome gentleman. There were pictures of me, too, even one of me shooting a basketball in high school. Jane got a kick out of that. I filled her in on her family tree: where our people came from, who we were, and what we meant to each other.

Lots of tears were shed as well. Jane asked me the painful questions that filled her mind: How could her father and I have left her in Ohio; Was she ever discussed between us after; Did we regret what we did? Jane grilled me repeatedly on the details, and I answered each query, each accusation, with honesty and humility. Jane deserved the whole unvarnished truth, and that's what I gave her.

For a while, I wasn't sure if there was anything I could say to ease her pain away. But after one particularly difficult, intense exchange, something beautiful occurred. Jane wiped her eyes, took my hand, and said, "I think I finally understand now, Ree. You did the best you could. That's all any of us can do. And I forgive you." I used to think "I love you" were the sweetest words ever spoken. Not any longer. "I forgive you" are equally as sweet.

Just as Jane and I had made amends, it was time for her to return home. On our last evening together, we were sitting outside as the sun was setting, bundled up in the crisp fall air. Jane turned to me and said, "You know, Ree,

I've been thinking. I own a one-story duplex in Cleveland and my tenant is leaving next month. How would you like to move to Ohio?"

"You mean live next door to you?" I asked, my eyes wide with wonder.

"Fifteen days isn't nearly long enough to get to know someone. What do you say, Ree? Do you want to be my neighbor?"

I can't think of anything I'd like more," I replied.

For the first time in our lives, we held each other in a long embrace. And it was the most magical feeling ever.

Now, it's time for another goodbye. Clementine has been so kind over the past couple of weeks, helping me pack what little I own and shipping it to Cleveland for me. She even printed off my plane ticket and arranged a car service to take me to the airport in Dallas this afternoon.

"You got everything, Mrs. Hadley? Boarding pass? Your medications?" Clementine asks.

"Yes ma'am," I pat my handbag, "it's all right here."

"Remember now, no matter what they tell you at security, you don't have to take your shoes off on account of your age, so don't you even try. I don't want you bending over and straining your back," she advises.

"Got it," I answer with a nod.

"Well, your ride should be here any minute, so you'd best be getting down to the lobby. Do you want me to wait with you?" she wonders.

"That won't be necessary," I say, shaking my head. "Thank you, Clementine. You've been a blessing to me."

I wrap my arms around her, and we hug warmly.

"I hate goodbyes," she admits.

"I do, too."

"Then why don't we say, 'See you later,' instead?" she suggests.

I grasp her hands as a smile crosses my lips. "See you later, Clementine."

Clementine

My backbone has finally come out of hiding. After weeks of shedding what seemed like a river of tears over Percy, I eventually wiped my eyes, blew my nose, and said adios to my non-stop pity party. I had every right to mourn, I realize, what with Percy's sudden passing and all, but it's not in my character to feel sorry for myself for so long.

That's not to say I'm completely back to normal. My eyes still well up on occasion without warning, and I'm sure there will be plenty of heartache for months if not years to come. Nonetheless, it's high time I picked myself up, dusted myself off, and dipped my toe into living life again.

My first task is to return to the house Percy and I called home for thirty-eight years. I ain't stepped across its threshold since that fateful evening when my husband washed up on Lake Worthy's shores. It was all I could do those first days after to keep from going under from sorrow; I wasn't good for anything, except breathing, I guess.

Ruth, bless her heart, made the initial pilgrimage to my homestead during this period, gathering clothes, toiletries, my Bible, things I would need to tide me over at her place for a while. As time passed, though, and my resolve was still shaky and frail, Ruth would stop by to collect my mail so I could at least pay my bills on time. That's the way it's been. Until now.

Cleo asked me yesterday if I could return Percy's VR headset to her, saying something about inventory levels and accounting she needed to do. I've got no use for it, so I figured this was as good an excuse as any to visit the house. Besides, Ruth said she'd meet me here shortly for moral support.

Yet as I stand on the stoop, staring at my blue front door, I'm overcome with jitters. I don't know what I expect to find in there, but I'm nervous all the same, my hands trembling so badly I can't fit the key into the lock. Maybe I should wait for Ruth.

"You're being downright silly, Clementine," I say to myself. "It's just a building with four walls. Grow a spine and get in there."

I take some deep breaths, in and out, in and out, till I'm calm enough to unlatch the door. It creaks a bit as it opens, adding to the anxiety that already eats at me. Tentatively, I take a step, and another step, then I'm inside.

I flip on a switch and the foyer brightens up. I peek around the corner into the den. No boogeyman appears, no ghosts come after me, nothing out of the ordinary happens. It's the same as it ever was.

My shoulders relax and I drop my handbag on the couch, then make my way to Percy's study. Knowing him, he stuffed the VR goggles into his closet somewhere among all the other junk he stowed there for decades. It'll probably take me hours to find it.

As I enter his study, the faint aroma of Percy's aftershave mixed with his own, unique scent hits me like a hammer, making my knees buckle. I grab hold of his desk to steady myself, waiting for the wave of grief to ease. Eventually, it does, thank Jesus, and gingerly, I open the closet door, bracing for an avalanche of clutter to come pouring out.

But it doesn't. Much to my shock and awe, all the bric-a-brac he hoarded over the years is gone. The shelves are organized, and in the front, clear as day, is Percy's VR headset. At some point, Percy must've taken it upon himself to sort this out and he didn't even tell me. What I thought would be an overwhelming chore turned out to be pretty simple. What do you know? Here he is, six feet under, and Percy's still surprising me.

I shut the closet door and pivot to leave, yet something stops me. I flip over the goggles and notice the Record button is on, making it possible for me to review what Percy did in the metaverse. I think on it a bit, mulling over whether I should leave Percy's secrets alone and let them die with him, or if I should satisfy my nosy nature. It don't take me long to decide.

I clip on the headset, hit Rewind, and away I go.

While I scan through his early experiences, each of them involves fishing: in lakes, in the ocean, in mountain streams, and jungle rivers. Good Lord, who knew you could catch a fish in so many places? Percy sure seemed to enjoy himself, because I can hear him whooping and hollering with delight at every turn.

Abruptly, his adventures change from trawling every type of water imaginable to the quaint outdoor space Cleo created for our residents at the Home. At first, Percy wanders about, taking in the pond and lush greenery that fills the area. Then, what I see next lays me to waste.

Percy meets Rebecca. Me—my Rebecca. There I am, in the pond, my shoes stuck in the muck, and here comes Percy to pull me out of the water. But he introduces himself as Gregory.

Percy was Gregory.

I rip off the goggles, crumple to the floor, and let out a moan, loud and deep, at the revelation.

"Clementine?" Ruth calls from the foyer.

In a matter of seconds, she's by my side. "What is it, Clem? What's wrong?"

I point to the headset on the ground. "I looked in there and watched Percy's experiences in the metaverse. Percy was Gregory. He was Gregory the whole time," I cry, choking out the words.

"He was? Oh, my Lord. You didn't have any idea?" Ruth asks.

"I thought Mr. Isaac was Gregory," I respond, shaking my head.

"Mr. Isaac?" she wonders, confused.

"I accused Mr. Isaac of it the other day. How could I have been so wrong?"

"Well now, Mr. Isaac must've done something to raise your suspicions, so don't beat yourself up about it. People can behave strangely in all sorts of ways, depending on the situation," Ruth soothes.

"Here I was, acting high and mighty when it came to Percy and another woman, kicking him out of our home and making him miserable, when it turns out the other woman was me."

I bury my face in my hands while Ruth comforts me through my tears; our newfound custom since Percy left this earth.

Cleo

During my time here on this mortal plane, I've had the privilege of being surrounded by folks who are wiser than their years, and who impart their insights to me on a regular basis. One such notable person is my dear Auntie Ella. In addition to her exceptional baking skills, Auntie Ella is also a very astute woman, especially when it comes to hair. She owns three beauty salons after all—The Weave Queen, Weave Queen North, and Weave Queen West—and has been a cosmetologist for twenty-five years.

As such, Auntie Ella has collected a good bit of wisdom in that time regarding the importance women place on their coiffures. Some of her most notable sayings are: "Invest in your hair. It's the only crown you never take off,"; "Life is more beautiful when you meet the right hairdresser,"; and my personal favorite, "No day is a bad day when your hair is looking fly."

Now, Auntie swears up and down that she created each of those maxims, although she does have a propensity to stretch the truth on occasion. Whether Auntie is their originator or not, she repeats them often enough they might as well be hers. Possession *is* nine-tenths of the law, so they say. But I digress.

I've brought up Auntie Ella to set the stage for the events that occurred this past week. And the foremost thing I did to prepare was to stop by The Weave Queen last Saturday to give myself a new look.

The Hen Brigade was already in session, with Auntie Ella trimming Miss Ida Mae's bob while Mama and Miss Clementine were doing their usual thing, sitting in styling chairs, thumbing through magazines, and sipping on Diet Dr. Peppers.

"Well Ruth, look what the wind blew in," Auntie Ella quipped as I breezed in the door.

"Hi there, honey," Mama said.

"Hey Mama," I pecked her cheek and dropped my handbag beside her.

Auntie Ella engulfed Miss Ida Mae in a cloud of hairspray, stepped back and admired her work, then nodded her head. "You're as beautiful as ever, Ida Mae. My work here is done," she pronounced.

"Are you here for a new weave?" Mama asked me.

"No, I think I'm going back to basics," I replied.

Auntie Ella whipped her head around, astonished by my announcement. "Does that mean what I think it means?"

A smile crossed my lips. "Yes ma'am. It's time for my Afro to make its triumphant return."

"Thank the sweet Lord," Auntie Ella exclaimed. "You look so much more attractive with your natural hair. Step right up and take a seat."

Auntie Ella wiped the chair down and I settled in.

"All right, Auntie. Do your thing."

Emboldened by my new hairdo, I needed all the confidence I could muster for my next big endeavor: having a heart-to-heart with Brian about us and our future together. I invited him over that evening for dinner—baked pork chops Mama cooked and sent with me after my hair appointment—and I paced the floor of my apartment until he knocked on my door.

"Hey Cleo," Brian said, squeezed my arm, and walked straight past me.

"Hey yourself," I replied warily. No kiss. No "Hey baby." Brian only refers to me as Cleo when something is amiss.

Brian planted himself squarely on my sofa, without removing his jacket. "We need to talk," he said quietly.

"Yes, we do," I agreed and sat beside him.

"I ran into Jonathan this afternoon coming out of Next Well. He was carrying some boxes to his car and asked me when you would do the same," Brian said evenly. "When were you going to tell me you got the Meta job?"

"Now," I answered meekly.

"I have to say, Cleo, hearing that from Jonathan threw me for a loop. I was so mad at you I couldn't see straight. Everything that I thought was true about you—about us— wasn't the case. Then it finally hit me: You've been telling me all along you're not ready for the next step—for marriage—and I wouldn't listen."

"But I am now," Brian continued. "I dug down deep, too, looking around at what I really wanted, and I realized that committing to you was just another item to tick off my checklist. It was something I thought I needed to accomplish. I was thinking with my head, instead of listening to my heart. When I looked at my feelings up close, I understood I've got more living to do, like you."

He took my hands in his. "This isn't a breakup, Cleo. I love you. But I know that things are going to be different between us. A new city. New jobs. We'll have to see how this all plays out. Okay?"

"I couldn't have said it better myself, Bri. I *did* have this whole speech rehearsed that I can't use now," I teased. "I imagined I'd be breaking your heart, but then you come in here talking sense. Ain't that something?"

"Ain't? I thought you gave up that expression?" Brian asked.

"Not anymore. It's a perfectly good word."

Monday morning, I strolled into Next Well right on time, rocking my Afro, ginormous hoop earrings, leather pencil skirt, and a tailored silk blouse. Dang, I looked good. The only thing that messed up my aura was the box I was carrying. Nothing's ever perfect, I guess.

To my surprise, Ingram was in our cubicle speaking with Jonathan. He must've gotten lost and asked for directions or something because Ingram rarely stops by to chat.

"There she is. Just the girl I wanted to see," Ingram said enthusiastically.

I glanced over my shoulder to make sure he wasn't talking to somebody else since Ingram's never been *that* happy to see me.

"To what do I owe the pleasure, Ingram?" I asked sardonically.

"I was filling Jonathan in on the exciting news," Ingram answered.

"What news?"

"Upper management had a change of heart. They want to go full speed ahead with your memory research. It seems there's a market for that, after all. I'm moving Quinn out of his office so you and Jonathan can have your own space," Ingram responded.

I looked at Jonathan. "You haven't told him?"

"I was waiting for you," Jonathan replied.

I turned my attention back to Ingram. "That won't be necessary."

"Why not? If you want a different office, I'm sure that can be arranged. Oh, and your budget will increase substantially, and there are some nice bonuses in the offing if you hit certain metrics. Won't that be nice?" Ingram offered.

Without answering, I set my box down next to the desk, swung my hand, and swatted my stuff into it. Well, I attempted to; most of it scattered across my desktop.

"It looks easier in the movies," I deadpanned.

"What the hell was that?" Ingram snapped.

"Cleo, let me show you how it's done," Jonathan said, and with one swipe, all his belongings scattered onto the floor. Granted, he only had a pencil holder and a day calendar on there, but it showed solidarity, nonetheless.

"Have you both gone nuts?" Ingram yipped.

"I'm going to make this simple for you, Ingram, so even you can un-derstand. Jonathan and I quit. As of this moment, we don't work for you anymore," I informed him, grinning ear-to-ear.

"Our letters of resignation should be in your inbox by now," Jonathan said to Ingram, then glanced at me. "Shall we go?"

"Let's," I replied with a nod.

Arm in arm, Jonathan and I strolled out of Next Well, and we never ever looked back.

Just like that, I'm unemployed, if only for a few weeks until my job at Meta begins. I'll have plenty to keep me busy, though, from finding a new apartment in Austin to packing my things and moving, and spending the holidays with family.

Much like Dallas, Austin is expensive. Thank the Lord for Meta's hefty signing bonus so I can afford the deposits I'll have to put down and the Christmas gifts I'll be buying since I left Next Well under less-than-stellar circumstances. Mama's always advised me to save for a rainy day. I'm glad I've got a little put away because it's about to come down in bucketfuls.

Brian has chosen to live in north Austin, but I'm thinking that an apartment closer to downtown and work is what I'm after. Regardless, it'll be nice to know a friendly face to help tide us over until we meet new people. Whether Brian and I stay together or drift apart, I will always love that man; he'll have a piece of my heart forevermore.

I'm excited about this new chapter in my life, and a bit nervous, too. When it comes to memory and virtual reality, the possibilities are endless. At times I wasn't sure if inserting people into the metaverse was a good idea, but I now believe it can do a world of good. Just look at Mrs. Hadley, reunited with her daughter after these many years, and Miss Margaret, who found peace and forgiveness in her own way. Then there's me, blessed with one last sojourn with my daddy to get my head on straight, and the chance to say goodbye. All due to virtual reality. It seems each of us is searching for something, whether we're aware of it or not. Maybe I can help folks find what they're looking for.

Clementine

Six months later

Of all of my shortcomings, and believe you me there are plenty, admitting when I'm wrong is at the top of the list. My headstrong nature makes it hard for me to look at myself with clear lenses. Instead, my pride fogs them up, obscuring who I really am. To put it mildly, "sorry" is a neglected word in my vocabulary.

But as I've thought about my life over the past months, the scales have gradually fallen from my eyes, leaving everything I've done out in the open and plain to see. In that time, I've realized I have many confessions to make and much forgiveness to seek.

Beginning with Percy.

What I did to that man near the end of his life is the biggest regret I'll ever know. We were together over forty years—a lifetime—and I let resentment get the best of me, allowing it to fester and rear its head in so many ways. I was jealous of Percy's free time in retirement, secretly wishing I could quit as well but was too cheap to let go of my paycheck. I envied Percy's hobbies that didn't include me—mainly because I never tried to like them—which left me bitter. And the thing that hurt the most: Percy's interest in somebody new because I failed to be who he needed me to be. All of this, combined with the mile-wide ravine already wedged between us from years of neglect, made for a stale, lonesome marriage.

And much of it was my fault. I should've loosened the purse strings and lived a little, creating memories I could look back on and enjoy. As Percy said, you can't take it with you. I should've adopted some children like Percy wanted to fill out our family. I should've fought for our marriage and not let it wither. I should've behaved like the person he needed me to be rather than wasting my time as Rebecca playing make-believe in 3D. I should've been kinder and gentler, not as sharp and critical. Yes, we had happy times, but there should've been, could've been, would've been more if I had tried a little harder. Shoulda, Coulda, Woulda: the mantra of regret.

It's too late now to beg his forgiveness. So instead, I get down on my knees each night, and ask the good Lord to send my Percy this humble message:

Percy baby, I know there were occasions when I did you rotten. I made so many mistakes that I lost count of them long ago. For that, I'm truly sorry and I humbly repent. I hope you can forgive me. If you believed anything I ever said to you, please believe this: You were my Alpha and Omega, my sunrise and sunset, and I loved you with my whole heart. Peace be with you, my one true love.

Apologies were meant not just for Percy. My dear friend Ruth is another who deserves one, plus my gratitude. I'm sure that poor woman had no idea what she'd gotten into while my grief poured out of me and wouldn't stop. I know I made Ruth's life a living hell for a while, with no complaints from her. She's been my rock through all this. I wouldn't have come out the other side in one piece without her.

And Ruth's support continued on. She helped me clean out my home and put it on the market with a real estate friend she knows. It sold quickly and at a fair price. It was a somber day when I handed over the keys, but when the sun rose the next morning, my chest wasn't as tight, and my breathing was a little easier like a burden had been lifted. Since then, my step has been lighter and my nature more carefree; I'm becoming Clementine again.

Ruth insisted that I move in with her. She wouldn't hear of anything else. Before I agreed, though, I drew up an arrangement between us that stipulated I would pay half the utility bills and all the property taxes and insurance for her home. Ruth balked at first, but I put up enough of a fuss, she finally put pen to paper and signed it.

Even though it's too late for Percy and me, I've decided it's high time to go on a few trips. This October, Ruth and I are taking a cruise up the east coast into Canada to see the fall leaves turn color. I ain't never been on a boat, or an airplane for that matter, so it'll be an adventure of sorts. There's a first time for everything I suppose.

One thing's for sure, I won't ever step foot into the metaverse again. I learned my lesson the hard way. Fantasy should stay within the confines of TV, the written word, and the corners of your mind. Venturing out into the virtual world is a poor replacement for real, human interaction, no matter how much we wish it could be. For me, it's best to leave it alone. Consequently, I have the other nurses shepherd the residents in and out of the metaverse so I'm not tempted, and I've returned my focus to romance novels once again.

Mr. Jeffrey, Miss Jillian's younger brother who took over as director when she got promoted to the board, is of a similar mind. He limits metaverse visits to an hour a day, plus he's created more activities for the memory care residents to enjoy rather than allow them to sit idly in their rooms. Mr. Jeffrey hasn't been at the Home long, but I think I'm going to like him. He's much easier to get along with than his uptight sister, that's for sure. My fingers are crossed it works out.

Which leads me to Mr. Isaac. After the dressing-down I gave him months ago, I rarely see him in the halls. If I happen to come across him, he turns tail and goes in the opposite direction. When we do interact, his gaze never meets my eyes, like a naughty puppy who's wary of its owner, afraid of what might be coming next.

I've felt guilty six ways to Sunday ever since that reprimand I gave him, but my pride has kept me from doing the right thing. Until now.

Last night, after I cooked up some smothered pork chops, cheesy grits, and ambrosia salad for me and Ruth's dinner, it occurred to me how much I liked feeding Mr. Isaac. The pure joy on his face when he would tuck into my food filled my heart with delight.

"What are you thinking about, Clem?" Ruth asked.

"Oh, I was just recalling when I used to cook for Mr. Isaac," I replied.

"You did a good job of it, too. I think he put on about ten pounds during that time," Ruth remarked as she pushed her plate away and patted her belly.

"I'm stuffed."

I glanced over and noticed she hadn't touched her ambrosia salad. "You didn't want any ambrosia?"

Ruth sighed. "Clem, I have a confession to make." She squeezed my hand and looked me square in the eye. "I've *never* liked your ambrosia."

What do you know? You learn something new every day. Ruth was faking it this entire time. She just didn't want to hurt my feelings. Percy was right all along.

Since I had a whole bunch of ambrosia left, plus a pork chop, I placed them into some Tupperware this morning for Mr. Isaac; a peace offering of sorts to help grease the skids for my long overdue apology.

I took a deep breath and knocked tentatively on his office door. "Mr. Isaac? May I come in?"

Mr. Isaac glanced up from his desk, his eyes wide, no doubt wondering what was on my mind.

"Yes ma'am. What can I do for you?" he asked hesitantly.

I stepped closer and set the containers on his desktop. "I brought you some lunch. A smothered pork chop and ambrosia salad—your favorite."

His worried gaze lightened a bit. "Thank you kindly, Mrs. Babineaux."

I sighed heavily and began my atonement. "Along with your food, I came with a confession to make. I was wrong about you and the metaverse. You weren't who I thought you were. I'm so sorry for treating you like I did. You are one of the kindest men I know, Mr. Isaac. I hope you can find it in your heart to forgive me."

A sympathetic smile crossed his lips. "I understand, Mrs. Babineaux. I do. I went through a lot of the same feelings when my Lily passed on. Grief is an odd duck. Everything's a blur and you're not quite sure which end is up. It makes you do funny things. So, you don't need to apologize. I figured our situation would settle out between us. You just needed time."

"Thank you, Mr. Isaac. I hope you enjoy the food," I said.

I turned to leave but thought better of it and pivoted back around. "Say, Mr. Isaac. Do you remember asking me out for coffee a while back?"

"Yes, indeed. Six months ago, to be exact. I believe that's what caused some of our troubles in the first place," he chuckled.

"Well, do you have any plans for your break? I can always use a cup after my morning rounds. Would you like to join me?" I asked.

"That sounds wonderful, Mrs. Babineaux."

"If it's all the same to you, Mr. Isaac, call me Clementine."

"Clementine. What a nice name," he said. "I'm Marvin."

"Marvin," I nodded.

And with our two little smiles, we began anew.

About the Author

Lori L Jackson lives in Frisco, TX with her husband and her faithful golden retriever. She enjoys tutoring and mentoring young adults, with some of their unique personalities serving as inspiration for her characters. When her nose isn't stuck in a book, she often hikes, putters around in the garden, and displays an ornery penchant for gossip whenever the opportunity arises.